# DEATH FROM ARCTIC SKIES

*Recent Titles by Leo Kessler from Severn House*

## *The S.S. Wotan Series*

ASSAULT ON BAGHDAD
BREAKOUT FROM STALINGRAD
THE BORMANN MISSION
FLIGHT FROM BERLIN
FLIGHT FROM MOSCOW
FIRE OVER SERBIA
MARCH OF DEATH
OPERATION FURY
OPERATION LONG JUMP
S.S. ATTACKS
WOTAN MISSIONS

THE HITLER WEREWOLF MURDERS

## *Writing as Duncan Harding*

ASSAULT AT ST NAZAIRE
ATTACK NEW YORK!
COME HELL OR HIGHWATER!
THE TOBRUK RESCUE
OPERATION JUDGEMENT
OPERATION STORMWIND

## *Writing as Charles Whiting*

## *The Common Smith VC Series*

THE BALTIC RUN
DEATH TRAP
HELL'S ANGELS
IN TURKISH WATERS
PASSAGE TO PETROGRAD
THE JAPANESE PRINCESS

PATHS OF DEATH AND GLORY
*(non-fiction)*

# DEATH FROM ARCTIC SKIES

An SS Wotan Adventure

Leo Kessler

This first world edition published in Great Britain 1997 by
SEVERN HOUSE PUBLISHERS LTD of
9–15 High Street, Sutton, Surrey SM1 1DF.
First published in the USA 1997 by
SEVERN HOUSE PUBLISHERS INC., of
595 Madison Avenue, New York, NY 10022.

Copyright © 1997 by Leo Kessler

All rights reserved.
The moral right of the author has been asserted.

British Library Cataloguing in Publication Data

Kessler, Leo, 1926-
    Death from Arctic Skies. – (S.S. Wotan series)
    1. World War, 1939-1945 – Campaigns – Norway - Fiction
    2. War stories
    1. Title
    823.9'14 [F]

    ISBN 0-7278-5239-6

All situations in this publication are fictitious and
any resemblance to living persons is purely coincidental.

Typeset by Palimpsest Book Production Limited,
Polmont, Stirlingshire, Scotland.
Printed and bound in Great Britain by
Hartnolls Ltd, Bodmin, Cornwall.

# Author's Note

A quarter of a century ago when I first came across the *von Dodenburg Papers*, as they are now called by contemporary historians, I accepted the facts as they appeared on those faded sheets of paper which he had written on his deathbed in Italian exile.

Many of his former troopers of SS Assault Regiment 'Wotan' wrote to me in response to the Wotan series and in consequence I have been forced to challenge some of those 'facts' in the sick man's writings, found so surprisingly in an Italian flea market.

Now with their aid, that of the Library of Congress and the NYC Public Library Service, allowed at last, thanks to the 'Freedom of Information Act', to reveal more of the truth (and certain individuals in the USA who a quarter of a century later still wish to remain anonymous), I have been able to tell the *whole* story of what happened to von Dodenburg. It is not a pretty one, but in those far off days there were no pretty stories, were there?

*L. K., Bolzano, Italy, Winter 1997*

# Book One

# *Into the Cage*

# Chapter One

"Haul ass, you lousy kraut bastards," the big sergeant yelled against the howl of the wind. "*Make schnell!*"

The guards herding the long column of prisoners ever eastwards took up the relentless chant once more in their pathetic German, "*Make schnell . . . krauts . . . LOS!*"

The column shuffled off, too weary, too hungry, too frozen to be still frightened of their white-helmeted guards who waded into them at periodic intervals if they thought the prisoners too slow slamming their cruelly brass-shod rifle butts into the Germans' skinny ribs or digging their bayonets into them.

Like some great, stinking serpent the prisoners wound their way among the frozen snow dunes, trying to find the road whenever possible, giving off an overpowering stench as they evacuated their bowels time and time again, leaving their steaming trail of wet, yellow faeces, for all of them were suffering from what they called the 'thin shits', because they had used the frozen, dirtied snow to quench their thirst.

*Obersturmbannführer* Kuno von Dodenburg, once commander of the elite SS Assault Regiment 'Wotan', fought his weary way forward with the rest of the POWs. His eyebrows were glistening white with hoar frost, his emaciated, pinched face an ugly purple, and every time he breathed, it was as if someone had plunged a sharp knife into his frozen lungs. All around him the survivors of the beaten army – tankmen in their black uniforms, sailors in floppy, beribboned caps, *Luftwaffe* paras in camouflaged coveralls and ordinary infantry in shabby ankle-length greatcoats – struggled to keep up. For all of them knew once they had dropped, they would remain lying there until they perished and the drifting snow covered their skinny bodies. This bitter December, their captors the *Amis*, knew no mercy.

Again the numbness caused by the freezing temperature had worn off and his wounds, although – thank God, they had ceased bleeding – had commenced hurting once more. The pain was almost too much to bear, but he was determined to keep going. Once they had reached the Reich and the makeshift *Wehrmacht* hospitals and camps on the other side of the border, he knew the rabble all around him would need leadership. Otherwise all of them would be condemned to an early death on the starvation rations their *Ami* guards allowed them. He had seen it all before when he had been a temporary prisoner of the Ivans – the Russians – the year before. For them to survive they needed someone to lead them and stand up to the guards. It was the only way to get out of the mess they had now found themselves in. *"March or croak, comrades!"* he had encouraged hoarsely more than once when they had been tempted to give up, lie in the snow and wait for death to take them.

He breathed out hard with exasperation and the next moment wished he hadn't. The icy breath ripped at his lungs like the blade of a razor-sharp stiletto. He knew there was no hope for him. Not only was he in the SS – "those Nazi bastards who murdered our guys in cold blood," as the big red-headed sergeant in charge had snorted more than once ever since they had commenced this death march to the Reich and the POW camps. "Remember that—" – but he was also the former commanding officer of the most feared regiment in the whole of the SS. "A Kraut Al Capone," he had told himself bitterly, "with a tommy-gun under each arm, only too eager to waste some poor innocent *Ami*."

In the American field dressing station to which they had taken him immediately after his capture to patch up his wounds, they had made it amply clear what the fate of *Obersturmbannführer* von Dodenburg of SS Assault Regiment Wotan was going to be. His wounds had been treated without benefit of any kind of anaesthetic. As the fat, harassed little Jewish doctor who had tended nervously to his wounds had whispered in Yiddish so that the rest of the place's nursing staff couldn't understand: "Sorry, Colonel, I've been ordered not to give you a shot. You'll have to grin and bear it, I'm afraid." He had wiped the sweat from his plump cheeks and continued his probing as if he was feeling the pain just as acutely as the tall, lean German officer with the harshly handsome, face stretched out on the stretcher in front of him.

Von Dodenburg had nodded, not trusting himself to speak, as the American doctor's scalpel had penetrated ever deeper into the raw, bloody wound, the blood pouring down his skinny ribs unhindered, for none of the aidmen were making any attempt to staunch the flow. Obviously they, too, had been ordered to make life hellishly tough for their high-ranking SS prisoner.

Finally it had been all over. Carelessly, an orderly had dusted the wounds with sulpha powder and bandaged them up, while the fat Jewish doctor tut-tutted and constantly shook his head, as if we were saddened by the whole bad business. His body lathered in sweat, despite the freezing temperature outside, von Dodenburg, exhausted, had fallen back onto the blood-soaked stretcher, But not for long.

It had been 'rounds' shortly afterwards. The tall, angry-faced colonel in charge had come bustling into the tent filled with wounded, both German and American, followed by his junior doctors and the sister in charge. Underneath the hissing white glare of the lantern hanging from the central pole of the tent he had stared in a bored manner at the check-list which the sister had presented him. He had seen it all before ever since Normandy. His concern was to get the 'bodies' (he always thought of his patients as 'bodies') capable of fighting again, fit for another spell in the line. Otherwise his sole concerns were his weekly booze ration of scotch and the nubile body of Nurse Smithers who was his current 'GI with the built-in foxhole', as the GIs referred crudely to the US Army's female soldiers.

Suddenly he started. Behind his steel-rimmed GI glasses, his grey eyes hardened and then became angry. "What the frigging Sam Hill is this, Finkelstein?" he demanded.

The fat Jewish doctor looked apprehensive. "What's that, sir?" he had asked timidly.

The colonel had glared at him. "Don't bullshit me, Finkelstein," he had snarled his face growing an even deeper red with anger. "You know what the Christ I'm talking about. I know goddammit, you're not one of us. But you can understand English plain and simple, don't yer!"

Tamely, ignoring the insult to his race, Finkelstein had nodded but said nothing until the colonel cried, "Put a 'sir' on that, Finkelstein!" he threatened, "Or I'll send you up to one of the fighting battalions and surgeons don't survive long up there," he had smiled maliciously, obviously noting the sudden look of fear on the junior doctor's face.

"Sir," Finkelstein said, red-faced and embarrassed at this dressing down in front of his patients.

"Good," the colonel had relaxed a little. "The trouble with you and your, er, fellow co-religionists," he pontificated, "is that you've not got enough fighting spunk. That guy," he indicated a semi-conscious von Dodenburg, who had raised his left arm and was showing the black tattoo mark of the SS under it, "is a big shot Nazi who has probably murdered a whole shoot of your, er, people. Yet you pussy-foot around with him when everybody knows that all the guy deserves is a swift polka at the end of a length of hangman's hemp."

Finkelstein said nothing, but looked at his feet in an embarrassed sort of way.

"And that's why," the colonel poked a finger at Finkelstein's plump chest as if accusing him personally, "you Jews have always been persecuted throughout your history. You've never learned how to hit back. You've always believed in turning the other goddam cheek – and see what it's got ya." He let his words sink in before adding, "Well, me, I'm a doctor, I know, but I'm also a red-blooded American, who doesn't forgive a wrong that easily. So I want that kraut dressed and out of *my* hospital in five minutes flat, or there'll be trouble – plenty of trouble for somebody." So saying he had swaggered away followed by his entourage, slapping his riding boots with the leather swagger stick that he affected.

Five minutes later, as the hospital commandant had ordered, von Dodenburg, swaying badly, his face twisted in a grimace of acute pain, was standing in the howling snowstorm outside. Opposite him, a worried Finkelstein looked anxiously at his one-time patient before reaching into the pocket of his bloodstained white overall and bringing out two packages. "More sulpha powder," he whispered so that none of the men inside could hear him, "and something to deaden the pain . . . Oh, yeah, and a few smokes." He tendered a dazed von Dodenburg a battered, half-full pack of 'Camels'. "The best I can do under the circumstances, I'm afraid."

Despite the acute pain that ran through his emaciated body

in electric shock waves, von Dodenburg was moved. "Thank you, doctor," he croaked and reached out his hand slowly, "Do you mind shaking the hand of an SS killer, Doc?"

Finkelstein took the hand a little hesitantly. "You're a sick man after all," he had said. "It's my job as a medic to treat you, whoever or whatever you are. Good luck, Colonel."

Von Dodenburg had wondered what *Reichsführer* Himmler, the head of the SS, would have thought if he had been able to see that little scene, with the snow whirling around the tents and the big, wounded colonel towering above the fat, undersized, obviously Jewish doctor. Now he grinned weakly at the memory. But at that moment he had had no time for amusement, for, abruptly, the head guard, the 'white mouse'\* the other guards called, 'Red', had appeared out of the snowstorm bellowing that cry which von Dodenburg was going to learn to hate, "All right, you kraut bastard *haul ass!*"

And duly, as the giant MP had raised his pick-handle as if he might strike him at any moment, he had 'hauled ass', leaving the little Jewish doctor to stare after him as he disappeared into the white, whirling mist, with what might well have been tears in his eyes.

But the American colonel commandant's attitude towards the beaten Germans, especially those of the SS, had made up von Dodenburg's mind. Ever since his surprise capture†, he had been unable to make plans: he had been too weak and miserable at the knowledge that his beloved regiment had been wiped out, save for a handful of survivors under Sergeant Schulze's leadership who had managed to survive the debacle and escape.

---

\* German nickname for the US military police on account of the white-painted helmets they wore.
† See L. Kessler, *Operation Fury* for further details.

His manner of release from the American military hospital, when he knew that his wounds needed far more attention if he wasn't going to succumb to gas-gangrene that stinking killer created in untended dirty wounds, had made up his mind for him at last. It wasn't because he was concerned about his personal future. He knew that in the end his life was forfeit; after all, he had commanded the most infamous regiment in the whole of the million-strong SS. But for the time being he wanted to do what pathetic little he could to help his beloved Fatherland in its hour of defeat. What had that big ox Sergeant Schulze said to him more than once before they had finally walked into the trap: "Sir, we've always had it drummed into us for these last years that we must learn to die for Germany." And he had inevitably stroked his pugnacious, unshaven jaw at that moment before adding, "Now we've got to learn how to *live* for our country!"

As that long column of stinking human misery trailed ever eastwards, leaving their dead and dying behind them, soon to be swallowed up by the raging snowstorm, von Dodenburg knew that that rogue Schulze, for all his undoubted faults, had been right. The days of dying on the 'field of honour' for Folk, Fatherland and Führer were over. Now one had to live. The question was – *HOW?*

# Chapter Two

The raging snowstorm had ceased now. From one horizon to the other, the new snowfield glittered and sparkled beautifully. A cold sun stood high in the hard, steel-blue sky. On the hills to both sides of the remote Eifel farmhouse, the firs marched up the steep slopes like spike-helmeted Prussian grenadiers. All was quiet and muted by the snow save for the distant rumble of the permanent barrage to the east where the Americans under Patton attacked yet again, being driven forward relentlessly by that 'cowboy general', as the Führer called him scornfully.

It could have been a scene from a pre-war Christmas card, with rosy-cheeked village children in woolly hats, dragging their sledges, heavy with holly sprigs and fir trees, back home to celebrate that most holy of German festivals, the family Christmas Eve.

But the silver, noiseless shapes of the *Ami* bomber squadrons knifing high across the hard blue sky, dragging their white vapour trails behind them, gave the lie to that. The Flying Fortresses, hundreds of them, were on their way to wreak vengeance on the Reich's already shattered cities, making the enemy pay for that great surprise offensive in the Ardennes which had come as such a huge shock to the Allied Supreme Commander, General Eisenhower, and his so-confident generals who had thought the war would be over, in the Allied favour, by Christmas. No, the war on the frontier of the Reich with Belgium still raged in its full fury, and many thousands more, both German and American soldiers, would die before it was all over and Germany was finally defeated.

Sergeant Schulze, who had led the handful of Wotan survivors to the safety of this remote Eifel farmhouse, where the animals lived under the same straw roof as the humans, had, however, forgotten the war for a time. As he was wont to say to his cronies in the Sergeants' Mess of SS Assault Regiment Wotan, "Life don't hold much for yer poor common-or-garden stubble-hopper, comrades, a little bit of firewater to gargle with and a drop of good Munich suds to wash it down." Here his wicked blue eyes always sparkled, "and then if yer really in luck, dancing the two-assed mattress polka with a big fine wench with plenty o' meat on her so that yer don't fall off the pit." And, to emphasize his point, he would let loose with one of his musical farts, celebrated throughout the SS NCO Corps.

Now Sergeant Schulze was engaged in that same delightful activity – the 'mattress polka' – while his survivors kept watch on the snowy wastes to the east, the way they would come, if they ever did come.

For two days now they had been in this farmhouse, inhabited solely by women, for their menfolk had long fled or had been swallowed up in the bloody maws of the war in Russia. It had been an ideal location for their, perhaps, hopeless vigil. The place overlooked the sole remaining road through the minefields down from the Belgian Ardennes into the German Eifel hills. If the prisoners were to cross into the Reich in the north, Schulze had reasoned it would be here and any crossing could be easily observed from the shell-pocked, red-brick, poverty-stricken Eifel farmhouse perched on the hilltop to the left of the snowbound road.

But for the moment the prisoners who might be coming

their way were forgotten as Sergeant Schulze carefully levered himself onto the bed just in case the wooden structure collapsed under his weight and that of Irmgard the oldest of the women on the farm and unfortunately the ugliest. Irmgard was fat and had the suspicion of a moustache under her large, usually dripping nose, which she wiped constantly with her manure-stained, big hands. Indeed, she was so fat that Matz had hinted darkly when it had became clear that one of them would have to 'pleasure' her as well, if they were going to keep enjoying the other, young farm maidens, "That bit o' beaver seems to be bigger every day that dawns. I swear somebody frigging well pumps her up at night, Schulzi!"

Now it had fallen to Schulze by lot to 'pump her up', "But not with a frigging bicycle pump," as Matz had chortled with relief when it was clear that he had not been given that task.

"I'm a virgin," she simpered as she removed her home-knitted woollen knickers to reveal the massive brown thatch below. "I've been saving myself for the right man, Sergeant Schulze!"

Under his breath, a somewhat desperate Sergeant Schulze sighed, "Ay, saving yersen for so frigging long that you're beginning to go off." He wrinkled his nose at the odour that her ample body gave off as she gazed up at him winningly.

Schulze loosened his flies. His member was beginning to stiffen. Her mouth dropped open as if in awe. "That's better than Felix, our bull!" she exclaimed. She reached forward and grabbed hold of it as if lugging at Felix's halter and at the same time opened her fat thighs invitingly.

Schulse gulped. "Oh God Almighty!" he said in wonder. "By the Great Whore of Buxtehude where the dogs piss through their ribs, I've never seen anything like it!"

She smiled, as if pleased with herself. With her free hand she stroked her great hairy thatch. "I'm not surprised, Sergeant, that you are impressed. I'll have you know that I've been saving it for someone like you for these forty –" she corrected herself hastily – "twenty years. I wanted the first man to take my body to appreciate what he was getting." She leaned back in what she thought was a seductive manner, pulling Schulze with her as she hung determinedly on to his organ. The bed squeaked alarmingly as if it might collapse at any moment.

Schulze looked in mute appeal at the flaking, dirty ceiling, as if half expecting some God to be sitting up there on the edge of a cloud, playing a harp as he prepared to rescue him from the awful fate soon to come. But if there was a God up there somewhere, at that particular moment he was looking the other way.

"Be gentle with me, my beloved," she sighed in a dreamy sort of way, closing her eyes, as if it were all a little too much for her.

Schulze gave one final curse against the fates which had condemned him to this horrible experience, perhaps the first time in his life since he had fingered 'Juicy Lucy' at his Hamburg *Volksschule* that he felt he wasn't really going to enjoy the 'mattress polka', and prepared to take her.

She gave a great sigh. "What an experience this will be, well worth waiting for twenty long years," she whispered as if to herself, as Sergeant Schulze started to insert what he fondly called his 'good piece of prime German salami.'

But this long-awaited answer to Irmgard's maidenly prayers was not going to be answered on this icy winter's day. For outside, some hundred metres down the slope next to the road, there came the shrill blast of the warning whistle – three blasts, to be exact.

"*Saved*," Sergeant Schulze exclaimed happily. He sat up

urgently, as Irmgard opened her eyes and cried, "What is it, my beloved? Am I too much for you?"

Schulze refrained from giving her an honest answer. Instead he hissed, reaching for his 'dice-beakers', his battered old jackboots which she had insisted he take off for this 'solemn occasion'. "It's the signal from Corporal Matz," he explained hurriedly, tugging the cold boots on. "He's seen what we've been waiting for all this time." He sat up and buckled on his pistol.

She blew him a kiss as he headed gratefully for the door, with the smelly pigs in the barn below rooting and snorting at the sudden alarm. "You will return?" she queried, tears in her cowlike eyes.

"Of course, my beloved," he replied with a courtly bow, now at his most gallant. "Who would be foolish enough to miss your great charms." To himself he said, as he fled through the door, "with tits like that, a man could be suffocated to death if he didn't watch out." And with that he was clattering down the wooden ladder, heading for Matz's wayside post.

Matz lounged against the snow-heavy, rickety fence. He had taken off his wooden leg. Now he was supported by a crude crutch made from an old rake from the farm and dressed in the rough clothing of one of the middle-aged men who had fled the advancing *Amis*. In his mouth he held a piece of dried straw from the barn. All in all he looked – well, he hoped he did – like a harmless village yokel who was too dotty to do a bunk before the *Amis* came looting and shooting in their usual fashion when they had drunk the local firewater, fruit schnapps.

Idly, mouth slack and dirbbling, he watched the long column stagger down the road, banked on both sides by piles of frozen snow, as if he couldn't quite understand what all these strange creatures, who paused all the time to lower their filthy pants to squirt yellow faeces into the mud, were doing here. In fact, his eyes were searching their miserable ranks for the first sight of the man they had been waiting here for days to rescue.

Involuntarily, Matz wrinkled up his nose as the first of the thousands of German POWs started to file by him, urged on by their guards who looked well-fed and warm in their thick parkas. Matz surveyed their miserable faces through half-lowered eyelids and wondered why the *Amis* hadn't moved their captives by truck. After all, they were suffering from that long march, too. But after a few moments he reasoned that the prisoners were for exhibition to the local civilians. They were there to show the Germans on the other side of the border just how throughly the *Wehrmacht* had been beaten this December in the Ardennes. Still one thing puzzled him. There was a high percentage of SS men among the POWs from all other branches of the service. He wondered why for a few moments. Then he gave up and concentrated on viewing the miserable, emaciated, unshaven faces passing by, Germany's final defeat written all too clearly on the captives's features.

A big, red-faced *Ami* NCO, who seemed to be in charge, came level with him. Somewhere or other he had picked up an arm-thick bull's pizzle and was using that joyfully now instead of the pick-handles which the others wielded. He waved the obscene article at what he took to be a one-legged peasant and one of his men yelled, "If you're gonna use that bull's cock on him, sarge, you'll need a jar full of Vaseline to do the job."

The NCO yelled something back, but Matz, who could only understand the *Amis*' gestures and not their words, was no longer listening. He had spotted him! There he was, tottering through the frozen mud, blood still staining his dirty bandages, looking as if he might collapse and die at any moment.

Tears flooded the little SS man's eyes. He wasn't an emotional man, but he had never seen the CO like this before. He was dying on his feet and if he, Schulze and the rest didn't do something soon, he knew that Von Dodenburg wouldn't last the week, perhaps even the day. They had to rescue their CO soon – *damned soon*!

Crouched behind the cover of one of the farmhouse's windows, trying to fight off Irmagard's importuning hands, which kept slipping into his pockets to seize his now flaccid organ, a worried Sergeant Schulze felt the same as Matz, lounging by the snowbound road below.

His mind raced as he tried to outguess the Americans. Where would they spend the night, for it would be then that they would have to make their attempt to rescue the CO? He flashed a look at the hard, blue sky. Already the sun was beginning to slip behind the horizon. It would be dark in another hour at this time of the year and he knew just how fearful the *Amis* were of the dark in enemy territory. By then they'd want to be under cover and their guards posted.

Greedily Irmgard nipped his organ once more and, sticking her wet tongue in his ear, whispered, "Beloved Sergeant, if you've got time I'd like to lose" – she hesitated for a moment – "my virginity before Christmas. It would be like a Christmas present to myself, you know."

Schulze sighed like a man sorely tried. All the same he pulled himself together – after all, they needed the farmhouse a little longer – and said sweetly, "Irmgard, my little cabbage, in due course you shall have the full benefit of Sergeant Schulze's undoubtedly very special love machine." He touched his flies briefly to make his meaning quite clear. "And I feel I must tell you this in advance. After Mrs Schulze's handsome son has worked his charm on a – er – lady, she never wants another man." He winked knowingly. Irmgard gave a shiver of delight . . .

# Chapter Three

"So this is Harrogate?" Colonel Schroeder of the US Army's Judge Advocate Branch, said, totally unnecesarily, dragging out the syllables in the American fashion.

"Sir," Major Sharpe of the British SIB snapped promptly, as he signalled to the PU car with its ATS driver waiting outside Harrogate's Victorian station for them. It had been a long trip from London, with the train packed with drunken servicemen going on leave and civilians going God knows where, for Sharpe wondered who would ever travel in wartime Britain given the choice. After all, it had taken them nearly twelve hours to complete the journey, with soldiers snoring in the luggage racks and even the lavatories packed, despite the stink, so that mothers were forced to pass their babies above the heads of the men in the crowded corridors in the hope that some kindly serviceman would ensure they would do their 'business' before it was too late.

The plump ATS driver saluted and they clambered gratefully into the warmth of the tight van. Hastily, Sharpe signed her ticket and ordered, "I049th US General Hospital, you know where it is?"

The ATS driver took her eyes off the plump American in his immaculate pinks and Saville Row jeep-coat. The Yanks, whatever their age, were always good for some buckshee fags and if you were lucky and played your cards right, even if it meant only letting them squeeze your knee, nylons as well. "Yessir!" she snapped promptly and thrusting home first gear, double-declutched and nosed her way into the slushy street.

Ashen-faced civilians moved slowly down the steep street leading from the station, as if they were finding it difficult to move. The Victorian buildings of the northern spa, which had once housed European royalty, were shabby and looked as if they hadn't had a coat of paint since that time. Outside a butcher's shop, with the legend *'Offal Today ... Ration Books A to H'* scribbled on the window in white chalk, patient housewives, with steel curlers showing from behind their flowered turbans which served in the place of hats, waited for their pathetic bit of pig's liver or half a kidney, not even talking to one another. They looked exhausted. At the corner an old, one-legged newspaper vendor with a Woodbine tucked behind his ear was crying something, a poster tied to his front like an apron. Sharpe read the headline from the *Yorkshire Post 'Rundstedt still attacking in Belgium'\** and sighed. There seemed no end to the war, it appeared to be going on for ever. And after the Jerries, there were still the Japs to be dealt with. Sometimes Sharpe thought it would have been better if the Germans had seen him off at El Alamein two years before. That would have been that. Still the Army's Special Investigation Branch was better than some postings he could think of, even if you had to deal with fat, self-opinionated arseholes like Colonel Shroeder of Eisenhower's staff, who appeared to look at the 'British', as he always called them, as members of a third-class nation. Sharpe smiled ruefully. Perhaps the Yank was right.

They started to climb the long hill which led to the

---

\* Field Marshal Gerd von Rundstedt, commander of the German assault in the Ardennes.

one-time private girls' school, which was now a Yank military hospital. As they did so, Sharpe remembered how the fat American ex-corporation lawyer (that's how he had described himself at their first meeting) had put him in his place straightaway, five minutes after he had stepped out of the Dakota from Paris at Northholt. The American had looked up at the tall major with the one arm, whose lean face was still tanned from the years he had spent in the Western Desert, and had growled: "Let's get this straight from the start, Major."

"Sir?"

"You have no jurisdiction in this matter. Your sole function is to get me from A to Z and open the necessary doors for me. Got it?"

"Got it, sir," he had answered, as he had stood there in the falling snow, smelling the American's expensive odour of good cigars and after-shave, and wondering what had occasioned the sudden lecture. Immediately, he took a disliking to the fat, conceited American who, apparently, he was expected to wet nurse. Still there was nothing he could do about it. These days the Yanks were 'calling the shots', as they phrased it, and that was that.

For a moment or two the American legal colonel became aware of the fact that Sharpe was minus one arm and it seemed as if he might make a comment about it. But he didn't. Instead he snapped, puffing away at that expensive cigar of his, "See about my digs, will you, Major. And pay particular attention to my briefcases, they've got my initials upon them. They contained what few papers and documents we have on this case and we can't afford to lose them, can we?"

Willingly he had agreed that they couldn't, though he hadn't the slightest idea what those documents were, however important, and what 'case' the fat American was talking about. But, as he had told himself at the time, it was all no concern of his. His role was to act, obviously, as an informed guide.

Now, with the first sad flakes of the new snow beginning to drift down silently outside the former girls' school, he nodded to the fat ATS girl, who had not succeeded in wheedling any nylons out of the American colonel, although he had sat very close to her in the front seat on the journey here. She put down the two briefcases and for a moment the two officers stood there in the great, icy hall in a state of slight bewilderment, breathing in the ether-tinged air and listening to a crazed voice somewhere in the makeshift wards, crying, "No, don't do that again . . . For Chrissake don't do that agen! Honest, I can't stand it!" There was something about that mad voice which sent an icy finger of fear tracing its way eerily down the small of Sharpe's back.

Schroeder was unmoved. He removed the great fat cigar from between his thick red lips and commented, "Section Eighter . . . Ready for the funny farm as soon as they ship him back to the States – and a darned good riddance to him as well. The Army's got too many of those guys these days, who simply won't frigging fight." He replaced his cigar and took a self-righteous puff at it.

Sharpe didn't know what a 'Section Eighter' was, but he could guess: some poor bastard who had cracked under the strain of combat and had retreated into madness as one way of getting out of the firing line.

"Yeah," Schroeder continued as the clerk at the reception desk, recognising the colonel's eagles on Schroeder's immaculate jeep-coat, pressed his bell urgently. "The rot's set in ever since the goddam krauts hit us in the Ardennes, they're going over the hill in their hundreds . . . their thousands, and General Ike" – he meant Eisenhower, the

Allied Supreme Commander – "wants it stopped tootsweet. That's why we're here . . . in a way."

"Which way, sir?" Sharpe began.

But he didn't receive an answer to his question, for in that instant, as somewhere in the wards the 'Section Eighter' screamed shrilly and then lapsed into silence, as if someone had got sick of his moans and had pumped him full of dope, an American doctor, followed by two gigantic and somewhat harassed assistants, all three dressed in white coats (though it was obvious to Sharpe they weren't doctors) appeared. The doctor was flushed and there was a trace of green spittle on his white coat, as if someone had just spat at him. "Sorry to keep you, Colonel," he said in a flustered manner, "one of the patients was a little – er – uncooperative."

Colonel Schroeder gave the medical officer a fake smile, "Understand perfectly, Doc," he said easily. "There are too many of those damned malingers about. The front's crying out for riflemen and those guys are trying for a soft touch in a nice, warm, safe hospital."

The bespectacled army doctor opened his mouth, as if he were about to protest. But obviously he changed his mind for he said in a neutral, professional tone, "I've got the personnel together you wish to see, Colonel. Understandably they are still a bit shaky after what they've been through. But they are capable of answering your questions."

"Swell," Colonel Schroeder said and flicked the ash from his cigar to the immaculate floor. "Then I suggest we get on with it. For the time being it's going to be routine. We'll interrogate them more thoroughly later on. But let's get it over with. I want to catch tomorrow's flight back to Versailles. Ike wants me to report to him immediately after the morning briefing."

The doctor was impressed, as Schroeder had intended he would be. "This way then, Colonel," he said urgently, extending his right hand like a head waiter ushering an important guest to a prime table in a restaurant. Schroeder followed him, with Sharpe trailing behind, wondering what the devil was going on in this remote provincial hospital.

There men were waiting in a small ward just off the main one, which to judge from the babble and moans coming from within was occupied by other unfortunate 'Section Eighters'.

All three men, one a lieutenant, rose at Schroeder's entrance, but Sharpe, used to making instant judgements of men, especially after he had been posted to the SIB, noticed no animation in their unusually pale faces. There was something passive about them, their eyes were blank, as if they might be under the influence of drugs.

"Second Lieutenant Barry, Privates First Class Hurst and Marcello," the doctor introduced the three men, all clad in clean uniforms devoid of unit insignia, "the only survivors that have been located so far, sir."

Sharpe frowned, puzzled. What did the MO mean? Survivors of *what*? he asked himself.

But Schroeder evidently knew what they had survived for opening his briefcase, he glanced briefly at his papers before saying almost immediately, "You're sure I'm going to be able to rely upon you?"

The young lieutenant, who, Sharpe now noticed, wore an unstained bandage around his wrist as if he might well have been wounded some time before, but by now the wound was beginning to heal, said tonelessly. "Yessir. I've talked it over with the guys. You can rely upon us to give you what we know, sir."

"Good," Schroeder turned to the puzzled British officer and said out of the side of his mouth, hurriedly, "these soldiers are the only survivors we have been able to locate of a German massacre of our troops on the second day of their damned offensive in the Ardennes."

Sharpe nodded his understanding though he wondered why the Yanks were making such a fuss. Front-line soldiers, or perhaps the second-line troops on both sides, made an occasional habit of shooting prisoners when the mood took them. He had heard of a good half dozen such cases before the German 88mm shell had put an end to his fighting career. Undoubtedly, if he survived that long, he would be investigating a lot more 'massacre cases' after the war, especially German ones once the Jerries had been beaten.

"All right!" Schroeder snapped, as if he were in a hurry, shivering a little in the freezing, unheated room that had once been a schoolgirls' cloakroom to judge by the coat-hooks lining the yellow-tiled walls, "Tell me what you know, please, Lieutenant."

A little hesitantly the young officer with the unstained bandage began his story. "We were cut off, sir. The rest of the regiment had been pulling back most of that morning and somehow the good word hadn't reached our company. We'd taken casualties – plenty of them – and then the Jerry tanks appeared on the scene." Suddenly the young officer coloured red and lowered his gaze, as if he were embarrassed. "Well, the guys started tossing away their weapons, taking off their helmets and raising their arms in surrender."

"Go on," Schroeder encouraged him hurriedly, as if he couldn't get out of that freezing cloakroom fast enough, "It could have happened to the toughest of fighting troops. What happened then?"

Mentally, Sharpe sniggered. What would the fat colonel from HQ know about fighting troops? He'd probably never heard a shot fired in anger during the whole of his military career.

"Well, sir, then the SS came swarming out of the woods, kicking those who were slow at raising their hands and started looting the guys of their smokes, watches, chocolate and the like."

"How do you know they were SS?" Schroeder asked sharply, as if it were important. "They weren't dressed in black uniforms were they, like a lot of guys think the SS wear?"

Sharpe knew what Schroeder meant. Many soldiers confused the German panzer troops who were clad in black and had the skull-and-crossbone insignia on their tunic with the pre-war SS who had also worn black.

"No sir, they were SS all right," the young officer answered. "They were dressed in the usual field-grey and they wore those black bands of the SS around their sleeves. I'd seen them before as prisoners, so I knew they were SS."

"Good," Schroeder's fat face glowed suddenly, as if he were pleased with the information. "And could you see what name was on those armbands? It wouldn't be 'Wotan' would it?" He leaned forward, abruptly tense, as if the lieutenant's answer would be very important.

"Well, sir. It all happened so quick and the—"

But before the lieutenant could finish his explanation, the door crashed open and a tall, dark-faced man stood glowering there, balancing his mutilated body on a stick, looking either drunk or mad, or perhaps both, for all a surprised Sharpe knew. "They was 'Wotan' all right!" he snarled wolfishly.

Startled, Colonel Schroeder turned. "What did you say, soldier?"

The one-legged soldier in the grey hospital issue dressing gown was obviously no respecter of rank, for he snarled once again, "You can fucking well hear, can't you, Colonel. I've just told you who the Krauts were – they were from that fucking 'Wotan' SS regiment of theirn."

"But how do you know, soldier?"

The one-legged soldier gave a demented laugh, his dark eyes glittering feverishly. "How did I know, Colonel?" he snorted. "I'll tell you how I knew. *I was frigging well there – that's how . . . !*"

# Chapter Four

Sergeant Rosenkranz, swarthy, with flashing dark eyes, was stirring another batch of waffle mix for 'my boys', as he called the young infantrymen of the 'Bloody Bucket' Division\*. "I'm not one your ordinary ragged-assed kikes," he would say to anyone prepared to listen. "No sirree, I'm a kike from Queen's, New York City, right up against Forest Hills where they have the ritzy tennis games. Get it guys!" and here he would invariably gesture with a waffle iron, or any other piece of chow-house equipment. "I'm one smart cookie."

All the same Rosenkranz, big, brawny and brainy, the one-time short-order cook on the East Side, had landed up in the infantry, though he had come to like – even love – 'my boys' in a way that only a devoted cook could. Now as he stirred another batch of the waffle mix in the big one-gallon can, he saw that the other cooks were getting progressively nervous. All the time they kept glancing at the burning dawn-horizon, the flames lurid above the green, fir-spiked hills as yet another German shall slammed across the border into Belgium and made the very earth tremble.

Finally Rosenkranz exploded, "What's matter with youse

---

\* Nickname for the 28th Infantry Division on account of its blood-red badge which looked like a bloody bucket.

guys? What ya creaming ya skivvies for? Even us hash-slingers," he indicated the other cooks in their dirty white aprons, most of them unshaven and probably unwashed, too, for it was bitterly cold that December Saturday in the Ardennes hills, as they prepared the usual 'shit on shingle' (hash on toast), "ain't that scared, brother!"

"But what are the Krauts up to, Sarge?" quavered a pale-faced teenage replacement, waiting with his canteen for coffee. "We was supposed to come up the line to this here ghost front to be trained for the real shooting war."

Rosenkranz laughed hollowly. "D'ya get that, guys? This clockwork cunt here really believes what the goddam Army told him. He ought to be Section-Eighted and sent back to the States."

All the same, the former short-order cook in a Kosher deli knew that there was something wrong, drastically wrong, up here. Right up to now the Krauts hadn't fired a single shot in their direction, ever since he had been posted to the battalion. Now all hell was being let loose and the Krauts were firing shells as if they grew on trees, which they certainly didn't for the hard-strapped enemy. "All right, youse guys, I'm gonna start the waffles now. The griddle's hot enough, I guess. And there'll be syrup for any guy—"

The rest of his words were drowned abruptly by the rattle of tank tracks. It was a tank advancing in low gear. He looked up, puzzled. A lone Sherman had broken out of the firs, snapping them off like matchwood, as it began to rumble down the slope, throwing up the snow in a gleaming white wake behind it. "What the Sam Hill's going on?" Rosenkranz exclaimed, noting instinctively that the mysterious Sherman's turret was closed as it advanced on the startled infantrymen, as if it were ready for instant action.

Next to him, a freckle-faced GI with his front teeth missing, who had been whistling the latest Bing Crosby hit

'I'm dreamin' of a White Christmas' stopped abruptly. He shouted above the racket, "Hey that tin can, guys, is coming from the frigging Kraut lines!"

A moment later his worse fears were confirmed. Suddenly, the mysterious Sherman's 75mm cannon cracked into action. A shell screamed, high-pitched and hysterical, through the freezing air. It was followed by an angry burst from the co-axial machine-gun and slugs slapped into the snow. Just behind the makeshift cookhouse, a log hut exploded in a great crump. Razor-sharp, red-hot shards of steel scythed through the air. Men went down screaming with pain and surprise. Suddenly there were dead and dying GIs everywhere. Their blood coloured the new snow an ominous scarlet.

Rosenkranz cursed as his waffle can overturned and the mixture ran everywhere. "Christ on a crutch!" he cursed. "Fuck this for a frigging game of soldiers!"

"Medic . . . Medic . . . !" the anguished cries for help went up on all sides as the mysterious Sherman fired again. "Medic . . . I can't walk. . . . The cunts have shot my leg off . . . !"

"*KRAUTS!*" Rosenkranz yelled urgently.

Already the first German infantry were crossing the snowbound skyline. They advanced deliberately. Their bodies were bent and they held their rifles at the high port across their grey-clad chests, as if they were moving against a high wind and were finding it tough going.

There was no mistaking them: Germans in the camouflaged tunics of the SS.

"Holy cow!" the shavetail first lieutenant in charge yelled. "Run for it, guys!"

The captured Sherman at the point of the advancing SS panzer grenadiers fired again. The young officer screamed as blood pumped from the sudden great tear in his skinny chest in a bright scarlet arc. Vainly and hopelessly he tried to remain on his feet. His hands clutched the air feverishly, as if he were climbing the rungs of an invisible ladder. Abruptly he pitched forward, dead before he hit the blood-stained snow.

That did it. His company immediately started to disintegrate. The infantrymen panicked. "We're bugging out!" they cried. Make a run for it, guys, while there's still a chance. *WE'RE BUGGING OUT!*"

Here and there men threw away their weapons and stood undecided. Others raised their hands. A few turned and, throwing away their M1 rifles, began to pelt through the snow to the rear. Mad with anger, his dark eyes blazing, Rosenkranz dropped his ladle, "Stand frigging fast!" he yelled desperately. "Hold the bastards!"

But no one was listening now to the enraged cook. The Sherman fired again. As men reeled backwards, swept off their feet by the force of the explosion, Rosenkranz realised it was hopeless; it was no use trying to hold the reinforcements. They were just wet-nosed kids, shitting their pants with fear. He had to save himself. Without wasting further time upon them, he, too, turned and started to run for the cover of the trees to the rear. Triumphantly, shouting among themselves, the SS swarmed forward and began to loot the abandoned US positions, yelling excitedly when they found cigarettes and chocolate, the like of which they hadn't seen for years.

*Obersturmbannführer* von Dodenburg, his face wolfish and emaciated, looked up from his situation map, as the prisoners were herded by him and his staff. Like very old and weary men the Americans trudged through the scuffed snow, littered with abandoned equipment. Their young faces were pinched, pink and petrified. A few had wrapped khaki blankets about their heads and skinny shoulders to keep out the biting cold. But the great majority of them were too frightened to do even that. Fear was writ large in their wild, staring eyes.

Sergeant Schulze, standing just behind the CO, chewing on a looted chocolate bar, knew why. The guards who had taken over from 'Wotan', and were to guard the new prisoners as they escorted them to the cages to the rear, were all members of an SS Penal Battalion. All of them had been virtually condemned to death by being assigned to this battalion. They were murderers, rapists, thieves, deserters – the lowest of the low who would never return from the front save feet first. And they knew it. The SS Penal Battalion troopers made their own discipline and, as Schulze whispered to his one-legged running mate, wizened little Corporal Matz: "Old house, I don't think them *Amis* is gonna get very far this day. It's too shitting cold to be herding slow-moving POWs along. Them murdering barn-shitters of the 666th will see them off, you can take that from me."

Matz nodded his agreement, but said nothing as he watched the frightened faces of the young *Ami* prisoners, as if attempting to etch their features on his mind's eye for ever.

"How are things?" von Dodenburg forgot the POWs and asked his operations officer, Major Stapelveld.

"Excellent," the other officer replied with a beam. "All positions taken. Now we can bring up the armour. One fly in the ointment, *Obersturm*, though." His smile vanished.

"And what's that, pray?"

"The tanks are already beginning to run out of 'Otto'." He meant fuel.

"Great Crap on the Christmas Tree!" von Dodenburg cursed, his harshly handsome face suddenly flushed with anger. "*That* already, and we've just started our offensive.

What in three devils' names are they up to at HQ? We—" He stopped short, his angry question never to be answered.

From beyond the trees on the opposite ridge there came the rattle of small-arms fire, like the sound of an iron bar run along a length of railing.

Behind the officers, the two NCOs looked significantly at each other. There was no need for words. Both of them knew what was going on. The men of the penal battalion, realising that the prisoners were going to be too much of a burden, were shooting the *Amis*. That atrocity, which would occupy generals, prelates, politicians and world opinion for many years to come from this freezing December of 1944, had commenced.

Crouched behind the cover of some snow-heavy bushes a quarter of a mile away, Sergeant Rosenkranz, along with 'VD' and 'Hairless Harry', two old heads like himself, listened grimly as the firing started to die down. "They're shooting our boys. Poor Bastards. And they're so young." VD had gained his nickname from his unfortunate habit of seemingly contacting what he liked to call 'a social disease' every time he went on leave to 'Pig Alley', otherwise known as 'Place Pigalle'.

"Yeah," Hairless Harry, who was as bald as a coot although he was all of twenty, agreed. "They're from SS Regiment 'Wotan' – we've got to remember that, guys," he added warningly. "I saw the arm patch on the first of the bastards when the firing started."

"Don't worry, Hairless," Rosenkranz said grinly. "I'll remember. Mrs Rosenkranz's handsome son'll remember this to his dying day and the bastards are not gonna get away with murder if I have any say in it. No sirree!"

Cautiously, very cautiously, VD parted the snow-heavy bushes in front of where they were hiding. They peered out, hardly daring to breathe as the firing ceased.

Now the rest of the enemy point came rumbling over the ridgeline opposite. Great 60-ton tanks, their huge overhanging cannon moving from side to side nervously, like the snouts of primeval monsters attempting to sniff out their prey. All around in the packed halftracks, young Wotan panzer grenadiers whooped and cheered excitedly as they rolled through the abandoned American positions, their tracks crushing the pathetic bits and pieces of American equipment. Obviously they were ready to drop over the steel sides of their vehicles at a moment's notice and ruthlessly mop up any opposition. They smelled victory in the air that was quite clear to the angry, secret observers.

But Rosenkranz was too angry to be worried about the intentions of the eager young German troopers. He pointed to the officer holding the map. "That must be their boss man," he hissed, his dark eyes full of malevolent fury. "Has to be. Mark his face, I'm gonna get that guy one day." He licked his wind-cracked, parched lips. "One day I'm gonna have the nuts off'n him for what happened here, if it's last frigging thing I ever do. There's gonna be no escape for him, get me?"

The other two nodded wordlessly. They couldn't speak. Rosenkranz's sense of hate was too overpowering, too elemental for words. It had to be accepted, like a fact of life.

"OK, let's go while the going's good," Rosenkranz ordered.

They rose, still in silence. Moments later the three hard-bitten old heads had vanished into the snowbound forest. Behind them they left an aura of sheer, naked, overwhelming hatred.


"So that's the way it was," the crippled ex-sergeant concluded, as they sat there in the freezing old cloakroom, with the whimpers of the Section Eighters and the soft howl of the wind outside, the only sound that disturbed the heavy clinical silence of the hilltop military hospital. "Later I beat up that Kraut SS colonel. But just when I was gonna hand him in – I didn't manage to kill the bastard* unfortunately – this," he pointed to his stump, "happened to me." He shrugged. "But anything I can do to nail him now, Colonel, for what he did to our guys, I'm your man."

For what seemed a long time, Colonel Schroeder didn't answer, while Major Sharpe stared at the dark-faced American, with the angry fire still burning in his eyes. "Thank you, Sergeant," the colonel said, "I'm glad I can rely on you." He turned to the senior survivor of the SS massacre. "Lieutenant Barry," he asked very formally, "can you confirm that which the sergeant here has just testified, namely that the massacre was carried out by an outfit called SS 'Wotan' under the command of a young German SS colonel?"

Barry seemed to take a long time to come out of his strange lethargy. Finally he said, "I guess I can't confirm 'Wotan', sir."

Schroeder flushed, obviously angry. "Well, what *did* you see then?"

"They were SS all right, sir. That I know. But I didn't see 'Wotan' or whatever their regiment is called, on their sleeve patches." The young officer's face looked pale, even frustrated now. "I think, sir," he added, "that the arm patch I saw had a number on it . . ." He let his voice trail away, as if he realised that he was saying the wrong thing. It wasn't what the colonel from Headquarters wanted.

Schroeder kept his temper with difficulty. "Yes, I understand," he said, though he didn't. "The shock . . . and everything. Naturally you would be in no position to take

* See L.Kessler, *Operation Fury* for further details.

in the details accurately." He looked at Rosenkranz, hoping obviously that the big sergeant would rise to the bait he was offering.

Sharpe followed that look and understood it immediately. Back in 1942, when he had had his arm shot off at El Alamein, he had come to realise later in hospital in Cairo that there were basically two kinds of seriously wounded men, especially amputees. There was the group that became more like a hunch of fearful old biddies, who wanted to be protected, felt hurt, out of the war, no longer concerned with the fighting.

Then there was the other kind, and for a while he himself had belonged to that group: men who were angry, bitter, were outraged that this terrible thing had happened to *them*. They had lusted for revenge, cost what it may. Rosenkranz, he was sure, belonged to the latter category.

Next moment the NCO's slight nod in the waiting colonel's direction confirmed what he had already guessed. Rosenkranz was prepared to do anything, say anything in order to avenge himself on the Germans who had done him such a grave injury – and any German, guilty or not, would do.

The big ex-cook would lie, swear black was white, in short perjure himself hopelessly and without hesitation in order to achieve his end; and Sergeant Rosenkranz would be a difficult nut to crack for any defence lawyer. Didn't he have the visible sign – his amputated leg – to show what terrible hurt he had suffered at the hands of the SS, whatever their formation?

Sharpe flashed a look at the fat colonel from HQ to check whether he had come to the same conclusion. But it was obvious he hadn't. Suddenly, after the young officer's disappointing answer, he had found the ideal witness he had sought ever since Eisenhower had put him onto this case. His next words confirmed Sharpe's thinking, for he said, "Sergeant, I'm going to check with your sawbones. If he says that you are fit enough to travel, I'm going to have orders out so that you can proceed to Versailles as soon as possible for further cross-examination. Would that be all right with you?"

"You betcha, sir. I don't need the medics' say-so. I'd even crawl there if it would help to nail those bastards who murdered my boys in cold blood, sir!"

Schroeder smiled, "Well said, Sergeant Rosenkranz." He looked at the other three potential witnesses, "That's the kind of guy the US Army needs in times like these. A guy who's not scared of standing up and saying his piece." He looked at Sharpe, as if for approval. But the latter turned his head away, already half aware that he was seeing the start of what well might be what the Yanks called a frame-up. It wasn't a pleasant realisation . . .

# Chapter Five

Schulze crouched in the dirty snow. He stared at the makeshift cage the *Amis* had thrown up for the prisoners. He had seen the type often enough before when the *Wehrmacht* had taken the Red Army soldiers prisoner by the thousand – the hundred thousand. There was the usual tumbledown farmhouse which would shelter their own people against the biting night cold to come. To the front of that there was a huge field, hastily encircled with barbed wire with machine-guns posted at each corner. Not that there would be much occasion for the *Ami* gunners to use their weapons. Their prisoners were too beat, frozen and starved to think of escaping. Their only war aim, Schulze knew from past experience in the Soviet 'paradise', would be to survive the night to come.

The *Amis* had 'fed' them, throwing them chunks of stale white bread and for those who had managed to secure one of the few cans, tins of spam and C-rations. The prisoners lay in the frozen mud as if they were too weak to walk, waiting probably for death. Otherwise they staggered around the compound beating their arms against their skinny chests trying to stay on their feet and keep warm. Other unfortunates lay dying in the yellow ordure next to the 'sanitation pits' the *Amis* had ordered the fit do dig, too weak to remove their stained, soaked trousers, slowly sinking into that unconsciousness which would be followed by death before the new dawn, abandoned by their comrades as too helpless to be cared for.

Schulze was not a sensitive man but even to him it was a heart-rending picture of the human condition at war and man's inhumanity to man. Crouched next him in their hiding place as they observed the camp, trying to spot von Dodenburg and waiting for the *Amis* to retreat to the warmth of the half-timbered, red-brick farmhouse, Matz whispered, "Remember that Ivan camp" – he meant a Russian POW camp – "where they sent in the two Alsatians to quieten the Ivans down, thinking that the Popovs would cream their skivvies at the sight of the hounds?"

Schulze nodded grimly. "Yes, I remember, Matzi," he answered. "Ten minutes later the Popovs threw out the dogs' furs – *empty*! They'd scoffed the frigging dogs, even the frigging bones, dead-stone cold!"

"Ay," Matz said. "And it ain't much better down there. There'll be scores of the poor barnshitters croaked it by dawn" – he paused abruptly and when he spoke again, his voice was animated by excitement and perhaps new hope. "There he is . . . the CO, Schulze."

"Where?"

"See the edge of the barn at three o'clock?"

"Got it, old house!"

"Lying in the shit with that other poor arsehole cradled in his arms," Matz answered urgently. "Fancy, Schulze, trying to look after somebody else in the condition he's in."

Schulze sucked his big, square teeth. "Yer right there, you Aspagarus Tarzan. On his last legs hiseen and looking after some other poor shit. Typical." He raised his voice as down below the big sergeant, swinging the bull's pizzle, posted the first batch of machine-gunners before retreating to the warm fug of the farmhouse. They could see from the grey smoke pouring from the chimney that whatever furniture the place had possessed was going up in the pot-bellied country stoves to heat their living quarters. "All right, the CO won't last the night under these conditions to my way of agreement."

"You're right there."

Schulze ignored the comment, as if his mind was fully concentrated on the problem at hand. "So there's no time to be lost. We've got to move if we want to rescue him before this night is out."

"Yes, wait till night falls and give the second batch of guards a chance to get sleepy and then we go in. We'll know where the *Amis* are all right. They're allus lighting cancer sticks and hollering to each other after dark and giving their positions away. Nervous Nellies, the lot o' them," he added contemptuously. "Real Christmas tree soldiers." He spat into the dirty snow.

"Thank yer frigging lucky stars they are," Schulze said. "We're in no position to tackle a mob of real soldiers, especially with the numbers we've got on our side. We've got to play this one cunning-like."

"With them clockwork cunts o' soldiers down there?" Matz said scornfully. "I could tackle that shower of shit with one hand tied behind me frigging back!"

Schulze ignored the scornful comment, as his mind raced while he worked out his hasty plan. Finally he spoke. "We'll get as close as we can, nobble the nearest M-G post just in case and then in and out with the CO like shit through a goose."

Matz absorbed the information for a moment before saying somewhat obscurely, "A diversion . . . that's what we need, Schulzi."

"What?"

"You heard, or have you bin eating too many big beans?"

"You'll be biting the end of my fist in half a mo,"

Schulze said threateningly, clenching a massive fist like a small steam shovel to emphasise the point.

"Up yours!"

Schulze took it in good part. "Can't, got a double-decker Berlin bus up there already*. Get on with it!"

"Irmgard," Matz said baldly.

"What about her?"

"She got a big pair o' lungs on her that could suffocate a man to death if he got caught between them and I 'spect she's got the usual sort of women's plumbing down below. Sort of take the *Ami* machine-gunner's mind off'n his popgun for a few minutes."

Schulze's big red face lit up. "Got yer, you evil, cunning arse-with-ears." He exclaimed in admiration, "Just let the *Ami* get a smell of her eau de farmyard and he'd have a revolver in his pocket like a howitzer!" He beamed in admiration at the little corporal. "Don't know where yer get 'em from – ideas like that – I swear I don't!"

Matz looked modest. "Some of us have got it up here," he tapped his forehead. "And others are called Sergeant Schulze!" His tone changed and became serious again. "All right, Schulzi, what's the drill?"

"This," his old running mate answered immediately and swiftly started to sketch in his rough-and-ready plan . . .

Slowly, as if his fingers were worked by rusty springs, von Dodenburg closed the dead youth's eyes and let the body slide from his grasp into the yellow, stinking faeces. Five or six metres away, a couple of ragged, wolfish-looking *landser* were squabbling over the dead man's hunk of bread,

---

* Berlin was the only German city with double-decker buses in the British fashion.

it, too, yellow with faecal stains. They rolled back and forth, tugging at the stinking bread as if it were priceless.

Von Dodenburg shook his head. So this was how it ended, he told himself sadly. This is what had happened to the Greater German *Wehrmacht*, that all-conquering army which had been the bane of Europe and which in a few short years had created an empire greater than that of Rome – a couple of ragged, lousy soldiers squabbling in the shit for a piece of bread. He closed his eyes momentarily and tried to blot out the scenes of despair and degradation all about him, wishing he were dead.

But at the back of his brain a harsh, cynical voice rasped, "It's not going to be that easy, Kuno . . . The Gods won't allow you to snuff it just like that, old house!" He frowned. The voice was right. Still, he knew instinctively that he'd better die soon. If he survived this march of death into the more orderly circumstances of a regular camp where there would be checks on people's identities, their outfits and what they had done in the great world-shaking conflicts before they had been captured, he knew that he personally would be in for trouble. The SS would be made a scapegoat, for the whole German people. The victorious Allies would not be able to indict the whole nation. Besides, they would be needed for the conflict to come with the Russians. But someone would have to pay for what the Third Reich had done to Europe since 1939 and he didn't need a crystal ball to know that the ones who would do the paying would be the SS, and in particular the members of its most elite regiment SS Wotan.

What was he to do?

For a few moments he was tempted to use the last of his strength and attempt to rally the men lying apathetically in the mud and faeces all around him. They vastly outnumbered their *Ami* guards, even if the latter were armed and they weren't. Besides they were on the holy soil of the Reich once more and he could tell from the hollow boom and thunder of the permanent barrage to the east of them they weren't more than twelve or fourteen kilometres from the front. A night's march, even in their condition, and they would be safe among their own people once more. Yet in order to succeed he would have to leave behind, at the *Amis'* mercy, the most vulnerable of their comrades – the wounded and the sick. He simply couldn't do that.

*"Well, then, what's the alternative?"* that harsh little voice at the back of his brain demanded with a rasp. "Will you just lie here like a bunch of old arseholes and wait for death, man?"

But before Kuno von Dodenburg could answer that single, overwhelming question there was a faint whistling sound coming from beyond the wire. The whistler was concealed from view by the evening gloom and the fir forest to the east of the camp. He frowned. Who out there could be whistling on a terrible day like this? What would occasion any German – no *Ami* would want to expose himself to the dangers of occupied Germany outside the camp's perimeter – to whistle in this hour of defeat? His frown deepened. What did it mean – and by now it was becoming clear that there was something vaguely familiar about the whistling.

Suddenly he snapped his fingers with abrupt animation as he recognised the tune. *"Clear the streets . . . beat the drum,"* the old words came roaring through his dazed head from those great days when they had marched from one victory to another. *"Here come the men of WO-TAN . . . !"* It was the famed marching song of SS Assault Regiment Wotan!

He felt new hope surge through his pain-racked, emaciated body, as he became fully aware of what he was listening to and its implications. One at least of his men, old men –

there had to be more than one of them – were out there. And he guessed why. They had spotted him. Why else whistle that marching song? And they were telling him that they were going to do something about it. Those unknown Wotan troopers out there in the growing darkness were going to rescue him and the others from this *Ami* hellhole before it was too late.

Hurriedly he pursed his cracked, parched lips, and then as an afterthought moistened them to make sure. Next moment he started to whistle that old familiar tune himself. Thus the unknown trooper outside would know that he had received that signal of hope.

Moments later the whistling beyond the wire had ceased once more and there was no sound other than the whisper of the wind in the skeletal trees and the soft moans of the dying. But von Dodenburg, his mind racing, heard neither. There was but one thought uppermost in his mind that shut out everything else.

*HE WAS GOING TO BE RESCUED AFTER ALL.*

# Chapter Six

The blonde 'Hyde Park commando' stretched out her long, silken-clad legs slowly, languorously. Colonel Schroeder swallowed hard and the fat hand holding his drink shook. With her legs spread he could see two things. One, she was wearing no panties, two, she wasn't a true blonde.

The whore smiled at him, as in the background Glenn Miller, who had been missing now for nearly two weeks, blared away and the young officers jitterbugged, as she said in the accent of North London: "You like it, Colonel?"

The colonel's hand holding the glass of scotch trembled even more.

The blonde emphasised her point. She wet her middle finger, her scarlet nail varnish making it look as if it were dipped in blood, and ran the glistening finger down the length of her dark thatch. "I'll give you a good time, Colonel," she promised huskily. "I know what you Yanks like best." She pursed her thick lips and puffed him a wet kiss. The colonel's hand trembled violently.

Sitting deeper in the darkness of the drinks' club, Major Sharpe smiled. Among other things, he told himself, the blonde 'Hyde Park Commando' whores, one of the many who swarmed all over London these days, was probably poxed up to her plucked eyebrows. She might well give the randy American a nice juicy dose of the clap. But he said nothing, enjoying this noctural drama as the colonel fought his sense of duty and decorum in front of a junior officer and his desire to get his wick up the whore's drawers, though in this particular case she was minus that unessential item of underclothing.

Sharpe turned his attention away from the randy American colonel to the tiny circle of polished wood called the dance floor, where elegant young staff officers danced with the whores to the records of Glenn Miller, playing the evocative tunes of that year 'The Little Brown Jug . . . In the Mood' and others which would become their lasting image of the great conflict when they were old and infirm and lived off their memories.

All of them looked ruddy-cheeked and very healthy, intelligent young men who were the products of America's Ivy League colleges and who had been too smart to allow themselves to be conscripted into the infantry, who now – undernourished, filthy and miserably cold – were dying in their scores, their hundreds on the other side of the Channel.

Schroeder stopped looking at the whore's dark thatch and followed the direction of Major Sharpe's gaze. It seemed that he was reading the one-armed Englishman's mind, for he said: "You think they're dodging the war, don't you, Major?"

Sharpe said nothing.

"And you're right," Schroeder said with a fat, knowing smile. "Because they're smart operators. It's something they learned at Dartmouth, Princeton, Harvard and the like. They're rich men's sons. They can think farther than this war. They'll go back stateside in one piece wearing the same medals as the poor suckers who did the fighting and if Daddy's rich enough and has the pull they'll go into politics. Their ticket will be 'We fought for your freedom' – that sort o' crap." Schroeder pulled a face, as if the whole concept was an absurd silliness. "With a bit of luck some of them will be congressmen in a few years' time, especially those young guys from the East Coast where the deals are made. A few of them will probably make it to the Senate." He leaned forward confidentially, as the blonde glanced at her nails in a bored fashion. All the same, she kept her long legs spread for the otherwise engaged fat Yank; business was business after all. "But all of them will end up rich, Sharpe. *Very rich*! That's the point of the whole exercise."

Sharpe made no comment. Though he did wonder why Colonel Schroeder was giving him this lecture in the middle of what was little better than a 'knocking shop', as the troops would have called the place.

"So what has this got to do with us and our particular problem?" Schroeder went on.

He answered his own question. "I shall tell you, Sharpe. First, I'm working in General Ike's interest and there will surely be a medal in it for me if I don't foul up. How can I foul up?" Again he answered his own rhetorical question. "By not giving him what he wants. At this moment what Ike wants to is to stop the rot – the thousands of GIs bugging out at the front, refusing to fight and surrendering to the Krauts." His sharp eyes took in the English major's face, as if he were trying to ascertain if the latter understood what he was getting at. He must have decided that Sharpe did for he continued, "What Ike wants is to show the average dough that it's no use surrendering or attempting to bug out because either way the Krauts are going to slaughter them. You understand? These Krauts, unknown at present, are going to have to be fall guys."

Now Sharpe nodded his understanding. He got it. Ike wanted to frighten into fighting any GI wavering in his loyalty because that was the only way he was going to save his neck if the Krauts caught up with him.

Schroeder paused and let his words sink in. On the chair opposite, the 'Hyde Park commando' was getting bored and fidgety. She kept closing and crossing her legs impatiently, as if she couldn't wait much longer for the inevitable. The fat colonel swallowed hard. His plump, soft face grew even redder, but he contained himself, for he evidently thought it important to finish his little lecture. And now Sharpe was convinced the man wasn't talking for the sake of it. He, Sharpe, was somehow to be involved in his devious scheme.

"But it doesn't end there," Schroeder went on, confident now that he had the one-armed Englishman's interest.

"How?"

"Like this. To be frank, Sharpe, I don't give a free fuck about what is happening at the front. Yes, you might look shocked. But that's the way it is. The whole of Supreme HQ is like that. Everyone's more concerned with his own future than the war. All of them from Ike downwards have got their eye on the main chance." He puffed out his thick, sensual lips scornfully, "Why even Ike, good old democratic Ike, the GIs' general, is aiming to become President of the United States one of these days. You mark my words. Yours truly is no different. If this business with the Krauts can get me my first star—" he meant the insignia of a brigadier general – "then it's worth a lot of extra effort on my part. Why?"

Again he answered his own question and Sharpe told himself these rhetorical pauses had to be part-and-parcel of a lawyer's technique. "Because that single star is going to open new doors for me in civilian life. The kikes, for instance," he smirked and added, "Jews to you. The star'll mean I'll move up another step in my business with them as a corporate lawyer. Didn't I fight for them in the big war?" He eyed the blonde cynically, "Well, sort of, I guess. But at the same time it'll put me in good with old money. To them, as a brigadier general, I'm not just a cheap shyster in the pay of the New York Jews. No sir, I'm a man who reached the rank of general in the United States Army. That'll look better on my card than attorney-at-law!"

"But where's this leading us, Colonel?" Sharpe asked, getting a little sick by now of Schroeder's harangue.

The fat American wasn't offended. He said easily, "I was wondering when you were going to ask. You see, we've got to make more of this than just a temporary wartime episode. We've got to make it into something which shows just how essentially evil the Krauts are. Look what they did to your guys. People must ask that question and when they do they've got to find out that the Germans have done similar evil things all over Europe during six years of war. We've got to use this case, Sharpe, to show to the world and, in particular, to the United States, that the Krauts are an abomination . . . that they were – and are – a unique race with the Mark of Cain on them. And the guy who has made this world-shaking discovery," he paused and grinned suddenly, "is no less a person than *Brigadier General Schroeder*," he emphasised the rank as if it were already his. "Lester J. Schroeder, Junior, that's what it is all about, Sharpe!"

In the two years since he had been transferred to the SIB after El Alamein, Major Sharpe had seen and experienced some very odd things. In that time he had been forced to plumb the depths of human degradation and brutality, and had met some self-seeking, cold-blooded cynics among the hard-boiled cops and legal men who dealt with military criminals. Undoubtedly there had been men among them who had pursued wrongdoers not for personal gain or the kudos of a conviction, but simply because it had been their duty to do so. But there had been others who had been out for personal gain and prestige. Secretly, perhaps they had hoped to win promotion through their success in the pursuit of criminals. But if they had, they had kept those personal hopes strictly to themselves. At least, there was no place in the SIB for office-seekers.

It was almost as if Colonel Schroeder was assessing the thoughts going through the Englishman's head – Sharpe told himself he'd have to watch the fat Yank – for he was shrewd, very shrewd, in his own fashion, because he said after a while, "Now, Major, how about you getting on the gravy train as well?"

"Me?"

Shroeder looked at Sharpe, staring pointedly at the missing arm, the empty jacket sleeve neatly tucked into the belt of his Sam Browne. "If you don't mind my French, Sharpe, you're slightly fucked up, you know. There's not much of a future for you in the British Army with that missing arm. I hope you don't mind my saying so, but there in not much use for one-armed infantry officers."

Sharpe flushed slightly. Schroeder had touched a sore point. It was something which had occupied him greatly now that the war seemed to be coming to an end: what was he going to do in peacetime? All he had ever known since he had gone up to Sandhurst in the early 1930s had been soldiering.

"But *might* be a future, if you could get a promotion to the rank of – say – colonel." He hurried on before the Britisher could ask questions. "My chief has talked to your chief and if you wish you can join the investigation team once we've wound up the preliminaries here."

"Doing what?"

"In the near future we've got to round up as many survivors of SS Assault Regiment Wotan – the more the merrier."

"Why?"

"Because we need their testimony. There's bound to be rotten apples among them who'd sell their own mothers if it would pay them to do so. And we'll need those kind of statements to nail the guy in charge of this Wotan outfit."

"You mean like the testimony of that cook in Harrogate?" Sharpe queried, a little cynically.

Schroeder ignored the comment. Instead he said, "Once we've cleared up the present mess at the front and start moving into Germany proper, then we break that country down into Zones of Occupation – Russian, French, American and British – and you know armies. They don't like to cooperate with each other, even if they are allies. They guard their rights jealously. We expect we're going to have some trouble finding the SS jerks we need in the future British Zone of Occupation. That's where you would come in, Major."

Sharpe looked at him keenly. "You mean a kind of liaison man for you in the British Zone?" he asked.

"Exactly, you could open the kind of doors that would make for quick action that would take more time by us, er, Yanks." He beamed at Sharpe winningly and across the room the blonde whore, hearing the word 'time' looked suddenly attentive. "What do you think? I've been assured, Sharpe, that there'll be a promotion in this for you, if you don't foul up."

"Even if we have to rely on false witnesses such as that chap back at Harrogate?" Sharpe asked, unable to resist the temptation to score over this fat Yank who seemed to know all the answers and all the angles.

"The luck of the draw, as they say," the other man replied easily. He fumbled with his flies while the whore looked on attentively. The colonel beamed at him, "American ingenuity," he answered Sharpe's unasked question. "A zipper instead of fly buttons. Makes for a quicker draw, if you follow me. Yanks don't have much time to waste. What's it going to be Major?"

Sharpe nodded reluctantly. "All right, Colonel, I'm with you."

"Good!" Schroeder said, dismissing the matter. Then he played with the new toy, rapidly zipping his flies open and shut, a pleasurable grin on his fat, flushed face. The blonde opposite stubbed out her cigarette, swung her long silken-clad legs round, giving them both a last glimpse of that dark thatch. "All right, girlie," Schroeder said thickly, "let's fuck."

On the floor the record was playing 'Chattanooga-Choo-Choo'. The blonde pranced about, wiggling her hips, and with her right hand she simulated a train driver pulling on the cord that worked the whistle of an American locomotive.

Sharpe grinned briefly. At least she wasn't bullshitting, she was in it for the money. But above the mellow, muted sounds of the Glenn Miller record and the shuffle of the dancers' feet on the tiny dance floor he could hear the chug-chug in the sky above London of what sounded like a broken-down two-stroke motorbike.

"VI doodlebug," he said to himself, recognising the sound. Then his grin deepened. Colonel Lester J. Schroeder Junior would soon be in dire need of that quick-acting zip-fastener when the doodlebug fell out of the night sky.

"Yessiree," he exclaimed *sotto voce*, imitating the colonel's fruity voice, "my zipper is going up faster than it went down!" With that Sharpe walked out into the cleaner, fresher air of the war.

# Chapter Seven

"Abe," the American machine-gunner guarding the eastern perimeter of the cage, breathed. "Willya get a load of that broad! Brother, is she stacked!" He turned his torch on the German woman who had appeared suddenly out of the night, whistling softly as if she might be out for a moonlight stroll in peacetime, not in the middle of a battle zone. "Je-sus, don't them tits make yer drool, buddy!" He smacked his wet lips.

Next to him, the loader whistled softly. He was impressed despite the freezing cold. In the circle of hard white light he could see the figure of a stocky farm girl, dressed in some kind of rough homespun. But it wasn't the awful dress which caught his attention, it was her stupendous breasts which bulged out from the material as if they might burst it at any moment. "Joe," he choked, totally forgetting the fact that this strange girl had appeared from nowhere long after the six o'clock curfew, and to cap it all was whistling for some reason known only to herself.

"Yeah?"

"Have you got any candy or Hitler's secret weapon?" he said, referring to a sickly, issue chocolate bar that the troops hated. "Boy, I've got to get up her drawers if it's last thing I—"

At that moment he was caught completely off guard as his helmet was tilted forward by rough, unknown hands and the hardwood club caught him a terrific blow behind his right ear. He didn't even groan. Even before he hit the frozen snow face-first, he was out like a light.

"What! . . . What the goddam Sam Hill," the gunner yelled, the torch falling out of his hand with the shock of the surprise attack. The two shadowy figures, one of them a giant of a man, the other half his size and limping badly, then fell upon him. "*Don't!*" The club smashed down on his right shoulder. He gasped with pain and fought off the sensation of falling. But not for long. The big man grunted. The gunner caught the flash of brass glistening in the light of the torch, casting its beam across the surface of the snow. Next instant his mouth and lips exploded in a welter of blood. Spitting out his teeth, stars exploding in front of his eyes, he pitched forward unconscious.

Routinely Matz started to search the two unconscious Americans sprawled in the snow, their breathing coming in the harsh gasps of severely injured men. "Knock it off, arse-with-ears," Schulze snarled. "Heave me any firewater they've got and let's get moving before the *Amis* catch us with our knickers down."

"Have a heart, Schulzi!" Matz began to plead.

"I ain't frigging got one," Schulze cut him off brutally. "*Move it!*"

As they abandoned the bodies and Irmgard disappeared into the night, her part in the escape plan over for the time being, the two of them started to lever up the barbed wire, potato-sacking protecting their hands against the cruel barbs.

With Schulze exerting all his tremendous strength, knowing as he did that time was of the essence and that they could be discovered at any moment – it needed only one of the guard to come outside the hut to urinate and they would be discovered – they had soon levered a gap in the wire large enough for a man to escape. While they did so they watched not only the hut but the prisoners as well, lying in the frozen mud, tossing and turning and moaning, a fortunate few of them slipping into a fitful sleep.

Back at the farm, they had already discussed the other German POWs while they had considered the escape plan. Schulze had been hard and final. "We can't take 'em with us. They're no-hopers anyway," he had said with an air of finality. "We're getting the chief out and that's that. If the rest want to make a run for it, they can. But we don't want them all over the place so that the *Amis* start a large-scale hunt for them. They might not bother about one of our people doing a bunk, but the whole lot –" he left the rest of the sentence unsaid, and Matz had looked at him, worried. "Yes, I get you, Schulzi, but what are we going to do once when we get the CO, out? Where do we go?"

Schulze had looked blank. "Let's worry about it when we get that far. First things first. Let's get him out . . . !"

They were now through the wire, nerves tingling as they entered the camp at a half-crouch, tensed for the first cry of rage that would set off the alarm. None came. Slowly but surely they worked their way through the mass of miserable humanity that had once been the cream of the Greater German *Wehrmacht*. Every now and again they paused and, hesitantly, whistled softly a few snatches of 'Wotan's' marching song. But so far there had been no response, though they knew from Irmgard that the CO was aware they were outside the camp and were sick and wounded as was von Dodenburg, that he'd guess they were attempting to get him out of the hell-camp.

Five minutes passed . . . then ten. They were making awfully slow progress and Schulze's anxiety started to increase rapidly. Their luck wouldn't hold out much longer, he was sure of that. Then suddenly he heard it, faint and a little out of tune, as though the man whistling their old marching song was finding it a strain to do so. "It's him," he hissed urgently, grabbing Matz as thought he might charge forward at the news and raise the alarm.

"Yer right. Coming from the spot where your fiancée," (he said the word sarcastically), "said he was earlier on."

"Now then, plush arse, don't take Irmgard's name in vain," Schulze said severely. "She might well become my fiancée in due course, it depends how good she is at the two-backed beast. I rather fancy to become a landed gent after the war."

"Yer, landed on yer fat arse!" Matz said unkindly and then added in a businesslike tone, "Come, digit out of the frigging orifice, let's get on with it, before them frigging Yanks tumble to us."

But already the train of events was being set in motion which would ensure that the Yanks did exactly that. PFC Jenkins, of the Fifth Provost Company, was the hardest man of a very hard bunch of redneck state troopers who had volunteered as one from their home state in order to avoid being conscripted into the infantry. He, like the rest of them, was a typical product of the prejudiced white trash that inhabited the rural areas south of the Mason-Dixon Line. Before he had dodged the draft in 1941 he had done his share of lynching 'nigras', as he called them; had chased 'them fancy-talking Jew-Niggers' of the National Association for the Advancement of Colored People back over the state line when they had been tempted to turn the local 'nigger's uppity' and ask for the vote; and had taken many a bribe from the local moonshiners in the traditionally 'dry' state. But since Jenkins had come to Europe he had developed another and much more profitable sideline.

"*Gold teeth!*" as he was fond of explaining to his cronies in the know about his morbid, illegal, activities. "All these here Europeans" – he had turned the word into at least four syllables in that slow Southern drawl of his – "have their mouths full of gold teeth. Worth a fortune back in the States to them Jewboys running the local hock stores." But there had always been one catch in his newly found source of income, as macabre as it was a very distinct possibility of being sent to the stockade or even Leavenworth in Kansas, if he were ever caught pulling out the gold teeth of the dead, and sometimes in his overwhelming greed the not-yet dead.

Now, a little high on looted German schnapps, confident that most of his comrades of the Provost Company were asleep in the warm fug of the German hut, he slunk out, his gloved paw clutching the vital pincers. He had already noted his next victims: two young grenadiers with single gold teeth and some kind of portly, middle-aged officer, who had a splendid gold bridge. All of them had been too weak to get out of the yellow, overflowing pit which served as a primitive latrine. Even as he had gone inside for the evening chow he had told himself happily they wouldn't survive the night and even if they were still alive in the early hours of the December morning – he had grinned to himself at the thought – it didn't matter a hill of beans. He'd ensure they wouldn't survive to tell anyone what he had done to their mouths.

The icy cold hit him almost a physical blow in his fat, evil, unshaven face. It was as cold as death, but that didn't worry him. He was too excited at the thought of the kind of dough he would make this night. Even the Jewboys wouldn't be able to trick him out of a fair-sized wad of greenbacks that the gold would bring him in the hockshops back stateside; and by now he was something of an expert at guessing the weight of the gold teeth he extracted. These had looked near to – give or take an ounce

– six to seven ounces, especially the dying Kraut officer's expensive bridge.

Warmed by the thought, he crept through the dark towards the latrine like a grey wolf. In his gloved hand he clenched the pincers at the ready. These days he had the technique worked out to perfection. A firm hold of the tooth at the base. Test that the pincers were gripping. A wrench to the right and then to the left. The crack and tear as the root broke. Another heave and out it would come, the gold gleaming against the dark red blood, to be popped into the jeweller's chamois leather bag which contained his other booty, teeth, rings, and a pair of large gold earrings with a piece of shrivelled white flesh attached to one of them that he had ripped from the ear-lobes of a dying Belgian woman. Sometimes at night, when the others were asleep, he would pull the leather pouch out from where it hung beneath his khaki OD shirt and gloat over his treasures, knowing that one day they'd buy him the freedom from taking orders from some fat-bellied, bird-brained officer of the State Police.

Suddenly he stopped in his tracks, every nerve jingling and alert, eyes narrowed to slits as he attempted to peer through the inky gloom and see what had caused the noise. *Nothing*. All the same, a sixth sense told him that there was something up there to his front. He cocked his head to one side and listened intently, then caught a faint whisper in Kraut. That wasn't particularly unusual, the whole goddam stinking place was full of the Kraut bastards. But the smell which now assailed his nostrils was overpowering the stench even of the Kraut shit. It was that typical cloying stink of the black, coarse tobacco the Krauts smoked in their little pipes – and all the tobacco they could find had been taken off their prisoners two days before. That way they had been more willing to barter their little remaining treasures – wedding rings, wristwatches and the like – for a handful of the greedily sought-after American cigarettes. So where did these unknown Krauts get their cruddy makings from?

A moment later he had the answer, as he also heard the chink of a weapon striking a belt buckle or the like. These were new Krauts from the outside – *and the bastards were armed*!

PFC Jenkins would never win the Congressional Medal of Honor for bravery. In fact, to use a phrase which he had picked up somewhere or other, "Brother, I'm the world's greatest devoted coward." All the same, he had to do something about these unknown armed Krauts who had appeared in their midst from nowhere, and do it soon before the shit hit the frigging fan.

Not turning, the Military Policeman backed off on tiptoe, aware now of the shadowy figures moving about some ten yards or so to his front. There appeared to be three or four of them and, farther on, he could hear other movement, perhaps outside the wire of the cage. Suddenly he felt very scared. He needed help. He heard of these Kraut werewolves* everyone was talking about: the German underground movement operating behind Allied lines, manned by youthful fanatics who would slit your throat without compunction. They were rumoured to do other even more terrible things as well as to their prisoners. "Let those homicidal cunts catch yer," they said apprehensively in the bars and messes of the Allied soldiers over beer and schnapps, "and they'll have the nuts off'n ya with a frigging blunt razor blade."

In his fear he stumbled. He caught himself in time, but he had been unable to stifle the cry of alarm he had made as he had almost fallen. The Krauts lurking in the shadows to his front heard it immediately. There was a cry of rage, a shout

---

\* A German resistance movement (Fraust).

of warning, a challenge. Suddenly scarlet flame stabbed the darkness viciously.

PFC Jenkins screamed shrilly, high and hysterical like a woman. Red-hot flame surged through his shattered chest. Blood rose up in his throat and choked him. He started to fall, one hand instinctively clutching the little leather bag beneath his woollen shirt as he went down.

Next moment, as he hit the shit, dead almost immediately, lights started to flash urgently in the MPs' house. An angry voice exclaimed loudly, "What the fuck's going on?" as a wild burst of fire erupted from the windows and the first flares began to hiss into the night sky. A dozen yards away a crestfallen Sergeant Schulze muttered, *"Holy strawsack, now the clock's really in the pisspot."* And it was.

# Chapter Eight

"*Fuck this for a goddam game o' soldiers!*" Sergeant Schulze cursed furiously.

As Matz bent down to raise an obviously very weak von Dodenburg, Schulze raised his pistol and without seeming to aim pressed the trigger. In the nearest window a dark shadow fell back screaming as the pane shattered. His torch went out abruptly. But the guards everywhere were waking up. Already an anxious, angry Schulze could hear them shouting orders as they tumbled out of the back of the farmhouse, protected from the fire of the two intruders in the compound. "How's he look, Matzi?" he demanded urgently, keeping his voice low so that the CO lying in the yellow mud and shit wouldn't hear.

"Not so rosy, old house," Matz answered gloomily as he took the strain and tried to raise the semi-conscious former CO of SS Assault Regiment Wotan.

Von Dodenburg must have caught his whispered answer, for as an American started blasting off a whole salvo of tommy-gun ammunition close by, the tracer bullets zipping through the darkness, glowing and lethal, he sighed, "Don't bother about me, Corporal . . . get the others . . . out . . ." He seemed to have the greatest difficulty in issuing even the simplest of orders.

"Don't talk like that, sir," Schulze said encouragingly. "It's gonna be roses . . . roses all the way, sir!" Schulze ducked as a vicious burst of slugs sliced the air all around him. "Nasty arseholes, the *Amis*. Try to shoot a poor stubble-hopper even when he's on an errand of mercy," he sighed and fired the next instant. The guard, crouching in the doorway some fifty metres away was lifted off his feet by the impact at such close range. He was slammed against the wall as if propelled there by some gigantic fist. "See, that's what yer get for being naughty—" Schulze never finished his sentence. A grenade exploded nearby. Red-hot slivers of metal, accompanied by yellow faeces, erupted all around the two SS men crouched protectively over the frail, wounded body of their former commanding officer.

"What bastards!" Matzi cursed in disgust. "They're even flinging shit at us now."

From outside they could hear the familiar high-pitched burr of a German Schmeisser machine-pistol. Hurriedly, a worried Schulze told himself the handful of survivors of Wotan were already being engaged by the *Amis*, who greatly outnumbered them. It was time for them to get out of the camp – at the double. "Come on, Matzi!" he urged, shouting above the crazy snap-and-crackle of the firefight. "Get cracking!" He reached down and gave a hefty tug at the same time as Matz began to raise von Dodenburg. Groggily the officer rose to his feet and stood there swaying as bullets cut the air all around.

Schulze, his broad face hollowed out to a blood-red death's head by the flares now shooting into the night sky, as the hard-pressed American MPs summoned help from the nearest friendly fighting units not far off, looked at his old running mate, Matz, in dismay. He said nothing but Corporal Matz knew what he was thinking. The CO was in no shape to make a run for it, especially now in the middle of this sudden battle. "What are we gonna do?" he asked a little helplessly.

"What the shitting hell do *you* think?" Schulze snarled. "We're not gonna leave the chief after all this. Come on – *los*!"

With his pistol clenched in a fist like a small steamhammer, Schulze threw his free arm round the skinny frame of his old CO. "Come on, sir! We're gonna make it. The boys are outside, waiting for you."

"Leave me, you big rogue!" Von Dodenburg pleaded miserably with the giant. "I've wasted enough of your lives in the last weeks. Save yourselves while you can. Don't bother about . . ." He coughed and staggered as if he had been wounded again, but he recovered almost immediately "Nothing," he choked. "Just thought I was going to black out for a moment . . ."

Schulze wasted no further time on talk. "Cover my rear," he commanded and then not waiting to check whether Matz had done so he grabbed von Dodenburg as effortlessly as if he were a small child and, with a grunt slung the weakly protesting officer over his shoulder.

Now, as the POWs yelled and cried in fear, some of them dropping into the noxious faeces in their desperate attempt find cover from the slugs cutting the air with lethal intensity, the two NCOs worked their way to the gap in the wire. Covering Schulze's gigantic back, Matz snapped off individual shots to left and right at any target that presented itself. But even as he did so he realised that his ammunition was running low and in the distance he could already hear the rattle of armoured tracks and the howl of motors fighting the icy night. "Great crap on the Christmas tree!" he cursed fervently. Everything was going wrong.

"*Tempo, Mensch*!" Schulze gasped, staggering on through the POWs, who stretched out their hands imploring, pleading with him to take them with him as well. But there was no time for that, Schulze knew. Time for the little band of hard-pressed Wotan troopers was running out rapidly. They'd be for the chop if they were not soon clear of the POW camp and up in the hills heading for their hiding place.

Again von Dodenburg, realising too that they were in a desperate state, cried "For God's sake, Schulze, leave me!" He forced some strength into his voice. "I *order* you to drop me and make a run for it . . . do you hear, Sergeant Schulze? *I'm giving you a direct order!*"

"Got two tin ears, sir," Schulze breathed, knowing that the CO was right. All the same he was prepared to take one last chance.

A burst of machine-gun fire sliced the air behind him. Matz stumbled and collapsed on one knee.

"*HIT?*" Schulze cried in alarm, staggering to a stop.

"No," his old running mate yelled above the murderous racket, "The shiteheels have just gone and shot my shitting wooden leg to ribbons!"

"That too," Schulze moaned and for one awful moment he was at a loss what to do.

Next moment his mind was made up for him. A grenade exploded only feet away. The big NCO staggered back, bleeding heavily from a myriad razor-sharp cuts on his face. Involuntarily, shocked by the suddenness of it all, he allowed von Dodenburg to slip from his grasp. With a gasp the CO landed in the mire. For a moment, while Schulze staggered wildly, trying to wipe the blood from his eyes, half-panicked that he had been blinded, he lay there gasping. But as Schulze discovered to his relief that the blood was coming from his gashed forehead, von Dodenburg said weakly, "Go, while there's still a chance. There'll be other opportunities . . . better ones . . . to get me out . . . *Now go!*" He forced iron into his voice, as if he were still back in charge, full of the vigour of youth – "All that piss and vinegar," as Schulze used to characterise it – "*MOVE!*"

Hardly aware of what he was going to do, Schulze grasped Matz. Together, with Matz hopping on the shattered wooden stump of his 'tin leg' as best he could, the two of them disappeared into the confused, glowing-red darkness. Behind them, lying in the mud, a completely exhausted von Dodenburg – it was as if an invisible tap had been opened and all energy had drained from his emaciated body – sobbed suddenly, knowing that he had come to the end of the road. There was no more hope for him now. Silently, his skinny shoulders racked with pain, emotion and despair, he started to weep like a broken-hearted child.

# Book Two

*Ike Takes a Hand*

# Chapter One

*Click!*

The icy white spotlight flicked on with startling suddenness. On the floor of that dark, dank underground cell *Oberscharführer* Doerr, lying on his blood-stained stretcher, stared mesmerised at the abrupt light. It was the first he had seen in days. Indeed since they had brought him from the makeshift hospital to this strange place inhabited by shadows, who neither spoke nor showed their faces but glided from place to place in their rubber-soled shoes like grey ghosts, it was the first sound he recalled hearing. Now, although the spotlight playing on the dusty concrete floor was powered by electric batteries, which under other circumstances would be virtually noiseless, he rejoiced in the faint purring of the light. Perhaps, as the wounded SS man he lay there, watching the light move slowly towards him, the spotlight's movement meant he was alive; that he wasn't merely dreaming.

Time passed leadenly, as the light came ever closer. But now, obviously, he knew that there were others with him behind that light in the dank cell.

Once more he heard the scampering of what he supposed were clawed feet, perhaps those of rats, which had badly disturbed him in his cell. But there was something else present, too. Now he could detect a distinctly sweet odour, perhaps some cheap after-shave lotion – and that of good *Ami* cigarettes. He gasped longingly, almost sexually. "Christ!" he muttered in the rough, tough fashion of the days gone by before he had become a prisoner and had learned to keep his mouth shut, if he didn't want to risk a blow with the metal butt of a rifle, "I'd give my right nut for a puff of that cancer stick!"

But there was no 'cancer stick' for *Oberscharführer* Doerr, late of SS Assault Regiment Wotan before the *Amis* had shot off his right arm the previous October in Aachen. Instead, a cool, detatched voice, speaking perfect German, intoned coldly, "You are *Oberscharführer* Doerr of the SS. State your regiment or division – *now*!" There was no 'please', no attempt to wheedle information out of him; no hint of a threat if he didn't answer. The voice was toneless. It said simply, without complications, "Tell me this information and don't waste any more of my time."

The big career SS non-commissioned officer considered for a few moments as he tried to penetrate the inky blackness behind the spotlight. The voice was German all right; native-born too. The way the unseen speaker pronounced his sibilants made him think he came from the north, to be precise, perhaps Hamburg. They pronounced 'S' like that up there on the coast. Finally he decided his tack – he'd lie. After all didn't all old soldiers – those stubble hoppers who had been smart enough to survive the debacle of Russia – lied 'the blue from the heavens', as they used to say in happier times. "Me and the SS," he said scornfully, telling himself that his voice sounded very strange after not speaking to anyone for days on end. "That'll be the day! Only Party arseholes and greenbeaks who haven't got all their cups in the cupboard joined the SS!"

He waited.

There was no sound save the soft purr of the electric motor and the uneasy scampering of those clawed feet once more.

Despite the dank coldness of the underground chamber, he began to sweat. He didn't quite know why, for he wasn't afraid. Perhaps it was the strangeness of it all.

"Why is it then," the northern voice said harshly, "that you've got your SS blood group, *Scharführer*, tattooed beneath your left armpit?"

His mind raced. He had been expecting that particular question. The *Amis*, he knew, hated the SS like poison. Back in the camp he had seen fellow SS men heat spoons and apply the red-hot metal to those tell-tale blue marks in an attempt to burn them away. But of course the burn itself was a dead give-away. "It was when I was first called up," he answered glibly, his answer already pat, "the frigging bone-mender who did my medical was blue as a violet. He had firewater coming out of his earholes, he was so pissed—"

"Get on with it," the voice of the unseen man demanded.

"All right, all right! So the drunken shitebag thought I was going into the SS and he had the orderly do the mark under my armpit . . ." He let his words tail away. Already he could sense that the man behind the spotlight didn't believe him.

"You burnt your paybook," the voice said after a few moments. "But *our* bone-menders have had a look at you. You've been wounded more than three times and you've got the silver wound medal so we anticipated that with the last wound you received the average doctor would have been slack – you wouldn't be much good in an ordinary infantry outfit. In your case that didn't happen. *Our* bone-mender said you obviously had first-class treatment, including penicillin captured from us at Arnhem. Only the SS has access to that particular drug. "For the first time the disembodied voice was animated, even angry. "All right!" the interrogator snapped, "Let's not piss about any more. Get off the pisspot and tell us what SS outfit you really belonged to. If your nose is clean, nothing will happen to you. I promise you that."

He hesitated, his mind racing. He was no fool. He knew by now from enemy propaganda radio broadcasts, in particular from the so-called 'German Soldiers' Transmitter, Radio Calais'\* that the whole of the SS was regarded by the enemy as nothing more than a gangster outfit. But at the same time he knew, too, that certain SS outfits didn't figure largely as criminal in Allied thinking. Mostly they were the SS alpine units which had fought in the remote Finnish forests and around Leningrad against the Russians. Somehow he felt he'd be safe insisting that he had belonged to an SS mountain division. He gave a quick prayer that he was right and took the plunge. "All right," he growled, like someone who knew that he was beaten. "Before I was wounded I was with the Sixth SS Mountain Division and then, as you know I copped one before the Division could take part in the fighting against you lot in the West." He licked his suddenly dry lips and waited.

There was a hollow laugh from behind the light. Suddenly someone, perhaps his interrogator, directed the beam right onto his face. He blinked hard and turned his head to escape the blinding, harsh-white beam. The light followed his attempt to do so. He thought he might protest, perhaps curse, "Take that fucking light out of my eyes, you arse-with-ears!" However, he didn't. There was something uncanny and insidiously frightening about this underground chamber that told him it might not be too wise to chance his arm. "Do you expect me to believe that?" the voice said scornfully. "We've examined your body with a fine-tooth comb while you were unconscious. If I remember rightly there were no signs on

---

\* A British black propaganda station aimed at the average German soldier.

the feet, the palms of the hands, the ears or nose that you'd ever had frostbite, which you probably would have had if you'd been in an SS mountain division. The closest you've ever been to frostbite, my friend, is a Langenese ice-cream." And this time someone else tittered in the darkness. His interrogator was not alone. There were others staring at him in the inky darkness, trying to assess his every reaction. He experienced a sinking feeling. This time, he told himself, "You're right up to your hooter in the crap, Karl!" What was he going to do, goddamnit to hell?

"On the other hand," the voice continued, "your whole body is permeated with the stink of diesel oil. No, my friend, you weren't with the mountain boys, you were with the panzers. Now then, who were you with? *Das Reich*, the Adolf Hitler Bodyguard – they were at Aachen in November where you were wounded and captured – the Hitler Youth?" The interrogator paused ever so slightly but *Oberscharführer* Doerr caught the hesitation. "Or perhaps SS Assault Regiment Wotan. Was that your mob, eh?"

Doerr felt an icy finger of fear trace its way slowly down the small of his back. They had him, the *Ami* bastards. They'd got him by the balls. *THEY KNEW. THEY'D KNOWN ALL ALONG THAT HE'D BELONGED TO WOTAN*!

"Well?" the voice demanded. The tone was even, calm, but there was an undertone of menace.

He tried bluster. "What can you do to hurt me anymore? You shitehawks have shot most of me away as it is. And it's no use threatening to cut my eggs off. I'll never—"

He never finished his challenge, for the voice of his interrogator interrupted brutally with, "You forget about the rats. Oh, yes we know all about your fear – phobia is a better word – with those long tails. We've been monitoring your cell and the few rats in it ever since you were delivered to us." He sniggered at the word 'delivered.'

Doerr groaned. He was a man who had been brutalised and hardened by the war. He had seen and done things in the last five years of the great conflict that he would have hardly dared dream about back in 1939. Once at Karkhov, in 1942, a man's innards, bloody, gory and dripping with a strange, stinking green fluid had wrapped themselves round his face when the tank next to his had been knocked out by a Popov anti-tank gun. A year later he had waded through the mutilated corpses of some comrades who had been ripped apart and tortured by the KKVD, the Popov secret police, and thrown down an underground tunnel. These things, with other events like them, had not affected him one bit. He had become hardened to shattered guts, severed limbs, the shit of the front mixed up with human gore. But rats . . . rats still made the small hairs at the back of his shaven skull stand up in fright and now his unseen interrogators knew it. He was terrified of the scampering, chattering 'longtails'. He knew, too, they wouldn't hesitate in incarcerating him in a locked cell together with scores of the dreaded creatures, allowing them to scamper across his helpless body, slowly picking up the courage to begin attacking his extremities with their razor-sharp teeth. He groaned.

It was the signal for the man behind the lamp. "Well?" he rasped, "Are you going to speak, you Nazi bastard, while you've still got a chance to do so, eh?"

"Yes, I'll speak," he answered weakly, feeling sick and revolted at the same time. He was going to do something he had never imagined he ever could: he was about to squeal on those comrades who had fought and died at his side over a dozen different countries in two different continents. It was the ultimate betrayal, worse than betraying his own aged parents.

"You belonged to Wotan before you were wounded and captured at the surrender of Aachen?"

"Yes," he answered weakly, hot tears of shame slowly trickling down his hard, lined, brutal face.

"Who is the CO of Wotan?" There was a slight pause as if the interrogator was running his mind over the names. "Was it *Obersturmbannführer* Geier?"

"No," the prisoner said. "The 'Vulture' as the troopers of 'Wotan' called their perverted, long-dead ex-CO, died at the front without ever winning those general's stars for which he had always craved throughout the war. He was killed at Monte Cassino in Italy."

"*Obersturmbannführer* Heinz?"

"No, he was just in charge temporarily," he explained lamely.

"Well, who is it, man?" the interrogator yelled in an outburst of sudden rage.

The prisoner hesitated for a fraction of a second, remembering how the harshly handsome CO had once risked his own neck to save him, holding off a dozen or so Popov ski-troopers while his mates had come out of their trenches to drag him in.

"*Obersturmbannführer* Kuno," he began and stopped short.

"Go on! *Los Mensch*," the interrogator urged. "Remember those longtails!"

Doerr groaned piteously, wishing he was dead already, and gave in at last, "Kuno von Dodenburg," he said, voice barely above a whisper.

There was a cry of triumph from behind the spotlight. "We've got him – *finally*! We've got the murdering bastard!" a voice other than that of the interrogator's exclaimed excitedly.

Suddenly the spotlight clicked out. Faintly but distinctly, Doerr lying there on the blood-stained stretcher, feeling drained and weak, heard as the voice of the interrogator commanded someone else in the darkness, "Take him out in the yard and shoot him. We don't need the SS bastard any more."

It was as if he were just a piece of garbage to be disposed of as useless.

Doerr closed his eyes in submission. The interrogator was right. He was useless. The whole of the SS was. The reckoning with Hitler's black guards had commenced.

# Chapter Two

Phones jangled urgently. Typewriters clattered. Self-important, elegant staff officers strode back and forth with files labelled 'Top Secret' under their arms. All the while, white-helmeted MPs posted at the doors of the great eighteenth-century headquarters clicked to attention and saluted. For here, as they said, "colonels were a dime a dozen". Somewhere, an irate voice was crying, "You've got to get that goddam regiment into the line by zero ten hundred tomorrow, or believe you me, Colonel, heads will roll! You read me loud and clear, yeah?" All was hectic, feverish activity, for the new offensive had already commenced. In the German Eifel the hard-pressed survivors of the beaten German Army in Belgium were pulling back fast, harassed and chased by a triumphant Patton, whose motto was, 'We're gonna go through those Krauts bastards like shit through a goose!'

Colonel Schroeder, squatting behind his desk in the HQ's Judge Advocate's branch, was unmoved by the hectic activity outside his office. The battlefield was no concern of his. He left that, as he often proclaimed to his cronies in the Senior Officers' Club, to "those goddam stupid death-or-glory boys from the Point. Let them get their foolheads blown off! After all, that's what we pay 'em for." On this early January day, in what people were now calling the 'year of victory, 1945', he was concerned with the latest discovery by his investigation team; and it had come along just in time.

Two weeks before, the Supreme Commander, General Eisenhower, had summoned him to his office farther down the ornate corridor. The broad smile which usually adorned Ike's face – at least for the newsreels – was absent. Grimly puffing away at one of the sixty 'Camels' he chain-smoked every day, he had growled, "Schroeder, you'd better get on the stick. We still don't know who carried out that massacre of our boys and *our boys*," this time he had emphasised the standard phrase angrily, "are still bugging out by the hundred. They *have* to learn what kind of ruthless bastards those Nazis are. Then they'd stick it out." He had stubbed out his cigarette angrily and immediately lit another Camel, saying, "Only yesterday I visited one of our front-line hospitals at Verviers in Belgium and you know there were a thousand of our guys – yes I said *one thousand* of 'em – in there with shellshock and self-inflicted wounds. All because they didn't want to fight the Krauts." He had stared hard at Schroeder's fat, well-fed lawyer's face. "We've got to show them what the score is with the Krauts, Schroeder. *You've* got to show 'em. Or else . . ." Eisenhower, flushed and angry as if it were all too much for him, had left the rest of his sentence unsaid, but the threat had been obvious. If he, Schroeder, didn't come up with something soon he wasn't going to be a happy man. For a moment he was plagued by the ghastly vision of being given a .45 pistol and being ordered to take over a line company.

Now everything had changed, almost overnight, thanks to the three German kikes. As he now explained to a silent Sharpe, who sat opposite him in the ornate baroque office of what had once been part of the palace of the French 'Sun King', "I call 'em 'the Marx Brothers'."

"*Marx Brothers*? . . . The chaps who are in the pictures?"

"That's the guys. They look funny, but that's about all. They're hard bastards and I wouldn't put anything past them if it came to getting info from a prisoner. They don't seem to have heard of the Geneva Convention, even though one of them was once a kike lawyer, before the Nazis kicked him out and he fled to the States."

"I see," Sharpe said woodenly, though in reality he didn't see at all. Outside an officious voice was barking, "Don't waste my time with that crap. If you want bodies, Colonel, trawl the repple-depples*. There's enough jerk-offs there trying to keep out of the goddam line. You'll find your riflemen there. Now haul ass!"

Sharpe waited while Schroeder obviously savoured his little triumph, making him wait. Finally he spoke, "These kike Marx Brothers I have just mentioned, Major," he announced, "have found out the name of the Kraut who commands those murdering bastards of SS Assault Regiment Wotan."

Sharpe pricked up his ears, all attention now, his keen eyes taut and ready for action, though he disliked this overstaffed headquarters and everything that went with it.

"Thought that'd get your interest, Major," Schroeder said. "Now we know who to pin it on. Not some little unknown jerk-off, but a ranking Kraut who was once Himmler's adjutant, worked at Hitler's side for a few months and now commands, or once commanded Wotan, the premier regiment of the SS." He lowered his voice significantly, as if it were a great secret he was now about to impart to the one-armed Britisher. "His name is Kuno von Dodenburg and he comes, so I've learned, from one of those old aristocratic Prussian families, Ju – what do you they call them?" he snapped his fat fingers in irritation.

"Junkers," Sharpe supplied the name for him.

* Reinforcement unit.

"Yeah, Junkers, those guys. Well, he's just the kind of fall guy we need, Sharpe, big Nazi, well connected. He'll look the part when we put him on trial for the massacre." Schroeder beamed with pleasure at the thought.

Sharpe attempted to bring the fat American lawyer down to earth, "We've still got to find him, Colonel. I assume we haven't as yet?"

Schroeder's smile still remained on his face. "I'm not worried about that. We'll find the bastard all right. There are scores, hundreds of SS officers coming into our cages now that Georgie Patton has started his campaign in Germany and your guys, too, farther north."

"Too many," Sharpe interjected, but Schroeder didn't seem to hear. Instead he said, pressing the bell on his desk, "But here, Major, let me introduce you to the kikes, the Marx Brothers." He laughed.

A moment later there came a polite knock on Schroeder's office door. "Come!" he ordered and it was opened immediately to reveal the three lieutenants standing there in what they supposed was the position of attention, though it was more like a caricature of that stance.

All three of them wore the crossed rifles of the infantry and had medal ribbons on their chests, more than Sharpe, veteran of two years' fighting in the Western Desert, possessed, but he knew the Yanks gave their soldiers a medal just for being able to fire a rifle, so that didn't impress him. And it was obvious they had never served at the front. They lacked that tense, fine-honed look of fighting men who had risked their lives every day.

Yet as Schroeder introduced Sharpe to them there was something about the three undersized ex-German Jews that was impressive, and a little sinisterly frightening as well. Of the three, Lieutenant McDougall, which was his cover name (though in Sharpe's opinion he made a most unlikely

Scot), was the most sinister. He was very dark with clever, saturnine eyes underneath a cowl of cropped jet-back hair which made him look as if he were wearing the death cap a British judge used to wear when sentencing a culprit to death. McDougall, too, was the most vocal in English, speaking only with a trace of his native German accent as he lectured Schroeder, after having dimissed the one-armed Englishman as someone of no importance. Not that the little interrogator had much respect for his superior Schroeder either. It was almost as if their roles were reversed and he, the subordinate, was in charge and not the fat American military lawyer.

"Let's face it," he snapped, "the Krauts are going to go underground. They've already seen the writing on the wall, even the – er – gentlemen of the SS." He pronounced the words with cynical emphasis. "We're already meeting quite a few of them equipped with false military papers, discharges from the *Wehrmacht* and the like and with diamonds, gold and other goodies for the next stage of their journey sewn into their uniforms."

"Yes, I guess the rats *are* leaving the sinking ship," Schroeder agreed. "But what are we going to do about it, McDougall?"

Next to the dark-eyed interrogator, the other two – Lieutenants Frazier and Rennison, the latter with his hair dyed a startling red for some reason, perhaps he thought he looked more Scottish that way – tittered at the Colonel's use of the cover name 'McDougall'.

"Redouble our efforts," the interrogator replied firmly. "Bribe one to betray the other, coerce, blackmail, threaten – *anything* to make them spill the beans."

"And the rules of land warfare, the Geneva Convention?" Sharpe interrupted, testing the water in a way, trying to find out what type of strange company he had landed with. "I mean, the prisoners can protest to the protecting Power if they feel their rights as prisoners are being violated. You know – Article Thirty-one." He quoted it by heart, it was one of the first rules he had learned when he had transferred from the infantry. He wasn't going to have some cocky, smart German attempting to throw the Geneva Convention at him when the man didn't know its rulings himself: *"On the request of a belligerent, an enquiry shall be instituted in a manner to be decided between the interested parties, concerning any alleged violation of the Convention."*

He paused and the three 'Marx Brothers' looked at him as if he had suddenly gone mad. In the end, after a shocked silence, McDougall, as usual acting as their spokesman, said: "You don't believe in that kind of crap, do you, Major?"

Schroeder beamed and chortled, his fat jowls wobbling, "That's my boy!"

Sharpe was suddenly angry. He had realised for over a year now, ever since the preparations for D-Day had started in earnest, that the Yanks were now calling the tune. Over those months in 1943 it was Britain and the British Empire which had become the poor relations. Still he had not liked the change. After all, while Britain had fought and bled alone, America had made money and the war – not President Roosevelt – had finally brought that great country out of recession. "Yes, I certainly do believe in that – er – kind of crap," he retorted hotly. "Remember, Old Jerry has still got a hundred thousand of our own men in his prisoner-of-war camps. He could turn nasty, too, and then it wouldn't be too rosy for *your* chaps. We've got to obey the rules whether we like it or not, Lieutenant McDougall."

The latter shrugged carelessly. "That's not my problem, is it, Colonel?" He flashed Schroeder a glance and without waiting for an answer, added, "Your POWs surrendered didn't they? They didn't fight to the end like we would have to do." He shrugged and dismissed the matter. "Forget it. Our problem is to find this Kraut colonel and put him on trial, wherever he's hiding at this moment."

"Hot dog!" Schroeder exclaimed enthusiastically, "That's the kind of goddam fighting talk I like, McDougall!"

McDougall's eyes swept the colonel's fat, flushed face disdainfully, as if the latter was something which had just crept out of the woodwork, and shouldn't have bothered to do so. But he made no comment. Instead he turned back to Sharpe and said, in that cold, emotionless voice of his, that spelled disaster and doom for those unfortunate enough to fall into his hands, "Major, that Kraut colonel has to learn that there is no hiding place on this earth for him . . . save the grave itself."

Sharpe shivered.

# Chapter Three

Matz squatted in the officers' thunderbox, just a pole stretched across a hole in the second-line reserve trench, with a piece of corrugated iron as a roof. It was an offence punishable with life imprisonment to use an officers' thunderbox, but as Matz had opined to Schulze, his old running mate, "Life imprisonment in Torgau" – the dreaded SS military prison – "has got a future in it. More than can be said for this kind of frigging life, or is it death, at the moment." To which Schulze, unshaven, unfed and lousy with the usual 'felt lice' of the front for these last three weeks, gave no reply. He simply didn't have the energy.

All morning the Russians had been trying to break through the defence of the Sixth SS Panzer Army south of Budapest in Hungary. Time and time again the Russian infantry had come in massed ranks, marching shoulder to shoulder, the thin winter sun's rays sparkling on their long bayonets, singing in that beautiful bass of theirs, before crying *"urrah"* and charging into the machine-guns of the waiting SS.

Once they had even attacked with a brass band, their flags waving bravely, officers trotting on their mounts to the front, gleaming silver sabres balanced on their shoulders. "*Slava Krasnaya Armya!*"\* they had bellowed in a deep bass,

---

\* "Long Live the Red Army".

their breath fogging the air in a grey cloud around their grave faces.

The hastily thrown together 'alarm battalion' of SS stragglers under the command of inexperienced officers, culled from Himmler's HQ, had waited tensely, peering down their sights as if impatient to open fire and get it over with, one way or another.

"*FEUER!*" the *Hauptsturmführer* in charge had bellowed urgently, as the massed Soviet ranks, packed shoulder to shoulder in their ankle-length grey coats, had broken into a trot, their officers lowering their sabres in a silver sparkle and pointing them in the direction of the waiting SS.

The German line had broken into a ragged volley of rifle fire. Almost immediately the machine-guns had joined in furiously, scything down the ranks of the Soviet infantry in savage bursts. The Russians went down everywhere, falling into the fresh snow in the same neat ranks in which they had advanced into battle. Still the survivors had come on, stumbling, tripping, cursing as they charged across the bodies of their fallen comrades.

Sweating madly despite the biting cold, the SS troopers had desperately poured on the fire. They knew that once the Popovs reached their trench line they would be finished. The Russians could use those long, old-fashioned bayonets of theirs with deadly affect. They poured on the fire with ever-increasing fury, with the Russians going down on all sides. The brass band disappeared, ripped apart by that merciless hail of lead, save for one trumpeter, bleeding from half a dozen wounds, who staggered on groggily, still playing his shining brass instrument until a burst of machine-gun fire had torn it from his suddenly nerveless hands and he had gone down on his knees like a boxer trying to survive a count of ten, fighting to the very end till finally he pitched forward in the scarlet snow – *dead*.

That final death seemed to take the heart from the Russians. One moment they were still advancing bravely, crying their bass "*urrah*", the next they had turned and were fleeing the way they had come, stumbling over the dead and dying bodies of their comrades, pushing and jostling each other to escape that murderous fire, throwing away their weapons in panic-stricken haste. Then, at last, silence, long and echoing, which seemed to go on for ever, returned to that cruel, remote battlefield.

For the time being the Russians had ceased attacking, but already the barrage had commenced once more and the sky was darkening over from the East, indicating that snow would fall once more. Then, under its cover, the Russians would attack once again. For they were desperate to break out into the *puszta* and continue that last final drive into the Reich.

Matters of such far-reaching importance did not occupy Matz as he squatted on the freezing pole above the hole piled high with frozen turds, straining till the sweat hung in pearls on his narrow forehead. All they had eaten in the last two days had been slices of bread so hard and frozen that they had been forced to cut it into slices with a saw after thawing it out the best they could over a miserable fire. It was not the best of diets for men whose stomachs had shrunk from a lack of food.

He waited for some kind of relief, muscles clenched as he forced the process for he, too, like the rest of the hard-pressed SS troopers, had heard gory tales of men who had sat half-naked on a crapper so long that their balls had frozen to the pole. It was a thought that made him shiver even more.

He tried to forget the straining and the possible damage to his 'family treasures', as he was wont to call his genitals. He let his eyes wander. Even in officers' thunderboxes there were sometimes amateur artists who livened up their waiting times in those noxious places with pornographic sketches and verses on the lines of *'It's no use standing on the seat, the crabs in here can jump six feet.'*

But the greenhorn officers, straight from the comb-out at Himmler's SS HQ had not been in the line long enough to know the rules of the game; they were strictly military, living by the tenets of the *Greater German Code of Regulations*, the Army's standard rule book.

He yawned and wished he hadn't. He felt a tugging at his genitals and realised they were beginning to freeze to the pole. He shifted his position hastily and told himself almost angrily, "Come on – *crap or get off the pot man*!" Then his eye fell on the rusting tin which had once contained 'Old Man', the standard army meat ration, supposedly made of dead pensioners culled from Berlin's workhouses. "As I live and frigging breathe," he said in awe. "There's even frigging paper in it! By the Great Whore of Buxtehude where the dogs piss through their ribs, *paper*! Them officers do frigging well live high on the hog."

He reached up a skinny hand, took off the outer mitten to reveal the leather glove below with the trigger finger cut away so that he could fire his weapon more easily, and took one of the neatly cut squares of paper from the can. The last thing he had read (apart from the instructions on how to use the latest contraceptive, trademark *'Vulkan'*, made from re-processed lorry tyres) was a tattered copy of *La Vie Parisienne* the French pornographic magazine. Even those primitive substitutes for lavatory paper were something new, despite the fact they came from the Führer's own newspaper, *Der Volkische Beobachter*.

"Fancy wiping yer arse on the Führer's own words!" Matz muttered idly to himself as he squinted at the square of paper. "Some of these new SS officers have no respect for the 'greatest warlord of all times'," he said, using the front-line soldier's contemptuous term for Adolf Hitler.

He turned the paper over until he got it right-side up. Suddenly he gasped, his reason for being here and risking his 'family treasures' in this malodorous place abruptly forgotten. Just below a large item headlined *The Führer Has Yet Secrets Up His Sleeve Which Will Win This War* – "Yer," he had commented cynically, "a frozen fart from the Eastern Front" – there was another, smaller one which caught his attention, reading, *Report From a Neutral Source*. But it wasn't the headline which shocked him into instant awareness; it was a mere three words: *'Wotan'* and *'von Dodenburg'*.

Desperately holding the paper up to the grey winter light, his eyes flew over the little report from 'Agentur Havas'. 'Today, it was reported' (it read), 'from a neutral source, generally regarded as reliable, that the former commander of SS Assault Regiment 'Wotan', Holder of the Knight's Cross with Swords and Oak Leaves—'

'ALARM . . . ALARM,' the urgent words cut into his reading. '*Die Iwan greifen an . . . Alarm . . .* !' Suddenly the officers' whistles were shrilling urgently and NCOs were bellowing their orders. Across on no-man's land the Russians were coming into the attack once more. Matz, busy buckling up his trousers and adjusting the straps of his 'tin leg', cursing fluently all the while as he did so, could hear the soft swish of many skis on the surface of the frozen snow and told himself that the Ivans were bringing up their elite Asiatic ski troops to finally overwhelm these stubborn SS giants. "Christ on a crutch!" he cursed, as he shoved the precious piece of newsprint into his pocket, "now the clock's really in the pisspot!" Then he was hobbling outside into the glowing greyness, unbuckling his machine-pistol, preparing for the inevitable . . .

Time and time again, the little yellow men in their wadded jackets came swooping in, crouched low on their skis, firing their round-magazined tommy-guns with one free hand, as they used a single stick to break off at the last possible moment before they hit the SS line. Many of them didn't make it. Already the snow-covered tundra was littered with their bodies, sprawled out in the careless poses of the dead – like abandoned toys. But still they came sweeping into the attack, again and again, seemingly unworried by their tremendous losses, as if they might have been high on drink or drugs, or perhaps both.

For a while it seemed their sheer weight of numbers would overcome the handful of defenders of the shattered, battle-littered SS trench line. Once they actually penetrated the forward trench. Carried away by the crazy, unreasoning blood lust of combat the SS rose from their positions and slammed into the little yellow men. It was man for man. No quarter was given or expected. When a soldier went down, he stayed down *for good*. Grunting and cursing like beasts, the two groups swayed back and forth on the rim of the trench, using bayonet, shovel, naked claws, gouging, chopping, hacking until the scuffed and dirty snow all around was covered with obscene gobs of blood; sawn-off limbs, the bones gleaming through the red mess like polished ivory; and dead men heaped up in steaming piles, like offal outside some crazy butcher's.

A slant-eyed Mongol sprang at a sweating, gasping Schulze, who was trying to hold the defenders, while their new commander cowered in his hole trembling violently. He aimed a tremendous kick at Schulze's crotch. "*Heaven, arse and cloudburst!*" Schulze exploded with a tremendous roar of rage, "you nearly had my meat and two frigging vegs, you fornicating slant-eyed chink piece o' turd." He lashed out with his own cruelly shod right boot. The Mongol screamed shrilly and his shining steel false teeth shot from his mouth as he lurched backwards, gasping through toothless lips.

It was Matz who restored the position Grabbing an abandoned MG42, he yelled, "On yer fuckin' shoulder, arse with ears!"

Schulze understood immediately. He flung the machine-gun, minus its triped, over his massive right shoulder and tensed. Matz didn't hesitate. He pressed the trigger. The air-cooled machine-gun burst into frantic life. Tracer sliced the air at over 1000 rounds a minute. The Mongols went down on all sides. Some of the still-advancing rear rank were blown off their skis by that tremendous volley of deadly fire at such close range. They floated through the air momentarily, still holding their ski sticks, to slam into the ground a moment later and lie there motionless, the blood jetting from their gaping, smoking wounds in bright red arcs.

That did it. The steam went out of the ski troops' attack. Yelling frantically in their own tongue, ignoring the angry shouts of their NCOs and the angry whacks with their sabres by their few surviving officers, they streamed back the way they had come, with the fire dying away until there was no sound save the moans of the wounded and dying.

It was while they were gobbling down the looted Mongol rations – dried fish, hard bread with plenty of salt in it – "Gives a fellow a real thirst," Schulze had proclaimed a little sadly. "I'd give my right bollock for a litre of Munich suds to wash this little lot down" – that Matz remembered the square of toilet paper.

Carefully he took out the 100g bottle* of pepper vodka he had taken from a dying Russian officer, helping him on his way with a hefty kick to his face – "Put the poor Popov

---

* Russian Army drink rations were measured out in grams.

bastard out of his misery," he had commented unfeelingly, and handed it to Schulze.

The latter's eyes nearly popped out of his face when he saw the precious pepper vodka had not been touched. "What's the frigging matter?" he exclaimed, staring at the bottle in disbelief, "you gonna be a frigging nun or something?"

Matz didn't take offence at this. Instead he said, "Put fifty grams behind yer tonsils . . . you're gonna need it, old house!"

Schulze didn't need a second invitation. His prominent Adam's apple working its way up and down his throat like an express lift, he swallowed the precious liquid, eyes flooding with tears as the fiery vodka struck his throat. Matz waited patiently, though his little dark eyes were fixed keenly on the bottle to ensure that Schulze didn't exceed his lot. "All right, sauce-hound," he said finally, "that's yer frigging lot. Hand over the juice."

Reluctantly, Schulze handed over the little brown bottle. With affected good taste, Matz gave a dry little cough, murmured, "Excuse me, yer frigging highness," and took a mighty swig himself.

"Greedy little bastard!" Schulze muttered under his breath and waited. Matz corked the bottle firmly and shoved it inside his tunic, carefully buttoning it up afterwards. "Yer never know," he said darkly. "There's a lot of robbers around, yer know."

Schulze said nothing, but waited. On the body-littered steppe a grievously wounded Mongol, trailing his steaming guts behind him like a snake, tried to crawl away.

"Shoot him!" the new company officer cried in an angry falsetto. "Shoot him before he gets away and reports our positions!"

None of the veterans took notice of his command. He

jerked out his pistol, fired three times and missed all of them. He looked away, pistol still smoking in his gloved hand, as if he was wondering who had fired.

"Officers," Schulze sneered, "I've shat 'em before breakfast. Now then, Matzi, where's the frigging fire?"

"Here," his old running mate answered. "Attach yer frigging glassy eyes to this, will yer?"

Schulze did so, mouthing the words aloud like a schoolboy learning to read for the first time, a look of disbelief and then hope crossing his broad face.

# Chapter Four

*Hauptsturmführer* Dietz looked incredulously at the two ragged 'old hares', who stank of cheap vodka, and repeated his words. "*Impossible*, Senior Sergeant Schulze, absolutely impossible! Every able-bodied man is needed at the front and you should be the first to know that, Schulze." He peered like a schoolmaster over the rim of the pince-nez he affected in imitation of his former master *Reichsführer* SS Himmler.

Again Schulze, growing angry and impatient now, for his stomach was rumbling loudly with hunger once more and the promised 'green fart soup', made from horse meat, had not turned up – as usual – slapped the piece of yellowing newspaper. "But it says here, sir—" he commenced.

Dietz cut him short. "I know what it says, Schulze. We officers are supposed to be able to read, you know. Besides, you should not take these foreign reports seriously. Who knows, they could be defeatist, aimed at lowering the morale of our brave boys. After all, the SS does *not* surrender."

"What do you think, that we shit through the ribs or something?" Schulze grumbled.

"I will pretend I didn't hear that remark," Dietz said severely. "I have made my decision. You'd better get back to my brave soldiers." He touched his single piece of 'tin', the War Service Cross Third Class, which he had won for devising a speedier method of counting and assessing the number and value of gold teeth wrenched from the mouths of unfortunate concentation camp inmates back in 1942. He smiled thinly, reassured that the treasured medal, awarded him by the *Reichsführer* personally, was still there. "I want you to ensure that the men know all the *Volkslieder*\* in the current *Soldier's Song Book*. He looked very stern. "There has been a degree of slackening off in that area and one never knows when some dignitary might visit the front and ask for a folk song."

"In this arsehole of the world, where they roll up the pavements and say good night at six in the evening?" Schulze snorted. Then he thought better of it and said to Matz, "All right, you Bavarian barnshitter. Let's sling our hook." Without saluting, the two of them, crouching low in case there was a Popov sniper about, went back to their own foxhole, with Schulze mumbling about "frigging folk songs" and "what a frigging war".

"Well," Matz said as they crouched there, warming their hands over the weak, flickering flame of the 'Hindenburg Light'.†

"Well, frigging what?" Schulze growled in an evil temper.

"What are we gonna do?" Matz asked simply.

"Give me a look at that bit of shitehouse paper agen," his comrade said by way of a reply.

Dutifully, Matz handed him the precious cutting.

Schulze spread it out in front of him, ignoring the obscene howl of a 'Stalin Organ', the Russian multiple mortar, which had now begun firing at their position. "Allied Headquarters in France reported yesterday," he read aloud, "that the holder of the Knight's Cross with swerds and

---

\* Folk Songs, usually part of the SS's training.
† A trench candle.

oak leaves, Colonel von Dodenburg, commander of SS Assault Regiment Wotan, is regarded as the perpetrator of the massacre of American soldiers in the first days of December's German attack in Begium. It is believed that he has become a prisoner in that country and is being actively sought by the Allied authorities so that he can be placed on trial for his alleged crimes. A spokesman for General Eisenhower commented that—" Schulze broke off and looked up.

To his amazement Matz saw that there were tears in the red-rimmed, weary eyes of his old comrade.

"What is it, old house?" he asked urgently.

"We've forgotten all about the CO living out here in Popovland, enjoying ourselves shooting yeller Chinks and supping their firewater." His voice broke as if he might begin sobbing at any moment. "We ought to be frigging ashamed of oursens."

Matz hung his head momentarily, as if truly ashamed of himself. "I know what you mean, friend Schulze," he said thickly. "But what with this thing and the other—" He shrugged his skinny shoulders, as if he couldn't bear to go on, but added after a few seconds, "But I hadn't looked at it like that."

"Well, you should frigging well had!" Schulze snapped waspishly, wiping a finger like a thick, hairy pork sausage across his eyes. "No matter. Whatever that four-eyed thin-shitter of an officer sez to the contrary, we're gonna try to do something about it, Matz."

"But what can *we* do?" Matz objected. "Two skinny-assed stubble-hoppers in Popovland on the other side of the continent?"

"Go right to the top, that's what," his comrade replied with sudden determination in his voice.

"*Right to the top?*" Matz echoed in wonder.

"Yer, don't yer hear right, you weak streak o' piss?"

"And who's that when he's at home, Schulze?"

His old comrades looked sternly at the little man. "Colonel General SS Sepp Dietrich, commander of the Sixth SS Panzer Army, that's who!"

Solemnly Matz crossed himself. "Well, I hope we'll make a pair of handsome corpses, old house . . . !"

The burly Bavarian ex-butcher's apprentice, who had been the first commander of the Adolf Hitler Bodyguard and who now led what was left of the once vaunted SS Panzer Army, the greatest force that the SS had ever sent into battle, was drunk. It wasn't something very unusual – Sepp Dietrich was normally drunk, though it was only eight this cold February dawn.

Even as the two of them sneaked through the warm kitchen of his farmhouse field HQ, which smelled of good German sausage and fried potatoes, they could hear him warbling somewhere above them on the second floor, with a frightened woman's voice pleading, "But please, General Sepp, do me a favour before your staff turns up, and put on your breeches . . . Oh dear what will they think of me, I wonder?"

Sepp Dietrich laughed coarsely and made an indelicate reply. There was the sound of a bottle being scraped along a table, followed an instant later by a long and deep gurgling. "Greedy arsehole!" Schulze grunted enviously.

"Rank hath its privileges," Matz commented, as if that explained everything.

Cautiously the two of them crept upstairs from where the sound of voices was coming. The door to Sepp Dletrich's bedroom was half open. Cautiously the two intruders peered in. The Colonel General, clad only in his vest, his teeth in a glass on a small table, next to the big bed, was staring down at his flaccid organ in a mixture of wonder and anger, while an enormous woman who seemed to be bursting from her sheer silk nightgown kept urging him to put on his breeches.

"But I did try, my beloved," he countered as if that was explanation enough for his lack of riding breeches.

"Yes, yes, I know, light of my life," the woman replied in a thick Magyar accent, thrusting one enormous breast back inside the thin material from which it had escaped.

"Get a load of all that," Schulze whispered in awe, "all that meat and no potatoes."

"It'd be like going up the north face of the Eiger – mounting that wench," Matz agreed, eyeing the huge woman, who was now busy preparing the dye to colour the General's moustache for the day; Sepp Dietrich was inordinately proud of his facial hair which was an exact replica of the Führer's own moustache. Matz changed the subject. "Are you gonna talk to him, Schulzi?"

The big NCO took his eyes off the Hungarian woman's ample charms, "Yer, I suppose I'd better. After all, I *am* the most senior man present, apart from the General naturally."

"Of course," Matz agreed hastily, a sudden wicked look in his little eyes. "I'll hop to it and see if I can find some fodder. These high-ranking officers do themselves proud. No fart soup and dead-men stews for the likes of them."

"Yes, you do," Schulze agreed, not much interested. He was much too concerned with making an impression on Colonel General Dietrich, who was now tucking away his flaccid organ. "Spanish fly," he was muttering to himself. "That's what I need – Spanish fly. I'll fly a plane to Spain today to bring me in a supply, then we'll see." He popped in his false teeth and beamed at himself in the big mirror just below the highly coloured pornographic picture of two crop-haired women doing something which Schulze thought was anatomically impossible.

"Sir," Schulze boomed, throwing the surprised Colonel General a tremendous salute so that the bed trembled, "Senior Sergeant Schulze reporting, with a request for the *Herr Generaloberst!*"

Dietrich spun round, startled, shirt tails flying. "What in the name of three devils . . . ?" he began, taking in the fact immediately that the big man opposite him, with a ruddy face that looked as if it had been hewn from granite, his brawny chest covered with every piece of 'tin' that a grateful Reich awarded its military heroes, wasn't one of his staff officers. Schulze didn't give him a chance to comment.

He launched into his plea at once, "With the General's permission," he commenced and then while Deitrich listened, obviously slightly puzzled at this request so early in the morning even before he had drunk his usual three or four dawn schnapps, his 'gunfire', as he was wont to call it, the big NCO told him what he wanted to do, now it was known that von Dodenburg was wanted by the Allied authorities.

Despite his bewilderment, Dietrich listened civilly enough, not taking in the strange panting now coming from the ante-room and what sounded like the hectic movement of rusty couch springs, though Schulze's face took on a slight frown as he became aware of it. Finally Schulze, standing rigidly at attention, listened as a thoughtful Sixth Army Commander stroked his dimpled chin, saying, as if to himself, "He was always an arrogant swine, that Kuno von Dodenburg, although all the same he doesn't deserve to be shoved against a wall by the *Amis* and shot out of hand." He frowned and Schulze waited expectantly. "All right, Dietrich said finally, as the strange rusty squeaking sound came to an end with a funny sort of sighing noise,

"Your request will be granted, Sergeant Schulze. But I can assure you that it is highly irregular."

Schulze beamed and prayed fervently that the missing Matz hadn't put his foot in it at this late stage of the game.

"You go and see my operations officer. He'll fill you in with what details we have. Then the quartermaster will supply you with passes, legitimation and posting orders. Tell him you are to report to the depot of the *Leibstandarte*" – he meant his old command, the Adolf Hitler Bodyguard. "There you will be given the necessary documents to enable you to travel to the front in the West." Dietrich lowered his voice, "And *behind* it, if you feel it's necessary to your quest. That will be on your own head."

"I understand, Colonel General," Schulze said, his heart racing, knowing that he was being given carte blanche with all the remaining resources of the *Leibstandarte* behind him.

Dietrich waved his hand in dismissal. Schulze noticed his nails were lacquered and polished and told himself the one-time Munich butcher's boy had come a long way.

"Thank you, sir," he rasped and turning about smartly marched out as if he were already on parade with the recruits at Berlin *Lichtefelde*.

Outside, Matz was waiting for him. He smelled strangely of something that Schulze could not quite identify at that moment and he was carrying a large wickerwork basket like some lady's maid about to set off on a picnic with her mistress. But Schulze was too eager to relate the great news to his old running mate to comment. Hastily he told him what Colonel General Dietrich had decided, ending with, "I don't know exactly what we can do about the old Chief, Matzi, but we're gonna have a damn good try . . . better than last one." He hesitated. "There's a funny pong of fish around here," he added. He looked pointedly at the pretty-looking basket Matz was holding.

"No fish in here, old house," he answered the unspoken question, obviously well pleased with himself. He pulled back the checked cloth covering the basket's content "Just a few things that the Countess—"

"Countess?"

"Yer, Dietrich's – er – girlfriend. This is what she rustled up for us poor old hairy-assed stubble-hoppers at the front. Venison, a small joint of ham, a bottle o' peach brandy and—"

"And what made her Holiness rustle up that kind of fodder for us?" Schulze interrupted him suspiciously. "Come on, you frigging asparagus Tarzan!"

"Can't you guess?" Matz stared at his nails in mock modesty.

Schulze's bottom lip dropped down comically. "Oh . . . oh!" he stuttered, "You . . . cunning little bastard!"

Matz gave a little bow. "Noblesse oblige, old house. Can't leave a well-born lady high and dry in her hour of need, can yer? If the general fails, his privates have to jump into the breech, if you follow my meaning." And then the one-legged little man was off down the stairs to receive their orders, swinging his pretty basket full of fodder, as if there wasn't a happier man on earth.

# Chapter Five

It had been an old trick, the simplest in the world really. From the one interrogator, the sinister one they called McDougall, he had found the hospital where they had taken the wounded *Oberscharführer*, who had revealed von Dodenburg's identity. If the place where they were tending the SS men, part of the great round-up of SS prisoners, could be called a hospital. It was a ruined barn in the bombed-out Eifel township of Bitburg, just beyond the Luxembourg border with an almost beaten Germany.

Outside, trucks and tanks had slithered through the mud, day and night, in a constant stream, heading for the last front, the Rhine, which Sharpe, up to his ankles in the goo while waiting for the irate American MP's signal for him to cross to the 'hospital', guessed would soon be under attack. Once that great natural barrier had been overcome there was no hope for the Third Reich, Hitler's Reich, which he had said would last a thousand years, but would be finished in a thousand hours.

So he had trudged through the mud and misery, past the countless sentries – for even though the prisoners were on their last legs, dying for the most part, the Yanks were frightened of the SS. Such was the reputation of Hitler's fanatical black guards.

In the entrance, which stank of urine, ether and human misery, he had been met by the harassed American doctor in charge, a couple of his German medical assistants and the tall, thin, totally frightened youth with glasses who was going to be his interpreter and who kept maintaining, "But I was called up straight from medical school last autumn. I didn't even get time to make the front before they shot away my hand," and miserably would hold what was left of his right hand, pus still oozing in thick, opaque gobs from the remaining fingers. None of the three doctors, the Yank and the two Germans, had taken any notice of him. There was death all about them twenty-four hours a day. What did it matter if the interpreter, who would never practise medicine now anyway, succumbed or not?

Sharpe introduced himself and waited a few minutes while an orderly passed carrying an enamel pail full of watery shit, followed by another with his hands cradling severed limbs and, balanced precariously over his right shoulder a sawn-off leg, complete with high jackboot. No one took the slightest notice of the two captives. There was horror all around them in this house of death. Such sights were part and parcel of their daily existence.

The interpreter, Hartmann, led Sharpe through the 'wards', if they could be called such: rooms lined with blood and faeces on stained straw, with dying and dead men packed together under filthy blankets, alive with grey lice, moaning and unattended save for, in one case, a harassed nurse with mad eyes, who was trying to stem the bleeding from a great red-raw stump of a thigh with nothing but paper bandages.

Sharpe had seen it all before just after El Alamein, when together with the 13,000 dead of the great desert battle there had been three times that number of serious wounded. But their condition had never been as bad as this, and there had been that wonder drug penicillin available which had helped to heal the most seemingly hopeless cases.

Finally, Hartmann led him into the rear ward, a former

schoolroom by the looks of it, with tattered maps still on the bullet-pocked white-washed walls and shattered pictures of Hitler with obscene slogans scrawled on them by the victorious Yanks. "The death room," the interpreter said simply. "Gas gangrene and the like."

Sharpe didn't need to know that. He could smell the nauseating stench of the gangrenous wounds where dirty clothing had been forced into the men's wounds. Surgery helped for a little while, but after a few days and with the wound getting ever worse another part of the patient's limb would have to be sawn away – and so on until there was no more flesh to be amputated and then the patient died.

"That's *Oberscharführer* Doerr," Hartmann said, pointing to the heap of blankets in the dirty straw at the end of the ward.

"For mercy's sake," a piteous voice moaned. "Don't move so heavily. The least vibration and I'm in agony—!" the plea ended in a broken-hearted sob.

Sharpe frowned. These dying men were Hitler's merciless killers, but now they were helpless and at everyone's mercy. It wasn't a pleasant feeling to know that he could do with them just anything he wanted, and no one would give a damn. He walked as softly as he could to where Doerr lay, eyes closed, moaning softly, carefully avoiding touching the stinking blankets of the other 'patients' which were alive with grey lice. Even in the freezing cold of that room of death he could see the lice moving, as if deciding to cross to the next victim when their present 'host' died.

"He's dying," Hartmann said tonelessly and without feeling. "His lungs are filling up with fluid. In the end he'll choke on his own body liquid."

Sharpe nodded and did some quick thinking. He knew, though perhaps Hartmann didn't, that Doerr might well be still saved if he were given a dose of the new penicillin, which was rationed and reserved for Allied wounded only. It was the blackmail he would use. There would be no other way to make the dying man (as he thought) give him the clue to von Dodenburg that he sought. Even in his dying moments, the SS sergeant wouldn't tell him what he wanted to know. The old SS oath would bind him, even now, to the day of his death. He wouldn't betray a comrade – *directly*. Sharpe decided to make the attempt.

He had learned the trick as a 17-year-old back in 1936 when he had failed his Matriculation at Wellington and in a moment of despair, knowing he might not get in at Sandhurst, had volunteered for the 1st Battalion, the Welsh Guards. He had been one of a squad of rookies, some middle-class volunteers like himself, others petty crooks who had been given the option by the sentencing magistrate to 'go down for three months' or volunteer for 'His Majesty's Forces'. To the latter the 'Kate Karney' (as they called the British Army) had seemed the easy option, one in which they could be fed three square meals daily and paid ten bob a week 'all found' and continue to carry out their habitual criminal activities. The Guards' NCOs had taught them differently.

It was then he learned the trick. An 'offender', one of the teenage criminals, would be double-marched up to the orderly room with the ramrod-straight sergeant chivving him with, "Yer for it now, boyo. It's the glasshouse this time, if you don't spill the beans! Yes, laddie. It's Aldershot for you, and they say them 'Staffs' – he had meant the guards – "are all on the old Vaseline. So yer'd better watch yer arse there!"

Naturally, working to some kind of perverted crooks' honour, the tough young offender would refuse 'to spill the beans'. But to his surprise, the orderly officer wouldn't sentence him to the dreaded glasshouse at Aldershot and its perverted guards. Instead, the teenage criminal would be let off with ten days or so 'jankers'. Naturally it had all been planned in the orderly room beforehand. In his exuberance at being let off, the relief that he wasn't going inside, the offender, now the pressure was off, would 'spill his guts', as the saying of the time had it, to all and sundry. Within hours of the trick having being played on the teenager, the hard-bitten Guards NCOs would know all they wanted; and in due course the 'wide boy' would end up in the glasshouse after all.

As a wise old quartermaster had explained it to the youthful Sharpe after he had been commissioned in the 'Ox and Bucks' just before the war: "Let up the pressure and there's a reaction. Suddenly they're light-headed as if they've bin hitting the ether bottle and they're telling everybody just what yer want to hear. I suppose, sir, it's like a geezer who's been condemned to death and then is reprieved. He can't stop talking – even if he is incriminating hissen when he does."

Now, as Sharpe nodded to Hartmann, he prepared to try the same technique on the gravely ill SS NCO. He said, "Tell him we know he is very sick, but there is some hope, I think."

Hartmann shook his head. "As a third-year medical student, sir," he said in his excellent English, "I must say to the contrary. You see, with his type of infection and the rundown physical condition he is in, the only drugs we have available, the sulphur drugs – are not effective."

It was what Sharpe had been expecting. He touched the phial of the precious drug, worth a fortune on the black market for its ability, among other things, of being capable of curing VD now rampant in Germany's shattered cities, and said carefully, "I think I could help there."

"You, sir?"

"Yes. We don't want this man to die, even if he does refuse to help us."

Hartmann's long, yellow face suddenly went sulky and Sharpe realised he, too, knew what was going on behind the scenes despite his protests about not having been a convinced member of Hitler's black guards. "Perhaps one day he might," Sharpe added carefully.

"How, sir?"

"I have a full dose of penicillin, the new wonder drug. You've heard of it, I suppose?"

"Oh yes. All of us in the medical profession have, sir. What a marvellous English invention!"

Sharpe ignored the intended flattery. He said, "I also have permission to allow the American doctor in charge to administer the penicillin to this poor chap," he indicated a semi-conscious Doerr. "It should do the trick."

Hartmann nodded eagerly, perhaps forgetting his personal misery for a while at the thought of being able to see penicillin actually being used. "Oh, that would be splendid, sir! But I must warn you, *Oberscharführer* Doerr will not be bought, even if it costs him his life—"

"There are no strings attached," Sharpe interrupted. "It's simply an act of humanitarian concern for a grievously sick person."

Hartmann fell for it, hook, line and sinker, just as Sharpe hoped he would. Hastily he bent and whispered something in Doerr's ear. The latter nodded weakly. He too had bought the idea.

Ten minutes later Sharpe was on his way again, nosing the jeep through the heavy traffic heading for the front, telling himself that with a bit of luck he'd know where Kuno von Dodenburg was to be found before the week was out. For as he had explained to Schroeder when he had requested the fat Yank lawyer to get him the precious drug, "Usually jailers think they're in full charge of a prison and that they know *totally* what's going on. After all, the prisoner is behind bars and cut off from the rest of the world. But it doesn't work like that."

"How do you mean?" the American had asked, obviously puzzled.

"Prisoners, especially POWs, have constantly changing links. They go with the very nature of being a prisoner of war."

Schroeder had still looked puzzled and Sharpe had enlightened him hastily, eager to put his plan into action. "You see, sir, a chap is captured. If he's an officer and somehow important, like these SS officers are, he is sent to an interrogation centre. Those places are manned not only by our guards and intelligence personnel, but also by the Jerries, cooks, orderlies, cleaners and the like. They are the permanent staff and whatever comes in often stays with them. What's important, gossip or otherwise, they can pass on to departing POWs who can take the info with them to their next camp."

"Got you," Schroeder had said, nodding his head. "Carry on."

"So, sir," Sharpe had concluded, "I hope in his moment of relief now that the penicillin means – hopefully – that he will live, he'll start blabbing to the others of the permanent staff and in due course what he has to say gets back to us."

"Do you mean," Schroeder had said slowly, "that you think this SS sergeant already knows where the war criminal von Dodenburg is?"

Automatically Sharpe noted the fat colonel's use of the term 'war criminal'. Even before there had been a trial, this unknown SS colonel had already been stamped in

Schroeder's mind as the guilty party. But although Sharpe had registered the statement he had said nothing about it. Instead he had said, "Yes, I think he does, and as soon as he's feeling better, he'll use the camp hospital's grapevine to convey the info to von Dodenburg that he is a wanted man. Perhaps the sick chap thinks he can warn this SS colonel to do a bunk while there is still time."

"OK, . . . OK, I'll go along with that," Schroeder had snorted somewhat angrily for a reason that Sharpe could not fathom, "but how are we gonna follow the route the Krauts will use to warn von Dodenburg, eh?"

Sharpe had looked easily at the fat American colonel and by way of an answer he made the Continental gesture with finger and thumb of counting money. "The Jerries have always been a corrupt people, sir," he had explained. "Now in defeat they are even more corrupt. As Mr Churchill has said recently about the collapse of Germany, 'The Hun is always either at your throat or at your feet'."

Schroeder had made no comment on the statement, save to grunt, "Well, I hope you're right. Bribe those SS guys as much as you like – promise them the earth cos we won't honour that promise – but find me that goddam SS colonel, *soon*!"

Sharpe had been surprised himself at just how quickly he had been able to follow the trail given to him by the SS hospital orderly he had bribed at Bitburg, to the little Moselle township of Wittlich, a mere twenty-five miles away. Exactly forty-eight hours later he was striding impatiently through the gates of what had been up to recently the *'Adolf Hitler Kaserne'* and which had now become 'Special Holding Camp Number Five', reserved, or so the American commandant had informed him minutes before, "Goddam home from home to a bunch of hard-nosed Nazi blacks*."

The commandant and his interpreter, this time a German-American, led him down the corridor towards the guarded ward in which the senior German officers were imprisoned. "Tough guy," the commandant commented laconically, working his stump of unlit cigar from one side of his mouth to the other, "Thank Christ, there weren't too many Krauts like him . . . !" He left the statement there, adding, "You'll see, Major."

The armed guard at the door of the single room in which von Dodenburg was being held, clicked to attention when he saw the commandant approaching. On any other occasion Sharpe would have smiled at the way an armed grand was needed for a single, bed-ridden prisoner. Not only did the American carry a tommy-gun slung over his shoulder, but he had a .45 in a leather holster at his side, and a looted German Walther pistol tucked into his belt.

"Okay?" the commandant asked in his laconic fashion.

"Kay, sir. But I'm keeping my eyes skinned. Wouldn't trust the bastard not to try to make a break for it when he goes to the john."

The commandant grunted something and turning to Sharpe said, "Okay, I'll leave you alone with Mueller here," he indicated the interpreter. "If you want anything, just holler."

He strode away and the heavily armed guard relaxed. For some reason, which he couldn't quite make out, Sharpe thought that this moment was of importance: something he would remember for a long time. In due course, he would be proved right, but on that cold March morning, with the permanent barrage only a distant rumble on the Rhine, he

---

* German POWs were divided into three categories: 'whites', the minority, who had no Nazi record; 'Grey's', the great majority who had a record but who were prepared to forget the past; and 'black's', dyed-in-the-wool, unrepentent Nazis.

was motivated by instinct: a strange feeling that his life, for better or worse, was changing.

A very skinny young man with cropped blond hair lay on the narrow, white cot. It was obvious that he had been very ill. There were dark circles under his ice-blue eyes and his cheeks were sunk like those of a very old man. He turned, again slowly, very slowly, as if it took a great effort of will-power to do so.

He looked at the men but his gaze was really concentrated on Sharpe's empty sleeve neatly tucked into his belt. Sharpe didn't need to be told. He realised instinctively that von Dodenburg recognised him as a fellow 'front swine', as the Germans called the veterans in a mixture of contempt and respect, and knew that he was dealing with his own kind.

"Von Dodenburg," the interpreter said stonily in German, "this English officer is here to ask you—"

Von Dodenburg waved him to one side weakly, as if the man were not there "I can deal with the major without you," he said. He looked hard at Sharpe as if trying to etch his face on his mind for ever, and added, "I've been expecting you . . . !"

# Chapter Six

"Will ya cast your glassy orbs on that frigging spectacle, Matzi!" Schulze cried in feigned amazement, as they paused at the great gate of *Leibstandarte*'s training barracks at Berlin-Lichtefelde. "Cardboard frigging soldiers to the man. And that in the midst of total frigging war." He pushed his helmet back and scratched the back of his shaven skull, while the two teenage sentries watched in wonder at the number of grey felt lice dropping from the stubble onto the frozen snow.

"Agreed, old house," Matz said. He stared at the squads of rosy-cheeked young recruits in their sweat-stained denim overalls as they marched, goose-stepped, practised saluting to left and right and crawled about the huge square, encouraged by the threats and hearty kicks of the beery-voiced old hares of NCOs. "'*Crap*', said the King and a thousand arseholes bent and took the strain for in them days the word of the King was law."

"That you can say agen; what a lot of slime-shitters, treating that frigging cannonfodder like that! Don't they frigging well know that the poor frigging greenhorns'll probably be looking at the frigging taties from below before this frigging month is out." He sighed wearily, as if at the inhumanity of man to man.

"Watch yer frigging language, Corporal!" a harsh yet female voice intoned in warning, "Don't yer frigging know that a frigging lady is in yer frigging presence?" They turned from the square, surrounded by the buildings still smoking from the previous night's RAF bombing attack on the German capital.

Smartly and a little awe-struck, Schulze whistled at what he saw, while next to him Matz crossed himself rapidly in the elaborate Bavarian fashion, "Get a load o" that mate, will yer – *all that meat and no potatoes!*"

Opposite them the huge woman, smartly uniformed in the walking-out dress of a senior NCO of the SS, drew herself up even taller, with a jerk of her wrist pushing up her left breast which seemed to have escaped from the bra beneath her tunic. "Well," she snorted and rubbed her other hand along the black trace of an incipient moustache beneath her big red nose, "what kind of Christmas tree frigging soldiers are you two? Don't yer frigging well know enough to salute a sergeant major of the SS when you see one? *Wird's bald!*"

There was something about the huge woman's tone of voice that made them comply at once, with Schulze whispering out of the side of his mouth in a suddenly awed tone, "Get yer turnip," – he meant 'head' – "in between them tits of hers and yer'd never know pain any more."

"Stop that talk in the frigging ranks!" the huge woman bellowed, her broad face flashing an angry puce, though Matzi guessed she didn't take the sudden rage too seriously; it was the kind of artificial anger which NCOs affected to frighten raw recruits. "Now mark this behind yer frigging ears and mark it right off, you couple of soft tails." She looked contemptuously at their flies to make her meaning quite clear. "I've bin ordered to take care of you two frigging heroes from the frigging front by *Reichsführer SS* Himmler hissen". She grinned suddenly, showing a mouthful of gold teeth. "I think he's got his monthlies, cos he don't feel like talking to yer personally."

Schulze, looking at Matz in slight bewilderment, said, "you said *Reichsführer SS*?"

"Yes, are yer deaf as well as daft? But we don't want to discuss that out here. You don't know who might be listening." She indicated the two awe-struck young sentries "I'll take yer over to the rest home for elderly noncoms. But I warn yer, I want yer to zip yer frigging lip over there. They're a delicate bunch, I don't want no bad language, or I'll have them swooning with shock on me agen." She laughed coarsely and turning, commanded, "Follow me, arse-with-ears." They followed even against their will admiring those huge shapely flanks beneath the tight grey material of the SS uniform. As Schulze was forced later to confess to his old running mate, "I think I fell in love with her there and then. What an arse, bigger than a ten-dollar horse's!" Coming from 'Mrs Schulze's handsome son,' as he always called himself proudly, that was the ultimate compliment.

"Suds," the big female NCO whose name they had found out as they attempted to keep up with her as she strode across the parade ground to the Senior NCOs' Mess, was Schonhals – "*Sergeant-frigging-Major* Schonhals, and don't yer frigging well forget it" – ordered drinks gruffly, "and a bottle of fire water," she added to the mess waiter in his white jacket, and then to the two old running mates. "That is if you two piss-pansies drink the hard stuff? Yer know there are too many warm brothers in the SS NCO corps these days. Yer never know d'yer?" she swept her hard gaze around the NCOs present, as if making sure that none of them were 'warm brothers', in other words homosexuals.

They, too, gazed at those hard-bitten, rakish, brutalised

faces and Schulze commented, "They all look hard dandies to me, Sarnt Major."

She laughed uproariously, as the mess waiter brought the drinks she'd ordered and said mockingly, "They'd have to be a lot harder than that to make my glassy orbs pop, Sergeant Schulze."

Schulze said nothing in reply. He thought it wiser as Sergeant Major Schonhals took a tremendous gulp of her 'suds' which emptied the litre glass of beer in one go, smacked her suddenly very red lips, wiped them with the back of her hand and belched as if in appreciation, then snorted, "That'll do fer starters. Now then, the two of yer. I know why Colonel General Dietrich – that old horned-ox of a Munich fart – sent yer here, as does *Reichsführer SS* Himmler. I have his full authority," and she thrust out that magnificent chest of hers like a tremendous feather pillow anchored there by the leather belt around her ample waist, "to inform you that he is backing yer up all the way – as the pavement-pounder said to the stubb hopper with the big prong." Again she laughed uproariously at her own wit and reached for the bottle of schnapps.

They eyed it apprehensively, wondering if they were going to get any share of the coveted firewater.

She pulled out the cork with her front teeth, spat it into the corner, poured a stiff slug into her own tumbler, then handed the half-empty bottle to a worried Schulze. "Give yersen a drink, and that little perverted banana sucker next to you as well. But don't down all the sauce. I need another drink before I eat my breakfast." So saying, she knocked back the fiery schnapps with more gusto than even Schulze could produce on an empty stomach.

She waited till Schulze had filled their two tumblers, chasing the schnapps down with her beer, then grabbing the bottle from them before they dare have any more, and they wouldn't have dared in the presence of female Sergeant Major Schonhals. "All right," she announced, "this is the crap." She looked from left to right to check whether any other of the NCOs was listening. Satisfied that they weren't, she went on with: "You've got the *Reichsführer SS's* permission."

"Permission – to do what?" they asked in unison.

"To rescue *Obersturmbannführer* von Dodenburg," she said easily, as if it were only a matter of opening a prison cell door.

Schulze whistled softly between his two front teeth and instinctively reached for the bottle to have another drink, necessary to overcome the shock of her bald announcement.

Hastily she grabbed it and snarled, "Keep yer frigging thieving flippers of that bottle." She eyed the two old hares threateningly, then relaxed. "We know where he is. We know how he's guarded and we know that the frigging *Amis* are not yet ready to try this officer. So now is the time to act."

"*Try him?*" Schulze asked, puzzled.

"Yes. But don't worry yer pretty head about that. Your job is to carve him out of his prison on the Moselle."

"Just like that," Matz quipped maliciously, eyeing the bottle still protectively clutched in the Sergeant Major's big fist.

"Zip yer lip, ape-turd," she said routinely, "or I'll frigging zip it for yer." She paused, finished her 'suds' and went on, "Have either of you two heard of the Werewolves?"

They shook their heads as one. "No," Matz said cheekily, "what are they when they're at home – the Führer's new secret weapon?"

Solemnly, Sergeant Major Schonhals nodded her head, which evidently again dislodged one of her massive dugs beneath her bulging tunic and with her elbow she forced it back into its cup.

Schulze watched the movement with narrowed eyes, telling himself he'd never seen a woman with so much wood before the door. "Christ!" he cursed to himself, feeling the old familiar stirring at his loins, "I daren't get up from the chair or I'd knock all the frigging glasses off 'n the frigging table!"

"They are a group of boys and girls, all from the Hitler Youth and the SS, who have volunteered to stay behind the enemy's lines. Now there's 5,000 of them or so in place on the other side of the Rhine."

Matz whistled softly, impressed. Schulze wasn't. Sourly he said, "Don't the poor silly shits realise that they are frigging cannonfodder? They'll all be dancing on air at the end of the hangman's rope if the *Amis* catch them. There's the death penalty for spying and sabotage you know, Sarnt Major."

She shrugged easily. "Tell that to *Reichsführer SS* Himmler," she responded and then her voice was urgent once more. "At all events, we're going to use these Werewolves to get out this *Obersturmbannführer* of yours. Himmler has given it the highest priority."

"But how are we gonna contact them?" Schulze asked.

The woman poked a finger like a hairy pork sausage at her massive bosom saying, "You *ain't. I am.* I know the Moselle-Eifel area like the back of my hand. I was brought up as an innocent little girl in the area."

Matz looked at Schulze in open-mouthed disbelief. His eyes read: *Her – an innocent little frigging girl*! She ain't been innocent since they took the three-cornered towelling pants off'n her you know what."

Schonhals caught the look and said hastily, "Oh yes, I was innocent – *once*. Before that fart of an uncle – he wasn't my uncle really, but we all called him that – took me for a ride on his bike into the country." Suddenly she was oddly embarrassed, stopping short and snorting, "Enough of that rubbish. Where was I?"

They told her.

"Right. So, according to the *Reichsführer*, we must make the rescue within the next eight to ten days. Why, does not concern you".

Schulze looked at the big woman, as if she had suddenly gone mad. "And how, Sarnt Major, are we going to work our way across the Rhine, which is now the front line, manned by hundreds of thousands of Tommies and *Amis*, and then get into the Rhineland with the facilities available to us, eh?" He looked challengingly at Sergeant Major Schonhals.

She returned his look calmly. "Very simply," she answered. "The *Reichsführer* has made special provision for us. At Hildesheim airfield there is a secret bomber squadron – the 1/KG 200 – which undertakes special missions, using captured enemy planes, Halifax bombers, Flying Fortresses and the like—"

"You don't mean," Matz interrupted her, his little wizened face aghast, unable to finish his question as the thought struck him a tremendous, frightening blow.

"I do. We *parachute* in!"

"Nobody's gonna get me to go for a walk in the air with my only support a bit of torn-off ladies' knickers!" Matz objected.

"It's either that or this." Melodramatically she drew her dirty finger across her plump throat, as if slitting it with a sharp knife. "You know too frigging much as it is, Corporal Matz."

Schulze intervened quickly. "All right . . . all right, so let's say we get that far. The flyboys drop us out of their plane somewhere beyond the Rhine. Who's gonna guide us through the enemy rear areas, packed with troops, to where they're holding our old CO. Go on Sarnt Major, tell me?"

She smiled at him sweetly, appraising him with eyes which were abruptly full of naked sexual interest. "I will, *dear* Sergeant Schulze," she simpered, head tilted coquettishly to one side like an innocent girl whose 'uncle' had not yet taken her for a ride on his bike into the country.

"*ME!*"

# Chapter Seven

The captured US Flying Fortress, still bearing the wing markings of the 8th Air Force to which it had once belonged before it had been forced down by a Messerschmitt over Germany, droned on with monotonous regularity. It was a fine, slightly sunny day and although the pilot had taken her up quite high prior to the descent for the paradrop, the 'team', as the three of them were now called by the members of the 100th, could see the ground below pretty clearly: the odd patches of snow still dotting the Sauerland heights; the thin black patches of industrial smoke from what was left of the Ruhr industry to their right; and the long toy columns of trucks and tanks heading for the defence of the Rhine, though even as the three of them watched they knew it wouldn't be long before the *Wehrmacht* troops would be making a mad dash for cover. Once the feared Allied *jabos* spotted them and came tearing in at treetop height, cannon and machine-guns blazing they'd be scuttling towards the woods and forest right and left of the *autobahn* leading south to the Rhine.

"Don't worry yer pretty soldier boys' heads," the mincing *Luftwaffe* dispatcher who painted his nails and smelled of perfume, warbled as he saw the look on their face beneath the leather flying helmets, "we've got the *Ami* insignia on this crate and all their secret call-and-recognition signals. We're a crippled Fortress coming back from a raid on

Magdeburg. When – and if – they make an appearance we'll feather a starboard engine and let off smoke as if we've been hit. We've done it before," he added confidently. He looked at Matz, ashen-faced, apprehensive (he'd never flown before) and air sick, and pouted his painted lips. "Shall I hold yer hand, soldier boy?" he asked. "You look like a nice sort of – er – fellow," saying the words as if they were of some special significance, known only to him.

"Go and shit in yer shako," Schulze snorted crudely. "He's not like that." He gave an apathetic Matz a deep look and added, "Well, I don't think he is at least."

Sergeant Major Schonhals, muffled up in her flying gear and the electrically heated *Ami* suit, turned from the open machine-gun bay. "Won't be long. I've just spotted the Rhine and the pilot's coming down. He says we're going to jump from 300 metres. That should get us down to the ground before anybody spots us."

"Without a parachute, Sarnt Major," Schulze quipped, though he had never felt less like joking. "That should get us down right toot-sweet."

She ignored the snide remark. "Once down we bury the chutes, the flying suit and get on our hind legs at double-quick frigging time." She looked grim suddenly, as if she had abruptly realised once again what would happen to them if they were caught. But if she did, she kept those dark thoughts to herself, lapsing into a preoccupied silence once more.

They flew on. The minutes passed in silence, save the steady throb of the Fortress's four engines. The homosexual dispatcher disappeared and Schulze thought he could smell the delicious odour of 'real' coffee being brewed farther up the fuselage in the galley. "Lucky assholes," he told himself. "Real bean coffee. Bet they've never been up to their hooters in shit at the front—"

He stopped short. Through the open .5in machine-gun blister on the port side he caught a glimpse of a small silver shape coming up from the waterlogged Rhenish plain below, ascending into the spring sky at an amazing rate. He felt a small finger of icy fear trace its way down the small of his back. It could only be an *Ami jabo*, a fighter-bomber. The enemy had shot the *Luftwaffe* out of the skies since the turn of 1945. Now whatever was left of 'Fat Hermann's boys'* would not dare to take to the heavens in daylight, especially near the Rhine. He held his breath and waited for what might happen next.

Then the lone American fighter was zooming at an incredible speed right over the huge captured bomber. For an instant Schulze caught a glimpse of the pilot's white blur of a face behind the gleaming sparkle of his cockpit. Then the fat-bellied silver Thunderbolt was hurtling even higher into the sky, trailing behind it a green signal-flare. Schulze held his breath. What did that flare mean?

Next moment the homosexual dispatcher came blundering down the fuselage, dressed in – of all things – some kind of cooking apron, with a pot of steaming coffee, complete with tin cups in his hands, stating, "Not to worry, fellahs . . . Everything is all right . . . He's checking us out . . . All routine, you can rest ass—"

The sudden crackle of cannon-fire made Schulze jump. Next to him, Matz cried, "What in three devils' name—" He never finished the sentence. Suddenly the fuselage was filled with the acrid stench of burnt cordite and the dispatcher was crumpling to his knees, still clutching his pot of coffee, blood arching in a bright red stream from his shattered chest through which the bones of the rib-cage glistened.

---

* Hermann Goering, the bloated, massive head of the German *Luftwaffe*.

"Hold on!" Sergeant Major Schonhals yelled, as up front the the pilot jerked the stick forward and the bomber's nose tilted downwards dramatically. Abruptly they were hurtling out of the sky, bound for certain doom and destruction.

Back in the fuselage in his little compartment, the sweating, frantic radio operator was sending out signal after signal in the hope that they might yet still fool their attacker into believing that they were a genuine US Flying Fortress in trouble. To no avail!

Once again the Thunderbolt came barrelling in, four machine-guns and cannon spitting fire. A series of glowing white 20mm cannon-shells tore the length of the top cabin. For a moment the terrified pilot relinquished the controls as the perspex canopy splintered into a spider's web of shattered plastic. Behind, the radio operator screamed and reeled back, dead, in his earphones the radio chattering purposelessly, for the Flying Fortress was doomed. Even the two laymen Matz and Schulze knew that now.

Sergeant Major Schonhals reacted immediately to the new danger, as the pilot regained his nerve and grabbed for the controls. Using all his strength, his shoulder muscles bulging through the material of his flying suit, he fought to pull the great bomber out of its death dive. To no avail and as Schonhal yelled above the howl of the engines still running at full throttle, *"Parachutes on!"*, the two old running mates were already fumbling with the straps of their chutes with fingers that felt like clumsy sausages enclosed in boxing gloves.

By now the bomber was tilted at an almost impossible angle. Strips of gleaming metal were shredding from it to flutter slowly to the ground far below. Still their merciless attacker came zooming in again, firing furiously, determined to finish off the crippled Fortress, trailing thick black smoke behind it.

Like men fighting their way up a mountain slope against a hurricane-force wind, Schulze and Matz, followed by the woman sergeant major, clambered hand over hand towards the open hatch, the terrific pressure forcing the flesh of their faces into grotesque masks.

"Keep . . . keep going . . . !" Schonhals gasped, her massive chest heaving as if she had run a great race.

Even in this moment of extreme danger and fear, Schulze said to himself in undisguised admiration, "By the Great Whore of Buxtehude . . . that woman has got real balls!"

At the controls, the pilot screamed. Then a sudden burst of cannon-shells ripped off his head, but it hung suspended in mid-air by the wires attached to the flying helmet, as blood pumped out of the neck of the torso in thick, scarlet jerks. The plane's nose dropped even lower. There was no escape.

"*March or croak!*" Schulze yelled, carried away by a crazy mixture of unreasoning panic and wild exuberance. Below them the green and brown patched earth flew by them at a terrific rate as they left the silver snake of the Rhine behind them.

"Mark or croak," Matz, his face ashen, as if he might be sick at any moment, echoed weakly.

"Don't fuck about!" Sergeant Major Schonhals snapped above the awful racket in that no-nonsense manner of hers. She rapidly sized up the two SS men. "You!" she cried at Matz, the wind tearing the words out of her mouth.

"What?"

"You first."

Matz looked down at the ground scudding by, now only 400 or 500 metres below. "I . . . I could hurt myself," he stuttered, now almost panic-stricken.

"Yer. I'll do the hurting if you don't position yersen at that frigging door *NOW!*"

Matz allowed himself to be shoved forward to hold on to

both sides of the exit door with white-clenched knuckles, with the howling wind plucking at him.

"Move it!" she yelled frantically, knowing that time was running out rapidly for the three of them. "If you don't jump now, we'll all be frigging mincemeat in half a mo!"

Still Matz didn't move. Losing patience with the terrified little man, she levered herself in position the best she could. Next moment she aimed a tremendous kick at Matz's skinny backside. His wooden leg cracked under that terrific impact. The bottom half fell to the metal deck. Next moment the little corporal vanished, carried away by the slipstream, arms flailing, silent screams wrung from his gaping mouth.

"What did yer go and do—?"

Schulze did not finish his outburst.

"*OUT.*" she yelled, raising her cruelly shod boot once more. Schulze didn't wait to be kicked. He waddled the last few paces to the door, hooked on to his static line, looked down and wished that he hadn't. Then, with his eyes tightly screwed shut to blot out the countryside rushing wildly past below, he flung himself out of the doomed Fortress.

Then he was falling at a tremendous rate. He felt his trousers suddenly go wet and hot with the urine of fear. It didn't matter, he told himself. He was going to end up on the ground as flat as a frigging pancake in a moment. Nothing mattered now.

"*Crack*!" the sound was like a pistol shot. He seemed to pause in mid-air as the shroudlines dug cruelly into his armpits and crotch. "What . . . me frigging balls—" The angry words died on his lips. Above him a creamy white canopy had opened and he was swinging from side to side gently, as he gazed up at the silk as if he couldn't quite believe it was there.

Slowly, very slowly, he started to drift to the earth.

To his right, the Flying Fortress screamed down. It struck

the earth in a mad flurry of soil and flame and rushed forward at a tremendous speed. All four props bent like the soft metal of a child's toy. A great wake of flying rock and torn metal followed it. The shattered fuselage struck a half-concealed rock. For a moment, it seemed to balance on its nose. But then, slowly, it dramatically crashed over onto its back. The fuel tanks ruptured and the air was suddenly full of the cloying stench of escaping gasoline. But not for long. With a great whoosh the fuel ignited and like a gigantic blowtorch the flame seared the length of the fuselage, burning off the paint in great popping bubbles. A moment later it exploded altogether. When the smoke and flame had cleared all that was to be seen of the great four-engined plane was a single wheel trundling crazily through the green spring corn. Suddenly all was quiet as the Thunderbolt hurtled high into the blue sky, turning its victory rolls, leaving a white vapour trail behind it across the bright wash of the heavens till it, too, vanished. Then there was a loud, echoing silence that seemed to go on for ever, broken now and again by the sharp crack of ammunition exploding in the burned-out Flying Fortress.

After they reached the ground, for what seemed a long time Schulze and Schonhals lay there tangled together like lovers locked in some final embrace of exhausted ecstasy. Suddenly – startlingly – white tracer zipped lethal and low across the shell-holed field into which they had landed. For what seemed an eternity, though which in reality lasted a matter of seconds, the two of them didn't react. Then Sergeant Major Schonhals pulled herself to her feet, crying as she did so "Ferk this for a ferking game o' soldiers! Here come the ferking *Amis!*"

She was right. Cautious, bent figures were approaching across the field dodging the shell-holes, brown against the green like the work of giant moles; and Schulze didn't need a crystal ball to know that they were looking for them.

Schulze sprang up. "Where's Matz?" he demanded, as the Americans spotted them and there was a crackle of wild small-arms fire coming their way.

"Over here, arse-with-ears!" Matz whined plaintively, "and the shiteheels have chopped me pegleg agen. Why do they keep on doing that?"

Schulze was in no mood to answer that question. Darting forward he grabbed the little corporal and tucking him under his brawny right arm like a bundle of rags he set off running for the cover of the nearest trees. A moment later Sergeant Major Schonhals followed, cursing wildly, with the slugs beating a tattoo of death at her flying heels.

# Chapter Eight

For a while Schulze had told himself the chase had died down. After all, planes were shot out of the sky every day. Why bother about a handful of fugitives now that the war was about won anyway? But he had been wrong. There seemed to be armed troops everywhere splashing through the waterlogged fields, shouting excitedly to one another and pointing the way that they thought the three of them had gone. At regular intervals flares hissed spluttering into the grey, lowering sky and more than once a little American artillery spotter plane came plodding in at tree-top height, speed just above stalling, obviously on the lookout for them.

Now up to their knees in stinking grey mud, they sought some respite, for as strong as he was Schulze was beginning to feel the strain of carrying his old comrade with his shattered pegleg. More than once, Matz had said, "Give it a rest, old house, willya? Yer can't carry me like this for ever. Dump me and get on." To which Schulze had grunted sourly in reply, "Knock it off, buggerlugs. I'm giving the orders here, *Kumpel*!"*

Sergeant Major Schonhals, as senior NCO, had shot the big man a look, but had said nothing. Schulze reasoned that she, too, was almost reaching the end of her tether, big and strong as she was.

---

* 'Mate', *Transl.*

By midday, hidden by a light mist rising from the Rhine, they were beginning to leave the delta, packed with assault troops waiting for the signal to cross behind them. Now they were toiling up a steep, narrow, winding road leading up into the Eifel hills. As a weary Schonhals had explained! "My guess is that the *Amis* will begin to thin out now. This should be the reserve area – the place where the rear echelon hang out. They'll be too scared of their own shadows to venture out of their billets once it gets dark. She flashed a glance at the grey sky, which was growing greyer in the wet mist. "And that won't be too long now to judge by that sky."

"There's many a frigging slip between cup and lip," Schulze told himself, hindered as they were by the little man, but he kept that thought to himself.

In weary silence they plodded on up the steep country in between the wooden hills, with the pines stretching up them in straight ranks like spike-helmeted Prussian grenadiers. All was silent now save the sound of their own laboured breathing and the keening of a wild bird soaring effortlessly over the trees in search of its prey. All the same, Schulze, with Matz asleep now, still slung over his massive shoulder, felt an uneasy sense of apprehension. He couldn't quite put his finger on it, but it was there all right and it worried him.

At 2.00 that dark afternoon, with the mist dampening their faces so that their features looked as if they were glistening with sweat, and as Schonhals was saying, "We're on the second-class road to Simmern, perhaps ten kilometres away now. With luck we can get our heads down there and something to eat, the locals are still loyal to our cause—" then it happened.

The Staghound armoured car burst from the forest trail to their right, throwing up a wake of soil and stones behind it, and caught them completely, totally by surprise. Astonished as he was, Schulze knew immediately that the *Amis* were looking for them. Why else would the six-wheeled US armoured car be out in the woods in the remote place far behind the main battle front? "Run for it!" he cried in sudden alarm, as the Staghound braked wildly to a stop, slithering in the muddy track, but with the turret gunner already behind the .5 in machine-gun and swinging it round in their direction.

Old hares as they were, they broke in two different directions to make his aim more difficult, perhaps even put him off his stroke. And even now in this emergency they kept their heads. Instead of clambering *up* the slope, which would slow down their escape, they sprang over the side of the road and began slithering and sliding *down* the lower incline, gathering speed as they did so.

But the black soldiers manning the Staghound seemed to have been expecting them to do this. As the first burst of tracer zipped over their heads in a lethal stream others on the deck of the armoured car opened fire. Slugs slammed into the trees. Wood chippings rained down upon the running figures. Here and there branches snapped like matchwood and fell. Bullets stitched the wet earth at their flying feet. "Couldn't hit a frigging barn door with a frigging bayonet!" Schulze yelled scornfully as he ran all out, Matz bouncing up and down on his brawny shoulder helplessly. Luck was on their side, he told himself joyfully. They were going to do it yet again. They were going to escape from this surprise ambush!

But for once Mrs Schulze's 'handsome son' was wrong, badly wrong. Crying angrily at the thought of their enemies escaping, the Negroes on the deck of the Staghound, which the unseen driver had brought to a stop so that they could aim better, started to take careful shots at the running figures.

Sergeant Major Schonhals was hit first. She screamed,

oddly feminine for her, faltered and then, gasping something which Schulze didn't get, staggered on. On the big sergeant's back, Matz tensed, his spine arched like a taut bow as the hot steel slammed into his shoulder. Schulze appeared to hesitate, but Matz yelled through gritted teeth, "Keep going . . . keep going, you silly shitbag!"

Then it was Schulze's turn. Something like a red-hot poker thrust with terrifying pain into his right calf. He staggered and almost fell, the agony was almost too much. Then, wounded and exhausted they were all round the bend in the downward track and the firing started to die away behind them. Perhaps the Negroes were too frightened to venture into the trees on foot, for the armoured car wouldn't be able to make it. Schulze neither knew nor cared. All he was concentrating on now, with the blood trickling down his calf, which was already beginning to stiffen alarmingly, was to get them under cover long enough to be able to patch themselves up. Then he'd see what else could be done. But even as the thought entered his fevered mind he knew that there was no future for them, alone in this Godforsaken wood with every man's hand against them. Finally, after six years of combat, they had reached the end of the line.


Sergeant Major Schonhals was dying. That was obvious. He had found the ruined stone woodcutter's hut half an hour before and without attempting to tend to his wounded calf he had hopped around gathering boughs and the like so that the other two could lie on something soft and perhaps a little warmer, too.

At first the big SS woman had been her usual tough self despite the gaping wound in her back through which were just visible her pulsating lungs and heart. "See to that little fart of a garden dwarf first," she had gasped. "The little shit needs it more than me . . ." But then she had begun to cough blood and his one field-dressing had been soaked with her blood within seconds. Her face suddenly pinched, the tip of her big nose white and narrowed, something which Schulze had always thought to be a sure sign of death, and she had started to wander off into a world of her own. Now and then she had moaned. A couple of times she appeared to have fainted, but when he had cautiously touched her her eyelids had flickered weakly and she had muttered something that he couldn't understand.

Once she had muttered for a while in a small girl's voice as if she had been that child who had not yet gone off with 'Uncle' into the woods. "I never wanted to be fat," she had gasped apropos of nothing. "Just sweet . . . have boys love me . . . Kind boys, nice boys, boys who didn't stink of alcohol and didn't want to stick their salami in me . . . No not them . . ."

"It's all right . . . all right," he had tried to soothe her, but she hadn't heard and continued her wild ramblings into the past. But about 4.00 that long, terrible March afternoon her ramblings had ceased and she had commanded in a rational manner, "I'm dying . . . I want you to say the Act of Contrition for me before I go, Sergeant Schulze."

Schulze shook his head wearily, his old cynical self totally absent as he felt the blood ebbing from him. Suddenly he was very faint and nauseated. He'd pass out in a minute, he knew that.

Sergeant Major Schonhals somehow raised herself. "But you . . . you must," she pleaded. "*Must!*" She fell back, completely exhausted by that last effort.

Matz looked from one to the other helplessly. Schulze's eyelids were flickering wildly. He was going to pass out at any time now and the huge woman was dying as she lay there. She seemed to have shrunk to half her normal size.

He cleared his throat and tried desperately to remember what the priest, *Vater* Johann, had taught them so long ago in that mountain *Volksschule*, with the crucifix over the door and all age groups from the mountain village grouped in one classroom. "I'll try," he said hoarsely, hardly recognising his own voice.

"Thank God!" she breathed, her massive chest, now shrunken, heaving in and out frantically. "Thank God!"

"Father," he began hesitantly, trying to get those almost forgotten words together, "I have sinned . . ."

Schonhals tried to clasp her hands together but failed lamentably. Next to her, Schulze gave a little gasp and passed out. Doggedly, fighting back his tears, Matz continued, *"Mea . . . culpa . . . mea maxima culpa . . ."*

Suddenly the big Sergeant Major, whose gaze had been riveted on his wizened, agonised face as she had attempted to say the last prayer with him, ceased in mid-word. She tried to say something, but failed. Next moment her head lolled to one side like a broken doll's and Matz didn't need to look any closer to know she was dead.

All was silent now, as he gazed at the two motionless figures. There was no hope for von Dodenburg now, he realised that. Slowly, sorrowfully, sad tears start to trickle down his cheeks. It was all over . . . and in the trees the wind blew softly and without feeling . . .


Twenty-five miles away on the other wide of the Eifel hills, von Dodenburg experienced the same feeling as they prepared to deal with him and he waited, his harshly handsome face revealing nothing.

The fat US colonel, with the well-fed, self-satisfied look of a 'rear echelon stallion' about him, was doing all the arrangements, watched by the other two: the one-armed

Englishman, who was definitely a front-line soldier; and the dark-eyed, sinister Jewboy, with that shaven cowl of jet-black hair that he wore like a skull cap.

"I'm not going to waste any time on you, von Dodenburg," Schroeder snapped, as the white-helmeted MPs bustled about the little hospital room getting the prisoner ready for transportation away from Wittlich Military Hospital. "By the time we've finished with you, you'll be singing like a goddam canary. Do you understand?"

Von Dodenburg understood all right, but he said nothing. he was already beginning to conserve his energy for the ordeal which he knew instinctively was soon to come. He flashed a glance at the Englishman, who saw the look and lowered his gaze, as if suddenly ashamed. Not the Jewboy however. There was a wolfish, eager look in his dark eyes, as if he could not wait to get his hands on the prisoner. Making a quick assessment of the situation, von Dodenburg told himself that it wasn't the two soldiers who were going to cause him trouble, even though the fat *Ami* colonel blustered a great deal in his self-important manner; it was the civilian dressed as a soldier. That's where the danger lay.

"Ready to roll, sir," the MP sergeant snapped. "Got all his duds together, sir."

"Thank you, Sergeant," Schroeder said, as outside on the barrack square the engines of the trucks and jeeps started up, for the *Amis* had brought a whole convoy, so it appeared, to escort him to wherever his destination was. He turned to von Dodenburg, sitting somewhat groggily at the edge of the iron cot, with the full chamber pot below it. Von Dodenburg had asked the orderly to empty it, but he had refused. He supposed it was another attempt to humiliate him in front of these tough, fit men who could make their way by themselves to the latrine. "I expect you want to know where we are taking you?" he asked, with a fat smile.

Sharpe frowned, McDougall's face remained impassive, revealing nothing. Von Dodenburg said nothing. He looked totally disinterested.

Schroeder's fat grin disappeared. He suddenly looked angry, "Well, I'll tell you where you're going, buddy," he snapped, his face abruptly flushed. "You're going where the rest of you Nazi trash is ending up. I think the name's apt enough for you jerks." He paused in order, it appeared, to give his words their full impact "You're going to Luxembourg . . . *to Camp Ashcan*. Now what do you say to that, eh, smartass . . . ?"

# Book Three

# *Schulze and Matz to the Rescue*

# Chapter One

Moodily, von Dodenburg stared through the barred window of the one-time Luxembourg hotel. Over the River Moselle was Germany, the vineyards marching up the slopes in the summer sunshine, still pitted with shell holes. Here and there an elderly peasant plodded along the tracks between the vines, following some skinny-ribbed nag, or pulling a *Rollwagen* slowly behind him. Otherwise the German side of the river seemed empty, as if the whole country had died with the shame of the great defeat of the previous May.

Von Dodenburg switched his gaze. He couldn't bear to look. His homeland was obviously finished. The victorious Allies would keep it subjugated for decades – perhaps centuries – turning it from an industrialised country back into the loose collection of agricultural states that it had once been in the Middle Ages. That, at least, seemed to be the American plan as they now took revenge on a beaten, downtrodden German people.

He looked at the grounds below. They were surrounded by high wire fences, guarded by tall, lean US military policemen in their white-lacquered helmets, all toting machine-guns and carbines, and looking as if they were just waiting for the first opportunity to use them on the prisoners. After all, this *was* 'Camp Ashcan', holding the former *Prominenz* of Nazi Germany, soon to be put on trial at Nuremburg for their alleged war crimes.

Gloomily, von Dodenburg, still skinny and pale, though fit once more again thanks to the efforts of the US doctors who had worked all-out on him. "Not because we love ya, Kraut," one of them had snarled in a moment of exasperation at a wound which stubbornly refused to close up, "but because we want to have you fit to stand trial for the murder of our boys last year – and by God in heaven, I hope when the executioner strings you up afterwards he does it slow and painful so that you can suffer like our guys did." He had made no comment. In the intervening months since the *Amis* had transported him to this riverside prison in remote little Luxembourg he had become used to that kind of talk.

He stared at the slow-moving figures below, moving round the circuit in slow motion, though they were all fit and well-fed, better than the average free German on the other side of the Moselle. All of them, former civilians and soldiers alike, wore some kind of *Wehrmacht* uniform, minus badges of rank. Even the 'Golden Pheasants*' the former Party bosses, had been stripped of their one-time finery and given the badgeless uniform of a simple private in the 'Greater German Army', as they had once boasted so pompously.

Von Dodenburg didn't feel sorry for them in their present state. They had never heard a shot fired in anger in six long years of war and they had grown fat and prosperous on the wealth of an occupied, looted Continent. It was different with the soldiers, though they, too, were mostly 'rear echelon stallions', who had fought the war from behind big desks, surrounded by fawning aides and adjutants.

---

* Party leaders, known thus by contemptuous German citizens and soldiers, due to their love of fancy uniforms adorned with plenty of gold braid.

There was Grand Admiral Dönitz, who had once brought Britain to her knees in starvation with his U-boat blockade of that island. Not far away was Goering, 'Fat Hermann', much slimmer now and wearing a simple uniform instead of one of the nineteen or so he had worn habitually during the great conflict. Not far off was Colonel General Jodl, pale-faced and cunning-eyed, who had directed the war for Hitler. Once they had been men with unlimited power, who with a snap of their fingers could send thousands, perhaps hundreds of thousands of ordinary loyal, 'stubble-hoppers' to their deaths in battle. Now they were impotent, powerless, with no pride, glad to scoop up and smoke cigarette ends thrown away by their guards. "Grey ghosts," he whispered to himself, "All grey ghosts . . . dead men from the past."

Von Dodenburg smiled thinly and, walking over to his simple iron cot without a mattress, sat down carefully on its metal frame. It was forbidden to do so in daytime and he knew he'd get a rocket from the guard if he were discovered there, but he needed to sit and think about the events of the past few weeks and what might happen next, now that his interrogators had failed to break him. Outside he could smell the delightful odour of good American tobacco. One of the guards was having an illicit cigarette while on duty. The German's stomach rumbled. He would dearly have loved to have had a smoke himself. But he had given up cigarettes once he had seen how the situation was going. Not only had he refused the cigarettes used as bribes by his interrogators, but he had also stopped himself from picking up the butts, long and fat and with lots of tobacco left in them, tossed away by the sentries. He couldn't see himself rolling his own from these American cast-offs. His dignity as an officer of the most elite regiment of the SS had not allowed him to do so. Instead he had given up smoking altogether. It was hard, as were most things in the life he led now as the key witness in the trial of the SS soon to come. That was what it would become, he knew that.

He licked his cracked bottom lip, where they had punched him repeatedly at his last 'interrogation', and tried to reconstruct what had happened to him and what it all meant for the future when the SS was tried in lieu of the German people. After all, they couldn't try a whole nation; therefore they would try only Hitler's Black Guards. They would become the scapegoats for the whole German people.

He forgot the 'grey ghosts' outside, as he called them to himself. They were no longer important. What was important was the reputation of SS Assault Regiment Wotan – that was the only homeland he knew these days – and the survivors, those young men who had fought to the very last when everyone else had long decided the war was lost and had given up. He couldn't allow such brave men to be sacrificed to save those fawning turncoats of Germans who would soon be serving the victors, toadying to them and their crazy whims for whatever gain it would bring them.

For a few moments he thought of the 'old hares', Sergeant Schule, Matz and the like. What rogues they had been! Yet they would have been the hard-bitten veterans who would have given some kind of backbone to any one of his 'greenhorns', who might waver under the tremendous pressures that would be soon applied to them. And he knew with the one hundred per cent certainty of a vision that was what was going to happen. After all, hadn't they subjected him to those self-same pressures – thankfully without success? Then he dismissed the thought. They had taken a 'dive', his 'old hares'. That's how they had become 'old hares' in the first place, he told himself, with a fond smile at the memory of his trusted veterans. They had known how to keep their heads below the parapet then; and presumably that's what they had done now in this time of defeat. That's why they had not ended up in the special POW camps like the greenhorns, facing a charge of murder. He dismissed his absent 'old hares' and recalled once more what had happened to him the first time they had transported him in the middle of the night in a sealed, guarded truck from Camp Ashcan, across the river and to the secret place of interrogation in the Reich; though he had guessed it was the old Roman city of Trier, the nearest large town on the German side of the Moselle.

They had arrived at dawn, as the down-trodden, half-starved workers in their dyed *Wehrmacht* uniforms of shabby blue overalls had been trudging off to whatever factories had been opened for production once more. No one had paid much attention to his truck, guarded by heavily armed MPs, and riding in jeeps to front and back of it. They had seen enough *Amis* in the last few months not to be curious about these well-fed young men from over the ocean, save for what they might get from them in the way of chewing-gum and cigarette butts.

Slowly the little convoy had rolled through the bomb-shattered surburbs, past the fading signs of the 'One Thousand Year Empire'. *'Hush, the enemy is listening'* ... *'Our Führer knows only work and duty'* ... and ... *'Wheels Roll for Victory'*. All of them seemed to belong to some mythical age of long ago.

They rolled into the centre of the unknown city. Black-clad women already stood patiently, even apathetically, with buckets in front of the water standpipes or little tarpaper food shacks, waiting for whatever pathetic rations were available this day. Everything had an air of defeat apathy, ruin about it – a grey city in a grey month in a grey year.

They turned into a former *Wehrmacht* barracks, with the decaying legend *'Adolf Hitler Kaserne'* above its gates. Already there were amateur whores waiting outside in their shabby blanket jackets and cork-heeled shoes, looking expectantly with professional concupiscence at the new *Amis*. But the guards weren't interested. There was too much VD around. They kept to their 'shack-up jobs', safe little 'schatzies' who could be relied on not to give them the dreaded pox.

The little convoy passed into the courtyard. Up in the barred windows, pale, half-starved faces looked down at the new arrivals without any particular interest. The guards jumped from their vehicles. A big sergeant slapped up the canvas of von Dodenburg's truck, his breath fogging the cold air as he cried, *"Kay, Kraut, let's haul ass!"*

Obediently von Dodenburg did as he was requested. There was no other alternative. Slowly, reluctantly, like a guilty man beginning his last walk to the gallows, he went to meet his captors. They led him through a maze of corridors, penetrating ever deeper into the heart of the prison, their boots echoing hollowly between the dimly lit stone walls, dripping with moisture. Once he tried to ask a question but the sergeant in charge rammed his billy-club into his ribs cruelly, snarling, "No talking, Kraut!"

Finally they stopped in front of a great oaken door that was at least a couple of hundred years old. The sergeant seized the rusty iron ring set in the centre of the nailed door, slammed it back and forth a couple of times and the sound echoed and re-echoed down those grim, silent corridors. Somewhere there was the unpleasant scampering of clawed feet as the rats bolted into the shadows in alarm. Von Dodenburg felt a cold finger of fear trace its way down the centre of his spine.

Slowly, very slowly, like the lid of a coffin being raised, the door squeaked open on its rusty hinges. A blast of icy-air hit von Dodenburg in the face. On the blanket-covered long table he glimpsed candles in their holders flickering, throwing great, grotesque shadows on the dripping stonework. It was like a scene from the Inquisition: silent, uncanny, ominous. Later, von Dodenburg reasoned that it had been carefully staged to rattle him. But at that particular moment he really *was* rattled!

They were all there, sitting or standing in the flickering shadows, as if they had been waiting for him a very long time. There was the American Schroeder; the one-armed Englishman Sharpe, looking worried; three other soldiers he didn't know and the three German Jews, all seated at the table, staring at him, their dark eyes revealing nothing save what seemed a bottomless, burning hatred.

For what seemed ages they all remained quiet, like characters in a waxwork chamber of horrors, frozen into immobility for all time.

Finally, with a slight cough that made von Dodenburg start, the one with the dark cowl of jet-black hair who they called McDougall (though von Dodenburg guessed that it wasn't his real name) broke the heavy, brooding silence. "Ah," he said in German, "the infamous Colonel von Dodenburg of the well-known SS Assault Regiment Wotan." He paused to let his words sink in before continuing, "Perhaps you thought we had forgotten you, my dear Colonel," the voice was silky with menace. "But we hadn't, oh no! . . . We wouldn't forget *you*." His voice rose slightly and became businesslike. "But let us waste no further time . . . Let us begin . . ."

The interrogation of *Obersturmbannführer* Kuno von Dodenburg had commenced.

# Chapter Two

"*Well?*" Sharpe asked and half sat up on the rumpled, sweat-soaked bed. Outside, some drunken soldier was coming back from a GI bar warbling the latest Bing Crosby complete with "*Spurs that jingle, jangle . . . DON'T FENCE ME IN!*"

"Knock off that crap, willya!" an irate, sleepy voice yelled. "Put a sock in it *for Pete's sake*, brother!"

She half smiled at the exchange and, sitting up on one elbow, her jet-black, tousled hair falling over one delightful naked breast, echoed his query. "Well?" She blew him a little kiss and the hard-faced, one-armed British major actually blushed.

Naturally she spoke excellent English, but there was no mistaking the inflection in that "Well?" English wasn't her native tongue. "Why don't you ask? It was good." She breathed out hard, as if with relief "It did *me* a world of good!"

Outside all was silent now. The drunk had staggered off. The only sound was the soft-shoe tread of an American rubber boot on the gravel outside the prison as a guard completed his round.

Sharpe sat back on the damp sheet and said hesitantly, "It's my arm, you see – since my wound." He looked a little helpless, as if he had gone through this type of explanation before but had still not got it right.

"Your *arm?*" she mocked him with those clever, merry

eyes of hers – of all the Yanks he had met in his job ever since he had begun to work with them the previous year, she was the only one who seemed the least bit happy most of the time – "I thought it was that monstrous thing at the other end that counted, Tom!"

"Oh, do be serious and listen," he chided her, feeling happy and satiated now after what had just taken place and not a little in love with this foreign girl who came from a totally different world from his. "One arm puts you off – er – balance when you're making love. You can get her right beneath—"

"The arse and give her a real good rattling, eh, Tom?" she interrupted him naughtily and winked at him as she had done the first time over Schroeder's fat shoulder when they had been introduced as future colleagues at his new office at US Army HQ in Frankfurt. "To be quite frank with you, Tom, I didn't notice. I was too concerned with – er – other things. Besides, if it'll please your male vanity, I do feel well and truly rattled." She swung her shapely, naked legs over the side of the bed. "I need to go to the john – quick!" she said and padded on her bare feet across to the little bathroom, her high, taut buttocks jiggling nicely as she did so.

She sat on the lavatory, legs askew, squirting out the urine in short, sharp bursts, grunting occasionally. "Oh – country contraception," she explained thickly.

"What?" he asked, lazily lighting a cigarette and frowning a little at the thought of what the morrow would bring.

"Oh, country contraception," she answered. "Can't have a goy – that's you – putting me with his gentile child!" She laughed and wiped herself. She rose and stared momentarily at her fine nubile body in the bathroom mirror. "Not bad," she said to herself and then turning to him asked, "You gonna spend the rest of the night with me, Tom?"

He shook his head and answered, "No, just in case the

Yanks – your lot – check the quarters. Wouldn't look good for a broken-down old limey to be found between the sheets with a high-ranking officer in US counter-intelligence. What would Colonel Schroeder say?"

"That asshole!" she said carelessly and taking up a cigarette from the pack of Camels, lit one for herself before he could do it for her. "He can go and take a running jump at himself for all I care."

He nodded his agreement, his lean, hard face wreathed in blue smoke. Somewhere over at the prison, its grey stone walls illuminated by the searchlights which played on them all night, a prisoner groaned in his sleep. "Poor sod," Sharpe said automatically.

She frowned. "War criminal," she corrected him. "Remember that – *war criminal*, Tom."

He shook his head and stubbed out his cigarette with an air of finality. "Not until they are proven guilty, Mary-Ann," he corrected her, feeling awkward as he used her adopted name 'Mary-Ann McIntyre'. In reality, she was Mariann Margolis. But like the rest of the interrogators over in the prison, she had changed it for security reasons.

She pulled on her slip, hiding her delightful, lush figure. "What does it matter? They're the SS, Tom – all those bastards are guilty, proven or not. I should know. Before the war I was at the receiving end of everything the black-uniformed swine could dish out before I went to the States."

"I understand that, dear," he responded hastily and touched her hand affectionately. "But if we're going to bring any kind of justice to this country, we've just got to do things legally ourselves. Do you understand, dearest?"

"Sure I understand, Tom. But what about the men – they've suffered. Not only here in the old country, but also when they moved to the States before the war. They were outcasts in Nazi Germany and they weren't much better when they came to America. After all they were kikes, Yids, Moxies, taking the bread out of the mouths of Americans, who were finding it damned hard to get a job themselves. You can understand just how bitter they were. Unwanted everywhere. And now back here they see the average GI playing footsie with the people who sent their folks into the ovens. No wonder they're bitter . . . want their revenge. And they're not inclined to wear kid gloves to get it, you know." She looked hard at him and paused to let her words sink in.

He understood, but yet he didn't. He still subscribed a little to the old public school ethic with which he had been brought up. "Play up and play the game, sort of thing," as he had mocked it in later life. All the same it was still part of his make-up. "Yes, I get you," he said hurriedly. "But I mean those new GIs that Schroeder had brought over from the UK as witnesses of the massacre back in December 1944. They're lying, you know that."

She said nothing, but she pouted suddenly like a spoiled, frustrated child who couldn't have its way.

"I mean they simply couldn't have seen von Dodenburg when they said they did. Why?" He shrugged a little angrily. "Simple. Because he wasn't there, that's why . . ."


They had led von Dodenburg into the underground interrogation room, the guards hearing rubber-soled shoes so that they glided in with their prisoner noiselessly. As usual they had placed a black hood over his head and a noose, with which they guided him, around the prisoner's neck.

The hood had been removed and as von Dodenburg stood there blinking in the sudden light, McDougall had immediately launched into his attack. "You can tell us any damn thing you like, von Dodenburg. But *we* know you're guilty. You shot the American prisoners down left, right and centre without mercy."

Von Dodenburg's face had remained impassive, revealing nothing of his inner thoughts. McDougall had pressed the buzzer on the rough, blanket-covered desk in front of him and the door had creaked open immediately. Two GIs appeared, as if they had been hidden behind the door, waiting for this call; one of them, a big surly fellow with angry dark eyes, limped.

McDougall rasped a question and the big man, who was the ex-Kosher short-order cook Rosenkranz, had wasted no time. Immediately he had pointed a finger at the puzzled prisoner, crying, "That's him, sir. That's the jerk who ordered our guys shot. K'd recognize him anywhere, sir."

Finally von Dodenburg's temper snapped, as McDougall had hoped it would. The weeks of torment had taken their toll. "I haven't killed any prisoners," he shouted in German, "and you damn well know it. If I had, I'd say so." He looked contemptuously at McDougall's dark, set face. "Do you think I'm afraid of dying, eh? *Do you?* God in heaven, I'd be only too glad to close my eyes for good and say that's that. I don't need to worry any longer. I've had six long years of it—" He looked wildly at his interrogators' stony, unfeeling faces. "What *could* you know about such things?" He controlled himself with difficulty, his shoulders heaving with the effort of his outburst. "I didn't kill the prisoners," he added in a voice without emotion, "and you know it."


As she dressed, Sharpe remembered that outburst and knew that the German had been speaking the truth, but how could he convince the girl who, of all those involved in the interrogation, was the most likely to show some compassion, some feeling, some sense of justice that went beyond her own personal problems and experiences? Yet somehow he knew, at least, that at the moment he couldn't. He gave up. "I'll see you tomorrow," he said, abruptly deflated.

"Yes, I guess so," she answered without any enthusiasm and then buttoning up her tunic she was gone.

Sharpe frowned. "You made a bit of a balls up of that, old chum," he said, talking to himself in the manner of lonely men. Still, he knew it had to be said. Someone had to convince basically decent people like Mary-Ann that two wrongs didn't make a right. What was going on with the German Colonel von Dodenburg was an abuse of power, an act of revenge or simple office-seeking, especially in the case of fat Colonel Schroeder, whom he suspected wouldn't give a twopenny toss if all the Jews in America were wiped out.

Sharpe lay back on the rumpled bed, single hand balanced under his head, his nostrils still assailed by the subtle fragrance of her perfume that lingered after the had left. It was well past curfew time for the Germans and by now even the GI bars with their drunken American soldiers would be closed. All was silent. He let his mind wander as he gave up on the problem of von Dodenburg, presumably asleep in his bare, icy cell only a hundred yards or so from where he lay stretched at this very moment. There seemed nothing he could do. The new British Government in London wouldn't be interested; they had more than enough problems on the home front to occupy them. The average man in the street wanted to forget the war and the fate of a Nazi colonel didn't interest them one bit. The only ones interested in von Dodenburg were those who strove to convict him and see him dance his last jig at the end of a length of hempen rope used by Master Sergeant Woods, the official US hangman.

He sighed. Why did he have a damned conscience? The Jerries had blown off his arm and put an end to his fighting career, the only job he had been trained for ever since he had reported to OCTU. If he 'kept his nose clean', as the fat Colonel Schroeder had put it, leering at him knowingly, and didn't rock the boat, he was sure of a half colonelcy. "Ike'll see to that, Major. I promise you." So why didn't he keep his conscience under control and his mouth shut?

Sharpe didn't know the answers to those questions. Outside, the clock in the tower which topped the 19th century Prussian prison began ponderously to chime midnight. He frowned. It was time to go to sleep. "What a life – if you don't fucking weaken," he snarled to himself, using the old sweat's time-honoured expression.

Slowly he drifted off into an uneasy slumper, crowded with severed arms, dripping blood; great hairy vaginas, wide-open so that they, too, appeared to drip blood; and dangling above those unattached bloody objects was a length of stiff rope, waving to and fro slowly like a live thing.

# Chapter Three

"All right," McDougall said in German, for among themselves they always spoke their native language, though they would be the last to admit it to anyone outside their little circle of 'emigrants', as they described themselves to their American colleagues in counter-intelligence, "this has got to be our strategy from now onwards. The war's over and Eisenhower is soon returning to the States, so the Army's no longer so much interested in the Wotan case. But," he leaned forward to emphasize his point, "the State Department is!" His dark, wolfish face looked angry for a moment or two, as if he were thinking of other things.

Outside the office window, the Bavarian sky was dark and leaden as if threatening the first snow of the winter.

"The fellows in the striped suits are beginning to have trouble with the Russkis. They're going to need the Germans soon, they tell us. Yes," he repeated the words as if he couldn't quite believe them himself. "Yes, Germany is to be our ally against the Russians one of these days. The boys in Washington reason that the limeys have gone commie already now that they've got a *sozi* government and the Frogs are weak sisters. De Gaulle and his gang couldn't fight their way out of a paper bag, a wet one at that. So it's got to be the Germans." There was a bitter note in his voice.

"So what has that got to do with us and the SS?"

Mary-Ann asked, as usual the quickest off the mark with the 'emigrants'.

"This. Try to convict the SS at double-quick time. Get it behind us, make them the scapegoats of the whole German Nazi pack and then the rest can be our allies with a clear conscience. Heaven, arse and cloudburst, the boys in Washington didn't need a Bismarck to teach them about *realpolitik*." McDougall let his words sink in, glowering at the window and the grey sky beyond. "So what have we to do?"

He answered his own question. "Our orders from that fat pain-in-the-ass Schroeder is get confessions quick so that the trial and the sentences can be dealt with before Christmas. In the New Year the Germans have to come up smelling of attar of roses – all sweetness and light."

"But how can we convict them when we don't know yet they're guilty?" Mary-Ann objected, puzzled. "Von Dodenburg hasn't cracked in the slightest degree."

"I know . . . I know," McDougall said, irritated beyond all measure by her words. "You don't have to write it on the fucking wall – excuse me. So we get rid of the bastard for the time being. We've got to find the weak sisters among his command who will crack, and crack quickly."

"Who?" one of the emigrants ventured, as Mary-Ann frowned at what she had just heard.

McDougall looked at the speaker, in control of himself once again. It was typical of him, something which made him feared by the men he interrogated, his ability to switch from a blind rage to calm, dispassionate reasoning in seconds. It was something that always upset the chosen victim. "The young for one," he said. "They are not hard like the veterans; they lack the backbone of the Nazi swine who had been with Wotan for years. The one-time fanatics, the kids from the Hitler Youth, the ones from the Party, who have now learned that Germany is not invincible and that their one-time Party bosses have feet of clay; that they beg and grovel for handouts and cigarette butts just like the rest." He looked around the circle of his listeners, all their eyes fixed intently on him. "But, above all, the ethnic Germans and those wretches who volunteered from the Occupied Countries to fight for Nazi Germany – the French, the cheese-eaters, the Belgies and the swine from the east. Threaten to send *them* back to the new masters in their old countries, the Reds, the Resistance and the like, and believe you me, *meine Herren*, they'll sing like the yellow canaries they are."

"But they're the little people," Mary-Ann objected. "What is to be gained from their confessions? Who cares about what they did or did not do, even if they were in SS Wotan?"

McDougall smiled deviously, obviously pleased with himself. "Their confessions will not be used against them . . . their confessions will be used to prove von Dodenburg's guilt. If he won't confess it, then they'll do it for him."

She nodded her understanding, her pretty face suddenly full of uncertainty and apprehension. "But in a way," she said slowly, seemingly formulating her ideas as she spoke, "that means character defamation. It still doesn't prove his guilt. It's all second-hand, unless you can prove that von Dodenburg gave definite orders to the man who confesses his guilt and carried out the crime."

McDougall smiled at her, his dark, saturnine face cynical. "Oh, come off it, Mary-Ann!" he said. "Grow up woman! What the hell do you think we are, a damned bunch of boy scouts . . . ?" And with that the discussions of the new 'strategy' came to an end.

The accused was taken into the underground chamber where

they were waiting; as was customary by now, he was hooded in a black cowl and was led by the noose tied around his neck.

They let him wait there nervously in the echoing silence for a while before the hood was removed so that, after he was able to focus his eyes, he could see the black-draped table with the crucifix displayed prominently at its centre as a symbol and a warning.

The spotlight which had been turned momentarily on his pale, worried face was switched off as suddenly as it had appeared. It illuminated the real noose hanging from a beam in the ceiling, the rope swinging slightly now in the breeze that had come from the opened door to allow the 'priest' to enter. Wordlessly, his hood pulled deep over his face so that the startled prisoner could see nothing of it, his hands hidden in the sleeves of his habit, he moved to the interrogators' table, the only sound the clacking of his rosary and other beads.

McDougall spoke, his voice deep and sonorous. "So you are Corporal Diefenbach? We've been waiting for you for, *a very long time!*"

The prisoner blanched. Why, he was obviously asking himself wildly, *why him*?

"You can tell us anything you like, Diefenbach, but we know you're guilty. We know you shot our men down in cold blood in the Ardennes. Diefenbach, you're a murderer. Now the time is coming when you must pay the ultimate penalty for your heinous crimes."

The prisoner wavered, every limb trembling suddenly, as if he might faint at any moment. "But . . ." he began. He didn't finish his protest. The door opened again. Two brawny GIs entered. Wordlessly they began to punch him. It was all done in a routine manner, as if they had carried out such beatings many times before.

McDougall nodded finally and the beating stopped. The men marched out, leaving the prisoner sobbing and shaking in the centre of the chamber. McDougall waited, taking his time, before saying finally, "You know the old German saying, Diefenbach, *mitgegangen, mitgefangen, mitgehangen*\*! If you want to protect your officers you'll hang with them. After all you were *there*."

McDougall let his words sink in as he sat there, obviously very pleased with himself. At the far end of the black-draped table, next to the hooded priest Mary-Ann looked worried.

"There is only one hope for you, Diefenbach," McDougall broke the heavy silence. The prisoner looked up urgently, eyes fixed almost passionately on the speaker. "Yes, a democracy like America is not interested in killing a young man like you." There was a grunt of assent from the other members of the 'court'.

Suddenly, Diefenbach's nerve broke. The boy who once, in what now seemed another life, had held back the attack of a whole battalion of US Sherman tanks with his lone Panther, broke into tears, his shoulders heaving, crying, "I'll confess . . . I'll confess! *Please, let me confess about the CO.*"

Night after night, day after day, the torture – for that was what it was – continued in that dark, dank underground chamber.


"It's working," McDougall chortled a week after they had started the interrogation of Wotan. "Ten confessions in seven days!" He clapped his hands and had the German *Sekt* brought in, beaming at his fellow members of the interrogation team while the white-tuniced POW poured out the sparkling German champagne.

\* Roughly: Went with, caught with, hanged with. *Transl.*

"But they're beginning to stick," Mary-Ann added a sober note later on after they had toasted their initial success. "Obviously the POWs have a grapevine among themselves. They know by now what's going on down here, gentlemen, and are being intimidated by the tougher ones to keep their mouths shut or" – she shrugged and those delightful breasts of hers trembled – "they don't believe we'll carry out our threats. My guess is that it won't be long before the confessions start drying up altogether".

"*Verdammte Scheisse!*" McDougall cursed bitterly in German. "I'm sure you're right, Mary-Ann. After all, they are alone with each other several hours a day. In that time they can get up to all sorts of mischief with comrades they regard as traitors. And it doesn't stop at just threats," he added darkly.

There was a murmur of agreement from the others and Mary-Ann didn't need a crystal ball to know what McDougall meant. Prisoners who were regarded as traitor were often 'tried' at the dead of night by a kangaroo court of their comrades. If they were found guilty they conveniently disappeared and she knew where they all went. A week or two later their suffocated corpses would be found in the great 'shit pits', as the latrine ordure channels were called by the POW cleaners. The 'traitors' would have been submerged in the noxious goo until they choked to death. That sort of thing could happen at this secret top-security prison once the other POWs became aware of the traitors in their midst.

McDougall found his voice again. "We've got to work harder and quicker," he snapped decisively, while our threats still work and they are more afraid of us than the kangaroo courts of their comrades. It's to be a production-line factory style affair from now onwards. There's no time to waste."

And the interrogators did not waste time, for they knew

they were engaged in a race to beat the prisoners before they started to take their own countermeasures. Suspects were brought in at all times of the day while the interrogation teams worked in two shifts, pushing themselves to the limit to get the confessions they needed to indict *Obersturmbannführer* von Dodenburg.

There were the usual beatings, the threats, the mock hangings, the base rumours of what would soon happen to the dear ones of the ethnic Germans if they didn't confess, the attempts to separate the other ranks from their officers— "after all, you only carried out their orders. The *officers* are the real criminals." The POWs were becoming ever more reluctant to confess and even when they did, they often went back on their word and refused to sign the written confession, which the prosecution would need in court if they were ever going to pin von Dodenburg down, break him under the sheer weight of this circumstantial and secondary evidence.

McDougall fumed. "Let's get the real young ones now," he ordered, "especially if they come from an Allied country or those occupied by the Russians. God in heaven, we'll break the bastard" – he meant von Dodenburg – "yet!"


It was thus that Roman Herzweiler from the Alsatian village of Wingen, French since 1919, but where most of the older villagers had been German-born and spoke German as their native language\*, made his brief appearance in the trial of Colonel von Dodenburg, to become briefly a footnote in the history of World War Two.

He was the youngest of the Wotan troopers, fifteen years old in 1944 when he had been captured in the Ardennes. He was

---

\* Ceded to France by Germany at the Treaty of Versailles, 1919.

medium-sized, rather too dark to be the ideal German Aryan type and handsome in a somewhat effeminate manner. Even now as he faced up to his interrogators, Mary-Ann could see in his manner and the way he fluttered the handkerchief that someone had given him that he would be ideal 'meat' for some homosexual – if he wasn't already – who could indulge him in the chocolate and candies that he probably craved.

One of the panel read out Herzweiler's brief military history – volunteer for the SS – action at Arnhem in September 1944; captured in the Ardennes three months later; under sentence of death for treachery in his native France. In other words, Mary-Ann told herself gloomily as she eyed the pretty boy, caught up in a situation that was way over his curly dark head, an easy victim for Lt McDougall. He'd confess all right.

McDougall wasted no time on the handsome, frightened, Alsatian boy; he knew there was no need to. As he exclaimed triumphantly afterwards to the rest of the 'emigrants', "The little prick was shit-scared right from the very start!" Immediately he launched into the attack. "You are accused of shooting at least *three* American POWs in cold blood last year. How do you plead?" His dark eyes bored into the boy's terrified face.

"No, no!" Herzweiler quavered, holding up both his hands and turning his ashen face to one side the way a peasant in his old village would do in an attempt to ward off the devil. "I didn't, sir! Honestly, I didn't." Already the first tears were flooding his terrified eyes and his bottom lip quivered, as if he might begin sobbing at any moment.

Mary-Ann looked at him, her mind racing as she told herself that this couldn't be allowed to go on. It was a travesty of justice. It shamed them all. But what could she do?

McDougall appeared to lose his temper. "Enough!" he

cried, springing to his feet as if beside himself with rage. "Guard, summon the court – and the hangman. We'll put an end to this damned lying here and now." Suddenly he leered and nodded in a seemingly significant manner to the huge guard with the beet-red face, brutalised by four years of war. "But before you swing, you Nazi swine—"

"I . . . I . . ." the boy stuttered.

McDougall cut him short with an angry wave of his hand. "Sergeant," he said in loud, slow German so that everyone would understand, "I'd like you to take care of the prisoner – *personally*."

The big, cruel-looking sergeant of Military Police licked his thick lips. "Yessir!" he said eagerly, his eyes, full of greedy curiosity taking in the trembling figure of the prisoner.

It was too much for Herzweiler. "I'll sign . . . I'll sign that *Obersturmbannführer* von Dodenburg ordered me to shoot American . . ."

But McDougall was no longer listening. He turned to face the panel, his features animated by a look of vicious triumph. "*Twenty-one*," he mouthed silently the number of signed confessions, adding under his breath, "Another nail in that swine's coffin."

The others looked pleased. Not Mary-Ann. She had had enough. The time had come to do something.

# Chapter Four

"She asked me if she could measure the length of my cock last night," ex-Sergeant Schulze said lazily, cutting himself off another length of fine black market salami and chewing on it thouthfully.

"You mean the virgin?" Matz, one-time corporal in the Greater German *Wehrmacht*, now unofficial pimp to the US 7th Army and well-known local black marketeer, said a little cheekily.

"Well, she sez she's never bin done . . . Tight as a drum between the thighs, according to her."

"Record for Germany today, I shouldn't wonder," Matz said as they huddled in the shelter of the wrecked former border post between Germany and France, its bullet-pocked walls engraved with the graffiti of the combat troopers! *"Hitler fucks sheep . . . Himmler's a pansy"* and the like, accompanied by crude pencil drawings of the alleged scandulous activities of the dead or vanished Nazi *Prominez*.

"Sez," Schulze continued lazily, "she'd like to compare the measurement with when I get a good old diamond-cutter on, rock solid. Do you think she's some kind of scientist – or sex maniac?" he added hopefully.

Matz shook his head firmly, "Ner," he declared. *"Amis."*

Schulze looked at him. "What d'yer mean – frigging *Amis*?" he demanded suspiciously.

"Ain't you got the sense you was born with? The *Amis* have gotten to her. Virgin, my ass!"

"Careful," Schulze said warningly, doubling a fist like a small steam shovel, "Yer talking about my intended."

Matz sniggered. "The *Amis* are allus going on about the size of the old love-tool. That's where she got it from."

Schulze scratched the back of his shaven head doubtfully. "D'yer think so, Matzi?" By now he knew a bit more about their occupiers. Their little racket – a nice one at that – had helped. The Frog smuggled in the porn, old tattered copies of *La Vie Parisienne*, in return for odd bits and pieces of grub they provided. They took the battered magazines, with their blurred photos of middle-aged ladies doing impossible things to each other, to Corporal Inigo Knightley, the *Ami* padre's assistant, who swopped them for cigarettes, nylons, even jerricans of petrol, all highly desirable commodities on the local black market. Why the weedy, bespectacled chaplain's assistant had got himself involved they couldn't fathom, even his name 'Inigo Knightley' seemed to be a source of ribald comment among the rough-tough GIs of the 70th US Infantry Division. But he did and Schulze and Matz lived well, very well on the proceeds in a starving, occupied Germany.

"I mean," Matz was saying in an oddly reflective manner for him as if he were giving the matter some thought, "why are the *Amis* so interested in the old joystick?. They never put it in the right place anyhow. It's allus gobble-gobble with them. I'm surprised there's any young *Amis* being born at all the way they make the two-backed beast—" He stopped short. "There's somebody coming up the trail," he said urgently.

Schulze forgot the strange business of the virgin and the tape measure. He swung round, hand reaching for his illegal pistol, possession of which might mean the death sentence if he were caught with it. A lone figure was plodding wearily up the forest trail between the snow banks, heading for the heights where they were waiting for their contact man. "Gendarme?" he hissed urgently.

Matz didn't answer for a moment, then he said, "Relax, yer big horned-ox. It ain't Father ferking Christmas either. Some sort of local civvie."

"What's it doing up here in this frigging weather?" Schulze demanded almost angrily.

"Am I Jesus, Schulze? How should I frigging well kn—" He stopped short, as he recognised the slight figure as the man came ever closer to their hiding place. "It's one of us."

"One of us – what?"

"A fella from Wotan," Matz answered.

Schulze blew out his cheeks in wonder. "What in three devils' names is he doing in this arse of the world?"

"Can't you guess, arse-with-ears! He's trying to cross the green border* into Froggie land."

"Got yer. Know him?"

Matz screwed up his eyes and peered down the trail for a few moments, while Schulze waited for his verdict. Matz had once had the keenest vision in the whole of Wotan and had been the Regiment's crack shot.

"Half Frog," Matz said. "You know, one of them booty Germans we recruited towards the end when the Regiment started to run out of bodies." He made an affected gesture. "I allus thought he was a bit warm."

Schulze didn't comment on the statement. Instead he said, "Wonder what he's up to? Do'you think he's got any news about the old shower? Sometimes I think I'd like to know."

Matz pulled a face. "That's all behind us now, old house.

---

* Green border, one that is unguarded.

We're up-and-coming businessmen, y'know. International traders, yer could almost say." He smirked.

"Yer, in frigging dirty books. That's a nice start of a career as businessmen I must say." He dismissed the idea with a wave of his big paw, still clutching the length of salami. "Anyhow, I'm gonna stop him, warm or not. Find out what he knows, if anything."

"What about the Frog?" Matz asked, looking across the border at the forest path the French peddler of dirty books would take to meet them.

"Who cares about frigging Frogs? A nation that makes love with its tongue ain't to be taken serious, comrade." And with those awesome words, he lapsed into silence, watching the lone figure toiling up the incline.

Roman Diefenbach was caught completely by surprise. He blanched, the colour draining from his flushed cheeks immediately at the unexpected challenge from the ice-covered boulders to the left side of the forest trail. "What—?" he exclaimed in fear at the first sight of the giant in a dyed, shabby *Wehrmacht* uniform, minus the eagles.

"Don't cream yer drawers," Schulze said, taking pity on the youth, who was obviously terrified. "It's us."

The boy's face reflected his relief at once, "Sergeant Schulze and – er – Corporal Matz. I remember you two".

Schulze smiled, but Matz's frown didn't change. "Ex-Corporal Matz to you, young fellah," he snapped sternly. "The war's over, yer know. Got to put all that shot and shit behind us in this post-war world. We're businessmen now, democratic businessmen." He sprang to attention, the hinges of his wooden leg squeaking under the strain and stretched out his right hand in the old German greeting. "*Heil Amerika. Ein Hoch President Truman!*"

The boy started. "Not so loud Corporal – er Herr Matz," he warned. "I'm a wanted man."

Schulze laughed heartily and made an obscene remark to Matz on the reason for Diefenbach being a 'wanted' man. Then he asked, "What yer wanted for? It's all over, ain't it. We've kissed and made up."

The boy ignored the nasty remark. Instead he answered Schulze's question. "I went over the wire . . . well, in a way, I did," he added mysteriously. "Because I wasn't prepared to be tortured into making accusations against the old CO."

"*Von Dodenburg?*" Matz snapped urgently, his role as a post-war 'international businessman' suddenly forgotten. "Is he still alive?"

"Of course he is," Diefenbach said. "They've got a whole bunch of us in a stinking prison. All the time trying to squeeze us into saying that the old CO gave the order—"

"*What order?* Dig it it out of the frigging orifice and talk sense, man!"

"Well, Sergeant Schulze, you remember when they shot the *Amis* in the woods in the Ardennes—"

"You mean them bastards of the SS Penal Battalion?"

"Yes, well the Yids who run the prison say we did it, and that Colonel von Dodenburg ordered us to do so."

Schulze gasped as if struck by a fist in his guts. "Well, I frigging live and die," he exclaimed, "I mean I know you can't trust a feller, who allows some old fart with a beard to saw the end of his dick off. But I didn't think that even that lot would sink so low." He sighed and shook his head like a man sorely tried by the iniquity of his fellow men. "Everybody knows that the CO was dead-set against that kind of thing." He pulled himself together with difficulty. "So now, what's the picture?"

They sat down together at the lonely spot at the top of the border mountain, with the cold wind coming in straight from Siberia. There was a hint of snow in the air and the sky had changed into a threatening leaden colour, but the two old comrades noticed neither the cold nor the threat of snow; they were too absorbed in the young SS trooper's story.

Finally, when he was finished, he shivered and rose to his feet. "Well, now you know, Ser – er – gentlemen. I'd better be on my way before the snow starts. I've got a long way to go by nightfall. And I don't want the gendarmes—"

He stopped short as, wordlessly and without any apparent effort Schulze reached out a big paw, grabbed his right arm and stopped him in his tracks. For what seemed a long time, the three of them posed them like figures frozen in a grotesque waxwork tableau.

"Why do you think that Yid woman helped you?" Matz asked finally. "Do you think she was after yer body? There's no accounting for women's tastes."

Schulze ignored Matz's question. He said slowly and thoughtfully, almost as if he was talking to himself, "So the old CO's alive and kicking after all – and I'd given him up for dead." His brow furrowed as if he were thinking hard.

Matz looked at him a little anxiously. He seemed to guess what was going through his old comrade's mind at that moment. "It's all finished, Schulzi," he said in a low voice, as a puzzled and worried Diefenbach looked from the one war-brutalised face to the other, wondering what was going on.

Schulze seemed to take a long time to react. "But we can't just forget, Matzi," he said in a tired voice, unusual for him. "I mean – can we?"

"Of course we frigging well can," Matz snapped hotly, eyes flashing with anger. "What the fuck was it all worth – all those poor lads who went hop, the years we spent right up to our hooters in crap, all that Nazi bullshit, which meant fuck nothing – nothing at all in the end." He spat the words, throwing spittle everywhere, the years of resentment, anger, fear coming to the surface at long last. "We did the best we could," he sighed wearily, his skinny chest heaving furiously. "We can't do no more, Schulzi." His voice trailed away to nothing as he realised that Schulze was only half listening to his impassioned outburst.

"We've got to do something," Schulze said with an air of finality. "We can't just let them hang the CO . . . You know . . . *Wotan!*"

"I know . . . I know!" Matz retorted hotly, trying to make one last attempt to stop his friend. "Wotan was our home. There were some good lads in it, I know that too. I enjoyed the good times, all that juicy gash in a dozen different countries. As a youngster I never even dreamed I'd see all that kind of woman. . . . The piss-ups as well! God, didn't we sink the firewater – *ouzo*, *whisky*, *vodka*, *Ami bourbon* and all the rest." His wizened face grew almost hysterical in his fever of anxiety that he might be dragged into it all again. "But there was a price to be paid, Schulze. I don't have to tell you that, you big horned-ox. Our lives weren't worth a wet fart in a pissbucket. Oh, sure, they gave us plenty of tin to stick on our manly breasts and pretend we were fucking heroes –" His words trailed away to nothing.

Diefenbach broke the uneasy silence, the air of near-hatred between the two old running mates. "What are you going to do, Sergeant Schulze?" he asked a little helplessly.

Schulze turned his big head slowly, very slowly. *"Do?"* he echoed, as if it were a very stupid question, which need not have been asked. "Why, what is there to do? We've got to get the CO out . . ."

# Chapter Five

She lay on the bed legs spread, exhibiting that splendid tuft of jet-black hair for him to admire, clad only in a sheer silk peignoir, slit down the middle. She caught the look on Sharpe's face and said, "Bought in Paris when I was young and virginal in '44. Fellow who bought it didn't come back from the Hurtgen fighting." She coughed delicately, while his keen eyes took in her lush body. "It hurt . . . I think I prefer to be an ex-virgin, vintage '46. One has fun."

He pulled off his trousers with a little difficulty due to his one hand, but she wasn't watching the clumsiness of his hand, she had other things in her eyes. "I see we have a visitor," she indicated the swelling in the front of his khaki shirt. "And he doesn't come from the bottom of the garden either!"

He laughed in the manner of a man who has grown accustomed to a woman in all ways and was easy with her, even at exciting moments like this – and Mary-Ann was certainly a woman who had no inhibitions. Sometimes when he thought about it (which wasn't often; these days he took things as they came), there seemed something desperate, even despairing about her love-making, as if this coupling might be the last, and she was going to enjoy it with every fibre of her being.

Awkwardly, he pulled the shirt over his head and completely naked stood at the end of the single army cot, the gnarled scar of his terrible wound clear for her to see. But unlike some women, that great, angry red scar where his arm had been sliced off at the shoulder by an 88mm German shell didn't seem to affect her. She accepted it the way she did everything else about him, including that "damned limey reticence of yours. Let your hair down, buster!" To which he invariably replied, "With this Army short-back-and-sides – that would be exceedingly difficult!" And then they would laugh together, not just like lovers, but two friends who had been together for years.

She opened her legs wider. He gave a little gasp at the sight. She heard the sound and said, her voice suddenly husky "Come on, Tom. Let's not waste any more time! You never know—"

But she never finished the comment, for already he had lowered his lean, muscular body onto her plump, lush flesh and was guiding himself into her wetness. She gasped and her head went back, eyes suddenly screwed, but, jaw jutting forward, face flushed almost angrily. "Do it!" she hissed the command through gritted teeth. "Do it, for Chrissake! I've been waiting for it all day!" She whimpered as he drove himself deeper into her and her voice abruptly took on a note of pleading, "Please . . . *please!*" Her spine curved tautly and then he was pumping away madly, seeing nothing, hearing nothing, his mind full of a crazy red roaring, the only thing he cared about now, his own urgent pleasure . . .

They lay on the rumpled sheet in silence, both of them damp with sweat. On their backs, smoking thoughtfully, they lay staring up at the ceiling and the cracks from the wartime bombings running back and forth. Outside, the GIs were heading for the mess hall. From the bed they could hear the rattle of mess tins and the ribald chatter, as GIs planned the night's entertain with their 'schatzis', as they called their German girlfriends\*.

\* From '*Schatz*', the German word for 'darling'. *Transl.*

"Funny," Sharpe commented, idly puffing out a stream of blue smoke from his nostrils, "A year or so ago they were killing each other. Now they go to bed."

She didn't respond. Her mind seemed to be on other things. Inside the prison the siren wailed. It wasn't the alarm. It was just to indicate that the prisoners were to begin their meagre supper. It would be the duty of the guards escorting them to ensure that they didn't see each other. Even when they had to pass in the dripping, narrow stone corridors, one prisoner would be forced to turn his face to the wall so that he didn't see who the other man was. It was all part of the treatment: a policy of isolation so that in the end, or so the 'emigrants' reasoned, they would be glad to talk to anyone, about anything.

"Schroeder's called off the search." She broke the heavy, brooding silence of the little bedroom. "But he's ordered an inquiry."

"What . . . what did you say?" Sharpe asked, startled by the suddenness of this unexpected revelation.

She repeated her information, adding, "You know, the search for that Alsatian kid who got away two days ago."

"You mean Diefenbach?"

"Yes, him," she answered, still smoking fitfully and not taking her gaze off the bomb-cracked ceiling.

He sat up, supporting himself on his one elbow and stared down at the expanse of her naked body, the large ripe breasts, tipped with what looked like brown plums. "Funny business. Still can't even make a guess on how he did it. He didn't look the type to make a break for it. No guts I'd say. McDougall felt the same, but he couldn't find how he did it." He shrugged a little carelessly. "Good luck to the kid in a way. I don't think he was guilty of any crime."

"Neither do it. That's why I helped him to get out of this damned hellhole of a place."

"*What?*" he exploded.

"You heard, Tom," she said, as calm as when she made her first statement.

He looked down at her naked body, forgotten now and what he had planned to do with her later. "Are you mad? Why did you do that, Mary-Ann. If Schroeder ever finds out—"

She held out her hand to silence him and pressed his wrist – it was tight and hard like that of an angry man preparing to punch somebody. "I don't think Schroeder will. He's got bigger fish to fry and time is running out for him. Why did I help the kid to escape?" She answered her own question. "I'll tell you. Because he was innocent and they were going to force him into saying anything they wanted him to, he was so weak. That's not my idea of justice."

"Mine neither," he agreed hastily. "But we've been over that before, Mary-Ann. Plenty of times. Don't you realise that you've left yourself wide-open for a court martial?"

"I've considered it," she answered easily. "But even if Schroeder did find out, I don't think he'd press charges. Too risky. I might blab too much and compromise what he's got in mind for von Dodenburg. After all, I am one of *them*." She meant the emigrants. "I've got just as many reasons to hate the SS as they have. It wouldn't look good to the Army or the State Department, especially if it were leaked to the stateside press."

She winked suddenly and surprised him. "And I would, believe you me, Tom darling!" Her voice rose and it seemed she had already forgotten her bold role in the escape of Roman Diefenbach. "Schroeder's set McDougall a deadline. It's all arranged with the Judge Advocate's Branch. Von Dodenburg is going to be put on trial a week before Christmas. Schroeder reasons that in the season of love and goodwill to all men," she sneered over the statement, "any failings on the part of the prosecution will be overlooked. The main thing is that von Dodenburg is convicted of war crimes in the name of the SS, and the rest of the German nation is let off the hook. The Russians are getting very uppity and the State Department is desperate to use the Germans, the *good Germans*," she emphasised the words cynically. "As if there is any such animal!"

For a few moments he was too shocked by her revelation to react: first, the escape of the young Alsatian and now the sudden preparations for the trial of von Dodenburg. Sharpe finally found his voice. "But McDougall won't get too far with the statements he has already obtained. A good defence lawyer would soon make short work of those, especially if it could be shown that they were gained under duress and it looks to me as if some of those who made the statements are beginning to waver."

"Exactly, but do you think that the authorities are going to allow von Dodenburg the cream of the American legal profession for his defence?" she sneered. "In a horse's ass". They'll give him a top-class German lawyer, but he'd be awed by an American court, the court of the victors as he will undoubtedly call it to his cronies, and more than likely his English won't be good enough for him to conduct the case in that language. So he'll be forced to use an interpreter. That will definitely cramp his style. As for the American defending counsel, they'll find him at the bottom of the pile, some shyster of an ambulance chaser, I'd guess." She frowned and sucked her bottom lip, sorely perplexed.

Time passed. Finally, Sharpe cleared his throat and said, "I don't know why you care—"

"Justice", she said softly.

"All right, then, for the sake of justice. But even if von Dodenburg and his mob are not guilty of this one, he will be guilty of other crimes against humanity. I'm sure of that.

How can someone who commanded a unit on the Russian front for so many months, where it was dog eat dog, not have committed a crime of that nature, Mary-Ann?"

"Take your point," she answered laconically. She hesitated. Finally, she blurted it out. "Don't think I'm saying this on account of his handsome kisser, Tom. I know he is one of those SS bastards who've terrorised Europe for half a decade. But—"

"Go on."

She looked at him in a guilty way. "I think basically he's a decent, honest man, a soldier first and foremost, like you."

"*Were*," he corrected her.

Instinctively she reached out and caressed him. "You still are, Tom, to me, even if you have lost your arm".

He was moved, but said nothing for a moment until finally he asked, "So what are you going to do about it?"

"I'm going to give him an even chance if I can. All right, he might be guilty, as the emigrants maintain he is. But he's gonna have a fair crack of the whip."

He laughed harshly. "You, a Jewess – and all this new business about Belsen, Dachau, Buchenwald and the like?"

"I know. I know! But they're talking about a brave new world, Tom. I mean, it may be all a load of bullshit—"

"Ah, language, Mary-Ann!"

She didn't seem to hear. "But after all we've been through, Tom, in these last bloody years, we've got to make an attempt, don't you think, an attempt to make a better world, even for alleged war criminals." There were tears in her dark eyes.

It had been a long time since Tom Sharpe had really loved a woman; he thought the bloody war had cured him of that kind of self-indulgence. Now he knew he had been wrong. He loved this hot-tempered Jewess with her burning, almost painful sense of justice, even perhaps on behalf of the wrong people. He pressed her to him. "I'll help you, Mary-Ann, in any way I can. Believe me, I will!"

"I know you will, Tom," she answered fervently, returning the pressure.

He frowned and patted the tears away from her cheeks. "But remember this, everybody's going to be against you. They might even say you're mad – a Jewess in the winter of 1946 trying to help a dyed-in-the-wool Nazi of the SS." He sighed, "God knows what will come of it, but we'll try, old girl."

He forced a smile. In an affected British accent, she replied," Thank you, *old boy* . . . !"

# Chapter Six

An officer barked out an order in German. His breath fogged a crisp grey on the icy air of the prison courtyard. It added to the sombre mood of the place. A deathly silence reigned, broken only by the cawing of the rooks, frightened by the shout, rising in protest from the black and skeletal trees. In the barred windows over-looking the central square not a face looked down. No one, even the most hardened of the prisoners, wanted to see what was going to happen next.

But one group of prisoners *were* being forced to observe the grim proceedings: the officers and men of the former SS Assault Regiment Wotan. They were drawn up to left and right of the podium on which was set the scaffold, made of good Vermont pine, as the hangman had assured the American officers the night before when he had arrived out of the gloom in his chauffeur-driven, looted Mercedes, stinking of cheap scent and even cheaper bourbon.

The officer in charge, a captain of MPs, tall and immaculate down to his gleaming jump boots, a hard, wary look on his lean face, snapped, "Gentlemen, may I have your attention please!"

The American officers, including the 'emigrants' in their Number One uniforms, turned their gaze somewhat warily to where the MP stood to attention underneath the gallows, the hempen noose motionless in the still morning air. Sharpe flashed a glance at Mary-Ann. Her dark face under her smart garrison cap revealed nothing. He wondered and then turned his attention to the Germans. Their emaciated faces also revealed nothing, but that of their one-time commander, *Obersturmbannführer* von Dodenburg, did.

Of all the people, American and German, present this morning, with the hoar frost hanging a brilliant white from the telephone lines, his features were the only ones to show any emotion: that of anger and outrage. He knew what this whole ceremony was about. It wasn't merely the execution of a teenage 'war criminal'. There was more to it than that. The hanging was to serve as a warning and a threat. To whom? To those who still wavered among the ranks of Wotan, especially his officers. That was its real intent.

"I will now allot you gentlemen your official places for the execution," the MP officer was saying, his voice revealing nothing, as if he did this – put a man to death – every day. But, Sharpe reminded himself, perhaps he did. "The official witnesses for the Judge Advocate's Branch will stand over there to the southern end of the scaffold. He indicated the spot with his raised gloved hand. Led by Colonel Schroeder, the official witnesses filed towards the designated spot like obedient schoolchildren. "No closer than five paces," the MP officer warned as an afterthought, "or there might be an unfortunate accident – that scaffold is reserved for *one* privileged person this morning." He smiled as if he had made a joke. No one smiled with him.

What the MP officer didn't tell them was that when in a few minutes the sergeant of the Hitler Youth Division was strung up he might well urinate some 3ft in his death throes, they often did. But they didn't stop there. Once he had seen a dying prisoner get an erection and ejaculate in the moment of death. It wouldn't do to have the official observers of the Judge Advocate's Branch pissed upon, the MP officer told himself.

He turned to Major Sharpe, a one-armed guy who was some kind of limey involved in this business. "You are in charge of the German POWs and accused, Major. Please ensure that there is no trouble."

Sharpe nodded but said nothing. Out of the corner of his eye he saw Mary-Ann bite her bottom lip, as if she was agitated by something.

The MP officer, his orders given out, turned stiffly on his heel and barked "Atten-*shun*".

All present, including some of the Germans stiffened, even if they didn't understand the command in English. Von Dodenburg drew himself up, skinny shoulders rigid, lean face a mixture of bitterness and compassion as the MP captain barked "Prisoner and escort!"

All eyes turned expectantly to the great door. Sharpe could now hear a soft mumble in Latin, mixed with the harsh tread of the giant MP guards. He thought, too, he caught the sound of sobbing.

The first guards appeared, marching into the courtyard slowly and solemnly. Behind them the Army chaplain followed, a purple stole thrown round the neck of his uniform. He was reading from his prayer book and at the same time encouraging the bent-shouldered, sobbing prisoner who would soon swing lifelessly from the scaffold in the centre of the square. The prisoner moved awkwardly, putting the dark-faced, Italianate priest off his stride, for the hangman had tied a brace board to the soldier's shoulders so that he couldn't crumple and collapse.

The hangman himself, Master Sergeant John C. Woods brought up the rear of the solemn little procession of death. His Texan face was brick red, and it wasn't from the cold. He reeked of drink from the vast quantities of alcohol he consumed prior to a hanging. Now, leering a little drunkenly at the youth he would soon 'promote the other way', as he always put it, he prepared for the task ahead.

They halted. The little Italian-looking US Army chaplain intoned his last prayer. "Have you anything you wish to say to me further, my son?" he asked in fairly good German.

The prisoner from the Hitler Youth Division shook his head wordlessly, as if he couldn't trust himself to speak.

Almost before the last interchange was over, Woods came up behind the condemned man. With a neat, experienced movement he slipped the black hood over the German's head. There was a stiffled gasp from the Wotan men. "Stand fast!" von Dodenburg hissed out of the side of his mouth, not taking his gaze off the hooded man.

He attempted to struggle but Woods's big fist slammed down on his right and then his left shoulder. The prisoner's struggles ceased. He was momentarily paralyzed.

With routine deftness, Woods lowered the noose over the hooded head and tightened it just above his left ear, as prescribed by US Army Regulation 633–15.

The spectators tensed. Schroeder smiled weakly. McDougall whispered to his neighbour, "This'll do it, I'll be bound!" Mary-Ann's hand flew trembling to her lips. Von Dodenburg forced himself to watch, face impassive. This, he told himself, was the way that the great glory of the New Order was going to end for them: the fanatical youth which had given its all these last six years for Folk, Fatherland and Führer. How ignominious!

Woods expertly threw the wooden lever of the operating mechanism. After all, he had done it often enough before, even in civvie street. The trap door clicked open and the prisoner gave one last great convulsion. Next moment it was hurtling through the hole without even touching the sides of the trap, coming to a stop with a violent jerk. But something bulged at the crotch of the shabby grey *Wethmacht* trousers.

The shocked observers gasped as a tell-tale stain spread across the flies, although the man was already dead. His seed had been spent – purposelessly – for the last time. Then the body just hung there, turning slightly, in awesome, frightening silence. The Hitler Youth man was dead and hardly anyone on that bare, winter square knew him. Slowly, very slowly, *Obersturmbannführer* von Dodenburg raised his hand to his bare, blond head in one final salute.

"Parade – rest!" the tall MP broke the heavy silence with startling suddenness. He waited till the spectators had shuffled to the position of 'at ease', then commanded, after looking at his watch to ascertain the regulation post-execution pause had been fulfilled, "Medical officer, make your examination."

A fat doctor came out of the doorway where he had been sheltering from the cold, approached the body, listened to the heart and then raising his hand, stated, "I pronounce this man dead!"

There was another shuffle. Somebody broke wind. M/Sgt Woods licked his thick, cracked, dark-red lips in anticipation of the stiff drink he would be swallowing in a minute as soon as his assistant had cut the body down. Afterwards, in the warmth of the prison building, they would force the rope away from where it had cut down deep into the flesh of the neck.

Colonel Schroeder turned to McDougall, a smile on his fat face. "That should do it, Lieutenant," he said under his breath. "A lot of 'em look as if they're gonna crap their pants at any moment," he gestured to the men of SS Assault Regiment Wotan. "Main thing now is that we get confessions and statements from the officers incriminating that von Dodenburg. The court'll believe them all right, especially when they are backed up by the statements we've already got from the rank-and-file."

McDougall's dark, brooding face beneath that black cowl of hair revealed nothing. All he said was, "We'll get him this time, sir. Now he's ours for the taking. The hanging did the trick." He curled his hand inwards, as if crushing a fly. "Yes, the bastard's days are numbered now . . . !"

After the savage hanging in that remote secret prison, things started to happen fast. Outside the snow began to fall in thick, fat flakes hour after hour, as if it would never cease, muffling every sound, even those of the nightly sobbing and the occasional blows. For now McDougall, trying to achieve the deadline set by an impatient Schroeder, who had decided to take over the prosecution in court personally, went all out in his fanatical, fevered attempts to pin von Dodenburg down at last.

More and more of the men signed confessions to the effect that they had been ordered by their officers to kill the prisoners. It seemed that all of them were prepared to swear black was white to save their own skinny necks, and a worried von Dodenburg could see now that some of the officers were beginning to waver – not the younger ones, they were still as fanatical as ever, but the older officers who had been with Wotan for years.

Two days after the hanging, O'Donnell was drinking coffee with McDougall in the officers' club, still decorated with the peasant murals from the Nazi period – great, blond muscular farmers swinging scythes and happy, barefoot peasant girls collecting in the wheat – and all the rest of the Nazi kitsch. When Mary-Ann came in for a break, she immediately could see that McDougall had been drinking. His eyes were sparkling and too alert despite the dark circles beneath them and his usually sallow cheeks were flushed. "Ah, the voice in the wilderness!" he proclaimed, pushing back a chair for her. "The voice of justice." His neighbour smirked, for she wasn't liked among the emigrants on account of her stance. But McDougall didn't notice. Instead he said, "Sit down, Mary-Ann. Good news, eh?"

"What?" she asked, helping herself to coffee and adding cream.

"We've got the last confession we're going to get from the rank-and-file. I'm expecting a signed confession from one of the swine's senior officers at any time now." Mary-Ann knew who the 'swine' was without being told – von Dodenburg. McDougall checked to see if anyone was watching, but no one was. Hastily he tipped the rest of the small flask of cognac into his coffee cup, although it was just past breakfast. Perhaps he was celebrating his little triumph. He took a drink, shuddered, and said, "You don't seem particularly thrilled by the news," looking at her in a quizzical manner.

She said nothing not wanting to be drawn any further. She didn't want McDougall to become so antagonistic that he'd have her thrown off the case. A word to that fat *goy* Schroeder would suffice.

McDougall leaned back and looked at her through half-veiled eyes, as if seeing her for the first time. "I know you don't like this whole business. Neither do I, if it's only intended to appease America and those fat cat Jews in New York." He laughed harshly, "You know what they say about that kind? A Zionist is a Jew who pays another Jew to send a third Jew – some poor *meschugge schliemel* – to Palestine."

Still she didn't react. But she wondered what he was getting at. Normally he wasn't so informative, especially with her.

"No, this is all intended for our future homeland – Palestine," he said.

"*Palestine?*"

"Yes," he snapped decisively. "The world has got to learn of the great injustice done to our poor people over the past ten centuries since the diaspora, or dispersal, and especially the wrong committed here in Germany by the Nazis. That's why we need a conviction, regardless of the methods used to obtain it. The Holocaust, as people are now beginning to call it, must be the justification for the foundation of a Jewish national state, however much that state will upset the balance of power in the Middle East."

"You mean that's what it is all about – a state that, as yet, doesn't exist?"

"Yes," he said solemnly. "Let the Americans think what they will, but we Jews have a responsibility only to ourselves. Europe didn't damn well want us, and it wasn't only Germany. It was France, Switzerland, Spain and all the rest of the Europeans. The Americans have tolerated us. So," he shrugged, "we must have our own state, where we are beholden to no one—"

He stopped short. An excited member of the emigrants was actually running into the officers' club, paying no attention to the stares of disapproval from the handful of MP officers present. "McDougall . . . McDougall!" he gasped, fighting for breath.

"What is it?" McDougall asked, speaking German, just like the messenger.

Chest heaving, eyes sparkling excitedly, the other man gasped, "It's Doctor Sigl," he meant SS Assault Regiment Wotan's senior medical officer.

"Go on," McDougall urged, leaning forward intently.

"He's signing . . . a confession . . . THAT VON DODENBURG ORDERED THE EXECUTION OF THE AMERICAN PRISONERS FROM THE US 99th INFANTRY DIVISION!"

McDougall whooped wildly, like a Hollywood Red Indian on the warpath. "We've got him . . . got him at last!" Suddenly, he broke down and began to sob great wet tears of joy and relief.

# Book Four

# *The Trial of Obersturmbannführer von Dodenburg*

# Chapter One

*"Haul ass . . . come on you Krauts . . . HAUL ASS!"* With that cry which von Dodenburg had come to hate, the MPs had wakened the accused, going from cell to cell banging on the nailed door with their white-painted clubs before peering through the Judas hole to check whether their charges were still there and alive. There had already been two suicides in the past week, with two officers hanging themselves from the water pipe with strips of blanket. They had not wanted to sign the 'confession' which would help to damn their former commanding officer. That had been four o'clock on that freezing December morning with the snow falling into the prison countyard as if it would never cease again.

They had been herded into the great shower room for their first shower in a month. To their surprise there had been hot water and real American soap instead of the German pumice-stone soap, which produced no lather. They had become accustomed to using it for years.

Still naked, but with bodies tingling and sweet-smelling after the cloying dankness of their cells, they had been shaved by POW barbers, each one under the supervision of a keen-eyed guard. Afterwards, the sergeant in charge had gone round personally counting and collecting the razors the frightened, awed barbers had used. Even at this stage, with the trial scheduled to start in four hours' time, Colonel Schroeder and McDougall were taking no chances with potential suicide candidates.

Breakfast had followed, the best they had eaten since they had been captured and gone behind the American wire. There had been scrambled powdered egg – plenty of it, a large piece of salt bacon and a piece of bread fried in its fat, of the kind the Americans liked. Best of all there had been real bean coffee instead of the usual substitute made from acorns – as much as they could drink.

The men of Wotan had separated into two hostile and embarrassed groups; the minority, who had refused to testify against von Dodenburg, and the others under Captain Sigl, who had. Someone remarked cynically: "And the condemned man ate a hearty breakfast," to which von Dodenburg had replied with a tired, cynical smile, "Eat while you can, comrade." They were all 'comrade' now, their old ranks forgotten. "You never know what the morrow brings." Even as he said the words, a harsh little voice at the back of his mind rasped, "Heaven, arse and cloudburst, Kuno, you know what it'll frigging bring. They'll play their silly little legal game – *and then they'll fucking hang you*!"

He finished the rest of his bacon in silence.

Just after six, the MPs reappeared, watched by Schroeder, who looked baggy-eyed and hungover, and a tense, sallow McDougall. The MPs passed through the prisoners, handing out large squares of cloth in black with a number in white on the front. Hastily the interpreter explained that the accused would wear these in dock to make identification easier for their judges on the court martial panel.

The young MP, one of the few who didn't wear the blue wartime combat infantryman's badge of the US Army, looked hesitant as he approached a waiting von Dodenburg with his particular number. "Colonel," he said, his young unlined face flushing with what appeared to be embarrassment, "the boss man – he meant Schroeder – insisted you should wear this identification number." He handed the folded cloth to von Dodenburg and waited until the German had opened it.

The colonel did so. He gave a crooked smile. The number was 13! The young military policeman looked even more embarrassed. He leaned forward and whispered, a hand covering the side of his mouth so that the two officers at the door couldn't see him speaking.

"I could try to switch the number if you like."

Von Dodenburg shook his head. "Thanks," he said in his now passable English. Ever since his capture he had been working on that language in the fond hope that it might be of some use to him, though now he doubted it very much. "But don't worry. I think my luck can't get any worse now, even with that Number Thirteen. Thanks again!"

"Knock off the guff back there!" the sergeant in charge snapped.

By raising his eyebrow swiftly, von Dodenburg indicated that the boy should be on his way. He fled, with von Dodenburg telling himself, as he bound the identification number around his skinny chest, that all *Amis* were not bad. There were some good, kind, unprejudiced ones among them.

At the door, Schroeder nodded to McDougall and disappeared at once. He thought it better to do so. The dark-haired Jew waited till he had gone before saying sharply, "You know what you have signed. We have your statements in black and white. Thanks to them you have received certain concessions." He flashed a warning look around the room. "It would be unfortunate if you didn't honour those statements in the witness box. I would be forced to take certain unpleasant mesures—" He broke off suddenly. Another American officer was approaching the mess hall.

The man was a middle-aged major, somewhat fat, with silver hair and what looked like a permanent benign smile on his red-apple cheeks. Behind his steel-rimmed GI glasses his blue eyes twinkled. He looked exactly what he was: a small-town lawyer, who had never defended anyone in anything higher than the local county court; a member of the local lodge, the high point of whose life was to go fishing for trout now and again and his weekly poker game at the back of the local saloon with the 'boys', middle-aged provincial worthies like himself.

Now to his surprise, Major McCarthy found himself thrust into a case that was already beginning to be featured in the *New York Times* and discussed in the Senate. It was all a little unsettling and, as he had written to his wife the previous evening, "Naturally I shall do my best. Whatever the Krauts are supposed to have done they deserve a fair *American* (he had underlined the word 'American') trial. I only hope I can do my best for them. Pray for me. Regards to Eddie and all the boys in the backroom."

Now he watched the main accused, each with a large number wrapped around his chest, which seemed to him to already single them out as special men, doomed even before the trial commenced.

"*Ihr Name und ehemaliger Dienstgrad*," Schroeder had commenced, speaking in German through the interpreter.

Von Dodenburg had waved him away and answered in English, "Kuno von Dodenburg. Former *Obersturmbannführer von Regiment Wotan*. Colonel, SS Regiment Wotan."

Schroeder had flushed angrily, taking this as a personal affront. Thereafter he had launched attack after attack – mercilessly – at the pale, haggard, blond German. In vain, McCarthy had protested at the tone of Schroeder's remarks, but the Court had turned him down again and again. It was clear that the panel thought von Dodenburg guilty, or had been ordered to think him so.

Now Schroeder was in full flow, detailing the preliminaries to the German attack in the Belgian Ardennes in December 1944. "We all know," he said confidently "what the German leader Hitler ordered his SS generals to do then. They were to cause as much terror as possible and break enemy resistance, i.e. American resistance, by every means possible. This criminal here—"

McCarthy had risen to object to Schroeder's use of 'criminal' but before he could do so the president of the Court waved for him to remain seated.

Sitting next to Mary-Ann in the well of the courtroom, Sharpe shook his head. "The major hasn't got a cat's chance in hell," he commented.

Mary-Ann answered, "I think he's not so dumb as he looks. He'll try his best, believe me!"

"This criminal," Schroeder repeated, savouring the word, "who had already shown what a barbarian he was in Russia, France and Italy, was just the man to carry out such an order." He paused for breath and continued his attack, his fat face flushed with triumph, for he knew the Court was with him. "Ambitious, one hundred and ten per cent a fanatical Nazi, Kuno von Dodenburg, he – of all the SS murderers – would stop at nothing in his attempts to please his beloved Führer."

"Objection," McCarthy said solidly.

The Court looked at him as if he were something unpleasant that just crawled out of the woodwork. Schroeder frowned.

"Did you say 'objection', Major?" the President asked severely.

"Yes sir, I did. These are minor matters, but I think it is important that we start by getting the little things right before we get to the capital crime."

"Go on then, Major," the President said.

"One, sir. Kuno von Dodenburg was *never* in the Nationalist Socialist Party. The Berlin records show that. Two, sir. So far not *one* single SS man, from private soldier to general, has been convicted of war crimes in the West. In Russia that is a different matter, but then, sir, I suggest that communist justice is not particularly impartial."

Mary-Ann dug Sharpe hard in the ribs. "I told you. The little guy isn't that dumb. The President can't praise the Russians for dealing with the SS. It isn't wise these days to praise anything Russian if you want to get promotion."

The President obviously thought the same, for he said in a low voice, "I shall make a note of that, Major." He turned to a crestfallen Schroeder and said, "You may continue, Colonel."

"Of all the SS murderers," Schroeder commenced, flustered, until the President ordered the clerk of the court, "Strike that off the record, please. Start again Colonel Schroeder. And please remember to state only facts, not suppositions and opinions. Right?"

"Yessir," Schroeder agreed, unhappily. He took a deep breath and started once more. "His record is well known and without any reverence to the past," he paused dramatically and raised a sheaf of papers on the desk in front of him, which McDougall was holding in readiness to give to him, for they had practised the procedure several times in advance, "these documents should suffice to show the accused for what he is, a cold-blooded murderer."

McCarthy looked up from his own papers sharply. Mary-Ann gasped and the President of the Court looked severe, as if he were preparing to administer another reprimand to the fat colonel.

"Yes," Schroeder said triumphantly before the President could speak. "Here I have in my possession affidavits from over twenty of von Dodenburg's killers and five of his officers stating categorically – and naturally on oath – that in December 1944, von Dodenburg, as CO of SS Assault Regiment Wotan, directly ordered his men to slaughter in cold blood, our boys who were helpless prisoners." He paused and glared at von Dodenburg opposite. The latter's face revealed nothing.

But the President's did. He, too, had his own orders – secret ones. They were, simply: find von Dodenburg guilty and do it fast. Now it seemed that the fat, pompous fool of a lawyer had gotten all the evidence he needed for Master-Sergeant Woods to string up the Kraut colonel.

Schroeder's words appeared to confirm his own thoughts when he thundered with fake indignation, his fat jowls wobbling with the effort, "Your honour, I ask this Court to waste no further time on this beast in human clothing, sitting opposite with the Number Thirteen around his neck. There is only one possible verdict the court can pass on the basis of these damning affidavits from his own men. That is – *DEATH!*" He sat down heavily like a man exhausted, leaving his words to echo and re-echo around the suddenly very still courtroom.

It was in the midst of this heavy, brooding silence that the young military policeman, who earlier had attempted to be kind to von Dodenburg, flung open the door of the court and cried wildly, "Sir . . . gentlemen, I'm sorry to disturb you. But—"

"What the goddam Sam Hill is all this?" the President of the Court snarled, as all eyes turned in the direction of the excited, embarrassed MP, who for some reason was carrying a sharp knife in his right hand. "What's going on, Corporal?"

"Sir . . . sir . . . There's been an accident," the soldier stuttered and before the President had time to ask what kind of accident had occurred he added in an excited flurry of words, "It's the Kraut – er – German, sir . . . that officer, Major Sigl—"

At the mention of the name of the chief witness against him, his one-time comrade and friend, von Dodenburg's face lost its arrogant calm. He shot a glance at the military policeman like everyone else in the court.

"Yes," the President prompted impatiently.

"We've just found him, sir," the MP answered and flourished the knife. "He was hanging from the steam-heat pipe in the washroom . . . I cut him down, but it was too late . . ." His voice tailed away to almost nothing. "He was dead, sir."

Von Dodenburg's heart leapt at the news, as he realised immediately that some God on high was looking after him. How, he didn't know, but he was. Thus it was that he was hardly aware, among the uproar that received the MP's announcement, of Major McCarthy's voice crying urgently, "Mr President, with your indulgence I ask for an immediate recess . . . Mr President . . . !"

Next to a suddenly pale-faced Mary-Ann, who was seemingly paralysed into silence by the news of Sigl's death, Major Sharpe, his brain working overtime, told himself that out of the blue he had been given another task: the investigation of the death of the chief prosecution witness.

On the raised bench, the President slammed his gavel down with such force that the head came off, leaving him to stare foolishly at the little wooden handle as he declared: "This court is recessed . . ."

# Chapter Two

"Let hold o' me!" Sergeant Rosenkranz snorted, as the MP tried to help him to the witness box, while the Court waited tolerantly for him to take his place. "I'm not altogether a goddam cripple!" He thrust his crutches towards the red-faced MP and putting pressure on his cane, the former Kosher short-order cook stumbled towards the box, watched by a smirking Colonel Schroeder, who could see that the big Moxie was having an effect on the Court already.

As he waited, Schroeder knew that he now needed all the help he could get. The apparent suicide of Major Sigl had almost put an end to his case. An hour after he was found dead hanging from the steam-heating pipe, his tongue lolling out of his puce-coloured face like a piece of scarlet leather, nearly all of the other witnesses started to go back on their word. One after another they had requested permission to see a fuming, violent McDougall to ask to withdraw their affidavits; and shout and cajol as he did, promising them the earth if they would stick to their testimony, the subdued Germans refused. Now he, Schroeder, would have to rely on the testimony of the American witnesses. They wouldn't go back on their word. They would make a favourable impression on the tribunal, especially as most of them wore the dark-coloured ribbon of the Purple Heart to show that they had shed their blood for their country. "The nigger in the woodpile is that damned Major McCarthy," he told himself grimly, as Rosenkranz approached the chair on the witness stand. "Why that creep goes out to bat for the murdering Kraut bastards I don't know." He took one final glance at the middle-aged provincial lawyer and then at von Dodenburg. Both their faces revealed no emotion, but he noted that von Dodenburg's knuckles were white as they gripped the bar in front of him. It was a sign of inner tension. The sight cheered him up somewhat.

Rosenkranz, who was minus half of his right leg, balanced himself in the box, refusing the President's offer to sit down. Instead he stood rigidly to attention in his well-pressed Class A uniform, the burly chest covered in medals, while Schroeder read out his military record carefully and slowly, ending with the impressive statement: "His divisional commander has recommended Sergeant Rosenkranz for the Congressional Medal of Honor for his bravery in the field. It is still going through channels, but the divisional commander is certain that Sergeant Rosenkranz will receive our country's top award for bravery on account of his performance with the US 99th Infantry Division in 1944." He let the words sink in while Sergeant Rosenkranz stared woodenly to his front and the Panel looked suitably impressed as Schroeder had known they would. For that reason, he had summoned the big greasy Kike as his first prosecution witness.

Schroeder waited till the court had settled down; he wanted Rosenkranz's statement to have the fullest impact possible. He nodded covertly at von Dodenburg, who was now obviously wondering who the big crippled sergeant was. A moment later he found out when Schroeder asked with deceptive silkiness: "Do you see in this court the enemy officer who ordered the execution – in *cold blood* – of your unfortunate comrades?" He put a quaver in his voice for the last bit. "After all, you and the two men with you were close enough to see everything, weren't you?"

Rosenbranz didn't hesitate. Over the months since the Ardennes battle and the massacre he had actually convinced himself that he had been close enough for that. "Yessir," he snapped promptly, "I saw everything." He turned awkwardly and pointed at von Dodenburg with a finger that trembled with surpressed rage and tension. "It was him, gentlemen – that Kraut—"

Von Dodenburg's pale face grew even paler. He seemed to reel back, as if struck an actual physical blow.

"He ordered the slaughter. I recall the bastard – excuse my French, Judge – as if it was yesterday!"

Schroeder smirked as he saw the effect of the crippled Yid's testimony on the Court. He gave a slight bow and said, "That's all I need from this witness, gentlemen."

"You may stand down," the President of the Court commenced, but McCarthy interrupted with a polite, "I wonder if the defence could ask a couple of questions, gentlemen?"

The President threw down his pen angrily, "All right, if you must, Councillor".

McCarthy took his time, while Rosenkranz stared at him, dark eyes hostile and angry as if he were asking himself, "Why was a goddam American defending the murdering Kraut bastard?" Finally he spoke. "Sergeant Rosenkranz, you have good eyes, I can see that."

The ex-cook glowered down at the lawyer, but said nothing.

"But I'm astonished at your tremendous memory, especially after what you – alleged – you saw take place in the heat of battle."

"Get on with it, Major," the President growled impatiently.

"Well, Sergeant," McCarthy continued without any apparent rush, "How long did you observe this defendant while he gave orders to his men to carry out the massacre?"

"Objection!" Schroeder snorted. "What does it matter if it took three minutes or three hours? It doesn't take much for a murdering bastard – excuse me, gentlemen – a murdering swine like that to tell his men to kill our fellahs."

"Of course not, you're right, Colonel Schroeder," McCarthy agreed gently, apparently unperturbed by the irate interruption. "But there is one thing that does worry me."

"And what's that, Major?" the President rapped.

"Is Sergeant Rosenkranz a fluent German speaker? If he *isn't*," he emphasised the words, "how did he understand the supposed order?" He sat down abruptly, his point made, with a mumbled "No further questions", while everyone in the courtroom stared at a suddenly deflated Rosenkranz.

"It was definitely not suicide," Sharpe declared as she watched him staring up at the steampipe that ran the length of the sweat-heavy shower room.

"How do you know?" Mary-Ann asked. Outside, the snowstorm still raged and in part that was the reason why they were in this place. Due to the condition of the snowbound roads leading south, no investigators had been able to reach them from US Army HQ in Frankfurt. So it was that the President of the Court had allotted them the task of looking into Major Sigl's 'suicide'.

"One doesn't need to be Sherlock Holmes to figure it out," Sharpe answered. "I got Sigl's height from his records, added it to the measurements of the length of rope he is supposed to have used and found that they didn't tally. He couldn't have reached that steampipe without help."

"Perhaps he might have climbed up on a chair to fix the noose?"

"Look around, Mary-Ann. No chair and that zinc-topped ablutions table over there with its iron frame would need more than one man to shift it." He shook his head with an air of finality. "No, he was helped. And if he wasn't helped," he added darkly "then he was *murdered*!"

She accepted the verdict calmly. "Do you think," she asked after a moment, "that explains why all of a sudden the prisoners started retracting their statements?"

He shrugged. "Could be. After all, they did so virtually all together, as if they had been told what happened to Sigl and warned that it might happen to them if they didn't keep their noses clean."

She swore. For a few moments they stood there as if transfixed, listening to the drip-drip of a tap leaking somewhere and the soft hush of the big wet snowflakes coming down outside. Finally she said, "Do you think, if you are right—"

"I am."

"—that it was an inside job?" she continued.

He nodded grimly.

"But how? The MPs guarding this place are specially picked. You know just how much they're on their toes, and somehow I don't think it could be one of the prisoners. Their spirit has been broken by the months of their captivity, Tom."

"Yes, I agree." He frowned hard, his mind racing as he considered.

She waited and then, growing impatient, said, "Well if it wasn't anyone from the *inside* it had to be somebody from *outside*."

"Yes, that's what I've been thinking too," Sharpe agreed. "But how could any would-be murderer get into this fortress? The only one with relatively easy access would be one of the guards – and they're all known to one another."

She pondered the problem for a while. "Okay," she said finally, "let's assume it was someone who could roam about the prison freely because he wore a guard's uniform, but how did he get in in the first place without being challenged by other guards who would have known him?"

He clicked his fingers as he saw what she was hinting at. "He had to be smuggled in in the first place."

"Yes, and what kind of German – it had to be a German –" she snapped, "would have easy access into the prison in order to smuggle him in?"

Major Sharpe cursed under his breath. "Christ, how would I know? Mary-Ann, this could become a full-scale inquiry." Sharpe looked at the falling snow almost angrily. "What a frigging Fred Karno's!" he exclaimed.

She didn't understand the phrase, but she got its meeting. "Yeah," she agreed, "What a frigging Fred Karno's . . . !"

It seemed that the Court had already forgotten the way that Major McCarthy had demolished Sergeant Rosenkranz's testimony. As the afternoon wore on and the snow continued to come down, as if God had decided to blot out the evil, wartorn landscape below, the Panel listened attentively to Colonel Schroeder's other American witnesses. Again they testified that it was von Dodenburg who had given that fatal order to massacre the American prisoners. But this time they stated they had watched from afar, though close enough to recognise von Dodenburg giving the orders.

In that mild manner of his, Major McCarthy raised an objection. He asked how could the witnesses know that the German colonel was giving orders of that nature?

The answer came not from the witnesses, or from Colonel

Schroeder, but from the President of the Court. The General snapped testily, "I know you are doing your best to defend your client, Major. But if we go into every little legal nicety we'll be here till hell freezes over." The President's impatience was all too clear. "If one moment von Dodenburg speaks to the killers and the next the killers – presumably private soldiers who couldn't make decisions without higher authority – start slaughtering our fellahs, then I think we can safely assume that von Dodenburg gave that order and, therefore, was the instigator of the massacre. Is that clear, Major McCarthy?"

The reprimand – and threat – were obvious enough. Wearily, McCarthy sat down and stared at the desk in front of him like a tired man who would have dearly liked to have gone to bed and forgotten it all.

In the dock, von Dodenburg felt pretty much the same. Schroeder had failed with his affidavits blackmailed from the Wotan troopers, but he was succeeding with the testimonies of the *Amis*, who had actually watched the 'massacre'. It was all too clear that he hadn't a cat's chance in hell. The Court was very definitely against him, the judge had already found him guilty. Suddenly he wished it was all over and done with.

But that wasn't yet to be. At the State Department in faraway Washington they had decreed that justice must be seen to have been done; the Ivy League graduates, in their Brooks Brothers' suits, who ran the Department had been very insistent about that. So the trial droned on, with here and there one of the Court dropping off to sleep with boredom, snoring softly until a glare from the President and a sharp nudge in the ribs from a neighbour wakened them.

Now that he had come to the conclusion that it was all a waste of time Von Dodenburg found his mind wandering; there was no hope for him. He remembered that snowy

March back in the late Thirties when they had marched off to begin a drive right across Europe. How young, how proud, how confident he and his young black-clad giants had been then. All of them felt as if they had been embarking on a holy crusade to rid Europe of its decadence, the decadence of greasy old men, and replace it with the New Order: the hope of Europe's Youth.

Now he was as old and as worn as those same old men he had once wanted to destroy. He, too, had betrayed Europe's Youth, sending them off on impossible missions for six long years, missions that could end only in death. The great dream had ended Now all that was left to him was to die and get it over with as soon as damned possible.

At four, the snow still falling silently and the courtroom lit by the weak flickering light produced by the hard-pressed local German electricity works, that ran out of coal nearly every day, the President called a recess. It was clear that come what may he was going to get to the end of the prosecution's testimony this day. Still, he could see, too, that everyone was flagging. Thus he ordered a ten-minute break.

To von Dodenburg's surprise he, too, was offered a chipped mug of strong *Ami* coffee, brought to him by the nice guard. Out of the side of his mouth the latter whispered, "With Major McCarthy's compliments, sir. Drink it please before the President of the Court comes back. He wouldn't like it." With that he went, leaving von Dodenburg to warm his skinny, pale hands on the hot mug. Then he took a first hesitant slip at the scaldingly hot mixture, his fingers moving round the enamel mug to avoid getting burned.

Thus it was that he discovered the little note taped to its bottom. He frowned. "What in three devils' names," he began, then thought better of it. Suddenly his heart skipped a beat as he realised that something – something illegal – was going on.

Carefully, very carefully, not taking his eyes off the Court for a moment, he edged his fingers under the mug to where the paper was attached, tugged it free and quickly palmed it.

A moment later his eyes were scanning the little pencilled message, before he popped the paper into his mouth and swallowed it before the routine of the hourly search. The text was simple. All the same, it caused his body to burn with excitement.

"*Halt die Ohren steiff,*" he read. "*Oma*" – his grandmother.*

"The big rogues," he whispered fondly to himself, as the President rapped with his gavel to indicate that the trial was recommencing. "They haven't abandoned me after all . . ."

---

* '*Keep your ears stiff, granny*', i.e. 'Chin up!' *Transl.*

# Chapter Three

It was two days now – and still snowing – since von Dodenburg had received that strange note from his 'granny', and as yet nothing had happened. In court it had been different. That afternoon, the President had found him guilty of war crimes and von Dodenburg had stood rigidly to attention while the American general had announced his verdict and the punishment: "The court sentences you to *death by hanging*!"

The silence had been impenetrable. Suddenly everyone was staring at the haggard, blond colonel, in his shabby field-grey uniform, as if they expected something world-shaking to happen next. It didn't. Von Dodenburg said politely and in a low voice, "Thank you, sir."

Without orders, von Dodenburg had turned smartly to the right. With a trace of his old pride, he had marched off with military precision, the MPs falling in quickly to his left and right as if they had been caught by surprise. Next to Sharpe, as if she were angry, Mary-Ann had dug her nails into the Englishman's one arm fiercely and painfully.


Two days later, von Dodenburg lay stretched out apathetically on his narrow wooden bunk, looking at the red jacket of the condemned man which he now wore. The *Amis*, it seemed, kept up the old Prussian custom of dressing the condemned in red jackets so that they could be easily identified among the mass of the other prisoners.

It was thus while he wondered if he had really received that cryptic little note attached to the mug of coffee, that the keys rattled in the big oak door and it swung open, the rusty hinges creaking noisily in protest. In the door frame stood the brick-faced, surly MP sergeant they called the 'Bull', hands on hips, his white-painted helmet almost touching the door jam. "Okay, Kraut," he bellowed, as if back on the parade ground, "Off'n that cot. You've got a visitor."

Von Dodenburg sat up quickly. "A visitor?"

"Yeah, what's wrong with you, you deaf?" Bull stared down at the German, his piggy, pink eyes full of contempt. "Ya grandma's here to see you."

"*Grandma*?" von Dodenburg caught himself just in time. His beloved *Oma*, the *Baronin*, had been dead at least a dozen years or so.

"Yeah, the CO out of the kindness of his heart, seeing they're gonna have a necktie party for ya purty soon," he grinned maliciously at the words, "decided to let the old broad see you. OK, follow me."

Von Dodenburg rose uncertainly, trying to hide the sudden nervous twitching in his left cheek. He followed Bull into the gloomy stone corridor which led to the room where visitors, usually legal ones, met their 'clients'.

*Oma* was surprisingly young to be a grandmother, von Dodenburg told himself. Big and blousy, her blonde hair concealed by a head scarf, she couldn't have been much older than her mid-forties. In no way did she resemble the average German grandmother in her black button boots. *Her* black dress was much too short for her massive flanks and instead of button boots she wore very high heels despite the deep snow outside.

"Kay," Bull anounced, "you've got exactly ten minutes.

You can embrace," he leered at 'grandma' knowingly, "now and on leaving. Otherwise there's no physical contact allowed." Again he leered. He sat down heavily on the wooden chair in the corner and, drawing his .45 placed it on his lap suggestively. "She's all yours, Kraut."

Von Dodenburg licked abruptly parched lips. What was he supposed to say to this bogus grandmother?

In the event von Dodenburg had to say nothing. The newly acquired 'granny' did the speaking for him. Taking the big man's handkerchief away from her red, bulbous nose, she gave one last fake sob and quavered, "How good it is to see you, Kuno, after all these years. But sad, too. How terribly sad!" she lowered her head as if she might start sobbing again, her big breasts trembling under her artifical silk blouse.

Bull, in the corner, his big feet parked on the wall, yawned, bored by this silly Kraut business, and closed his eyes.

"What in three devils' names is going on?" von Dodenburg hissed urgently, not taking his gaze off the big military police sergeant for a moment.

The fat woman made a warning face. "Calm down!" she whispered. "Don't make the big *Ami* bastard suspicious." On any other occasion von Dodenburg would have chided the fat woman on her use of definitely ungranny-like language. Not now. He was too intrigued by what this strange visitor had to say. "A good friend of yours – *from the old days*," she added significantly, "has sent me. He wants to help you before it is too late." She looked at the red jacket of the condemned man, but said nothing.

'*Wotan*' von Dodenburg felt like shouting out in delight. Instead he whispered, "Who?"

She shook her dyed blonde head. "He told me not to tell

you. These terrible days you can't be sure of anyone. No name, no pack-drill."

He nodded his understanding.

"But you can rest assured that he'll be coming to see you soon, as soon as he bribes the *Amis*. They'll do anything for a nice piece of juicy gash." Von Dodenburg's mouth dropped open at the surprising phrase coming from a woman. "Sell their own frigging grandma for it!" She chuckled softly. "Not this particular granny, mind you!"

In the corner the MP started to stir. Their time was about up.

"One thing," she said urgently, "You mustn't be one bit surprised when he turns up here to give you your final instructions. Promise that."

"Yes, I promise . . . I promise!" he swore urgently. "But how is he going to get into this hellhole?"

She smiled. "You know him. He'll get in anywhere." Her smile broadened as if at some very private and personal joke.

In the corner the MP looked at his black market gold wristwatch.

"Holy strawsack, but how's he going to get into here," von Dodenberg persisted. "Women, I understand. Even the *Amis* can't be that hard-hearted. In fact they're quite a sentimental bunch as far as aged ladies go. But a man!"

She laughed softly. "Surely they wouldn't stop your nearest and dearest relative from coming to see you, now that you're wearing the red jacket?"

"What—"

"OK," the Bull cut him off sharply. "Time's up. Come on, Granny! You've had your say."

Stiffly, as if every joint in her body ached, 'Granny' rose to her feet. "Father's written," she said in parting. "He's trying to come and see you before it's too late, dearest Kuno." She raised her handkerchief to her eyes, as if she might burst into tears at any moment and in the same instant pressed her cheek against Kuno's. He recoiled, startled. 'Granny' had definitely not shaved this morning . . .

"*Is it good?*" Mary-Ann grunted fiercely. "Say it's good, damn your eyes!" She squatted astride Sharpe, her naked body glazed with sweat, her dark eyes wild and demented, her breath coming in short harsh gasps. She thrust down hard once more so that the bedsprings protested against their weight. She stopped abruptly, her face contorted even more. Her nubile body was racked with shudders, as if she were in acute pain. Her spine arched like a long bow and a deep, satisfied sigh that seemed to go on for ever came from somewhere deep down in her sex-racked body. Next instant she collapsed on his naked chest, her breath sharp and hectic as if she had just run a great race.

Satisfied more than once, needing no more, feeling that pleasure that always comes after good sex, as if it will never be as good ever again, he stroked her long, matted dark hair lovingly. Outside it was still snowing, muting all sound. They might well have been the last people alive in the world. "Domination?" he queried quietly, indicating that she was on top of him and not the other way around.

"No," she gasped, trying to regain control of her hectic breathing. "Fornication!"

He laughed shortly and reaching out the best he could with his one hand he felt on the stained night table for the packet of cigarettes and silver Ronson lighter she had given him for his birthday – 'to light a little flame in your heart, dearest'—and lit two cigarettes.

She rolled over on her back luxuriously and carelessly so

that for an instant he caught a glimpse of that delightful place between her thighs and accepted the cigarette. Gratefully she breathed out a stream of blue smoke.

"So she got away from you – gave you the slip, eh, Tom," she said without rancour.

"Yes, it was the bloody snow. I slipped as I started to cross the street after her. Went arse over tit. By the time I'd righted myself she had disappeared into that warren of ruins opposite the prison. Not a hope in hell of finding her in there, especially with this bloody snow."

She leaned over and gave his limp penis a gentle squeeze. "Couldn't be helped. Besides it gave us more time for this, eh!"

He nodded thoughtfully. "All the same, despite the fun and games, I would like to know what the old biddy was up to. His *grandmother*! What a load of old bullshit!"

"Bullshit indeed," she agreed.

They were silent for a while. He placed his good hand on her left breast and playfully tweaked the nipple. She didn't respond. Probably she was thinking about the old biddy he told himself.

But he was wrong. When she spoke, she asked, "What are we going to do, Tom?"

"Do?"

"Yes, about us."

She spoke slowly, as if she were formulating her thoughts with difficulty. "This business with your – er – old biddy, as you call her, has convinced me."

He sat up, puzzled. "Convinced you of what?"

"That everything here in Germany is rotten – rotten to the core. Our side, if it is *our* side, and naturally theirs. I just want out."

"You mean quit the service?"

"Yes." She nodded solemnly. "I'm sure McDougall

wouldn't exactly object. In fact that particular sly gentleman would be only too glad to see the back of me. I'm a thorn in his flesh."

"Agreed," Sharpe said, suddenly worried as it came to him that he wasn't going to be able to function without her. She was the first woman he had ever felt anything about, save sex, for years. I suppose, he told himself, people might call it love. "But what would you do?"

She looked at him, as if seeing him for the first time. "What do you mean?"

"Where would you go? Back to America?"

She shook her head. "No, I don't think so. I'm a foreigner there really, you know. The Americans took us in and all that, but I don't think they really like us. We look foreign, we talk foreign, we eat foreign. We're a constant reminder to Mr Average that the world is not as Mr Norman Rockwell portrays it – roses around the door, Mom and her cookies—" suddenly she sounded bitter and cynical – "the kind of place where people love one another. Well they goddam don't!"

He ignored the bitterness. "Well, what's the alternative – Europe?"

She tapped her forehead with her index finger in the Continental gesture for madness. "Are you *meschugge*, Tom? Live in Europe, after what happened to us Jews? And it wasn't only in Germany. The French were just as bad." She shrugged and dismissed the matter without completing her thought.

"Where then?"

"Palestine, Tom." She took his one hand and grasped it hard in her own, as if willing him to agree. "There we'd get a new start, even if we had to work in the fields in some Godforsaken *kibbutz*. It'd be a fresh, clean world, a chance for *both* of us."

"*Both of us*?" He laughed a little hollowly. "Don't you

know what's going on in Palestine at this very moment?" He answered his own question. "We and the Jews are going at it hammer and tongs. The general public know little of the kind of bitter underground war both sides are fighting out there, with the Arabs in the middle." He laughed a little harshly. "Can you imagine how I'd fit in in the Jewish community? A British officer and in Intelligence to boot. Your Haganah would have my guts for garters very toot-sweet."

She nodded thoughtfully and said, "I see what you mean, Tom." For what seemed a long time she stared through the dirty window at the white snow falling outside, blocking out the prison courtyard where soon Master-Sergeant Woods, with his bourbon, big cigar and length of hempen rope, would put an end to the meteoric career of *Obersturmbannführer* Kuno von Dodenburg. Finally she sighed and whispered, "Perhaps tomorrow we'll come up with a solution, Tom." She didn't sound very convinced.

He forced a laugh and said as lightly as he could, "Remember that song Bob Hope and some woman used to sing back in the Forties? *"No more money in the bank . . . no more little kids to spank . . ."* For such a hard-bitten combat soldier his voice was light and quite charming, *"So what's to do about it? . . . Let's put out the light and go to sleep . . ."*

He reached behind his head, switched off the light and everything went black. She gasped and then like two lovers abandoned to an unfeeling world, they made love.

## Chapter Four

The chaplain had tried his best. Mild-mannered and speaking in his hesitant German he had said to von Dodenburg, "My son, you will be starting out soon on a long journey . . . But it isn't one into darkness. Regard it as a journey into light, love and understanding." The American padre had smiled a little hesitantly at the condemned man in his red jacket.

In the old days when he had renounced his own Lutheran creed in favour of the pagan one of the New Order, von Dodenburg would have laughed in the weak, ineffectual face of the cleric. Not now. Instead he said mildly, "I know you are doing your best, padre, and I thank you for your efforts." He shrugged a little helplessly. "But I'm afraid there is going to be no love and understanding for me where I'm going. More likely intense heat and hate!"

The padre had tut-tutted, but he knew when he was beaten. Before going, he had exchanged a few words, left behind some sort of uplifting religious leaflet beneath which he had hidden a few contraband cigarettes, for which von Dodenburg, very nervous and tense with the waiting for 'father', was grateful.

"I shall pray for you, my son," he had said from the door, giving the man in the red coat his blessing.

Now it seemed that that prayer had been answered. For ten minutes later Bull appeared, sneering, "Don't think the sky pilot did much good for you, Kraut. Can't see any halo."

He pretended to peer around the freezing, grey cell before saying, "Yer old man's here. Ya've got ten minutes. OK?" He turned and cried to the guard farther down the corridor, "Let's have the old Kraut."

There was the sound of feet shuffling down the loud-echoing corridor. A few moments later, accompanied by a hacking cough, a big, bent civilian appeared, eyes hidden by tremendously thick-rimmed old spectacles, body clad in a black market shirt made from a GI blanket, with a leather strap wrapped round his battered left boot, the sole of which was flapping and threatening to come off at any moment.

Von Dodenburg caught his breath. With a sheer effort of willpower he contained himself just in time. "You!" he gasped.

In the corner, Bull, balancing himself on the wooden chair, carbine between his knees, turned his attention to the cartoons in the current issue of the soldiers' newspaper, the *Stars and Stripes*.

Slowly, as if it were an effort, the big civilian handed over the bunch of drooping winter violets. "For you, my dear boy," he said somewhat sadly. "Your mother sent them. Grandma sends her best wishes as well." He winked solemnly and von Dodenburg answered, knowing that Bull didn't speak that much German. "My love to her – and tell her to get a better damned shave next time!" His emaciated face lit up. "Christ on a crutch, Schulze, you old rogue, what a sight for sore eyes you are!" At that moment he would have dearly loved to embrace the big ex-NCO, but he knew that it was impossible with Bull present. Instead he asked sharply, "What's the drill, you horned ox?"

"Knocking shop, sir. You are looking at the proud sole owner – well, that little Bavarian barnshitter Matzi's part owner as well, I suppose – of the town's sole class knocking shop. Special exhibitions – donkeys and lesbians for our new friends the *Amis* – God rest their souls." He looked very pious.

"Get on with it, Schulze!"

"Sir. Get yersen in the dock. I've got some castor oil. That'll give you the thin shits long enough for the bone-menders to put yer in dock. Wouldn't look good for you to be shittin' yersen all the way to the gallows would it, sir?"

"Oh no," von Dodenburg answered, as if it was the most reasonable thing in the world, and neatly palming the thin metal phial, full presumably of castor oil, calculated to give him the 'thin shits'. As soon as Bull had taken his 'father' out he would slip the metal tube up his rectum. It was the safest place to hide the contraband from the nightly American search. His guards had peered up his rectum, and found nothing, daily for so long that they had given up doing so.

Minutes late, before a sobbing Schulze was led out by the Bull, he whispered, "The Popov medic is one of us. He'll tell you the rest once you're inside the dock." He used the soldiers' slang on the Eastern Front for 'Russian'.

"Popov?" von Dodenburg began, puzzled. But Schulze, the tragic 'father', had already been hustled outside.

Two hours later Schulze, huddled next to the roaring pot-bellied stove, surrounded by his men, including von Dodenburg's aged *'Oma'*, now well-shaven and dressed in shabby civilian clothing, explained his plan. "The first thing is to get the old CO into the hands of the bone-menders. That's the least defended place in the hospital. After all, the only people the *Amis* send to the dock are those who are about to snuff it, to look at the taties from below. So why guard the place?"

There was a murmur of agreement from the handful of shabby Wotan survivors who had come from all over

Southern Germany to help in the rescue of their beloved ex-regimental commander before it was too late.

"Once the Popov gives us the wire, that von D is in the dock," Schulze continued, "we go into action that very night as soon as it's dark. Everything's got to be done and dusted before curfew starts at 0200 hours. We don't want to chance bumping into an *Ami* patrol looking for curfew-breakers." He raise a huge fist, "And anyone who fucks up, answers to Mrs Schulze's handsome son."

Matz pretended to shiver. "Oh, ex-Senior Sergeant Schulze, how masterful you are! I swear if I'm gonna give my virginity to anyone it'd be you. Can I feel yer muscle, darling?" he added wickedly.

"Yer'll feel the toe of my frigging dice-beaker, if you don't watch yer frigging step, Matzi. Now, no muckin' about. Let's frigging well get on with it." Without waiting for the others' reaction, he continued hastily, as if time was running out rapidly. "With a bit o' luck the people inside under von Dodenburg will be able to take care of the side gate. But from then on, we're in charge. Once he's out, we scoop the CO up and let the others who have volunteered to come out with him do a bunk – after all, we don't know if they can be trusted now they've let him down once."

'*Oma*' sneered: "In a pig's ear, Schulzi! Once you're a squealer, you're allus a frigging squealer. Our sole obligation—"

"What high-falutin' language you do use, Grandmama!" Matzi interrupted mischievously.

'*Oma*' ignored the comment, but continued doggedly, as if it were an article of faith, "You know what I mean frigging Matzi. Our first obligation is to the old CO."

"You're right there," Schulze agreed, opening the door of the stove and throwing in another precious black-market log. "We've got to get him out of this place toot-sweet before the

*Amis* start turning the town upside down looking for him." Strangely enough he winked at Matz at this juncture, as if there was something secret between them. The others didn't notice, as he came to his final point. "Of course we'll be armed. I've got a dozen Lugers hidden beneath that pile of logs," he indicated the wood stacked neatly at the back of the bomb-damaged cellar which was their black market HQ, "as well as a couple of machine-pistols, plus five mags of ammo per weapon." He saw the the sudden worried look on their hard faces, brutalised by years of combat. "I know . . . I frigging well know," he exclaimed hastily. "I know what the *Amis* will do to us, the bastards, if they find us armed." He looked around at them almost angrily. "But if any of you weak sisters want to become nervous nellies, shut up now and back out before the fun and games commence. I don't want any aspagarus Tarzan going damned soft on me after we've started."

He waited.

"Well?" he demanded finally, his big face hollowed out to a scarlet death's head in the flames coming from the little stove, with its pipe poked through the ruined wall of the cellar.

One by one they shook their heads. Some murmured, "What the frig d'yer take us for, Schulzi?" . . . Others snorted angrily. "Get off'n my hairy arse! We'd never let the old man down . . ." Matz brought the whole matter to a close with a hasty, "Piss or get off the pot, Schulz. Don't let us hang around like a nun waiting for her nightly candle. When's tea dance gonna start? I've not cocked my flipper over a piece of female gash for almost 24 hours. If this goes on, I won't know where to put it no more." He looked suitably aggrieved.

"You mean with that little bit o' dried-up gristle hanging between yer legs? A thing like that wouldn't even make a virgin blink. I feel ashamed to admit that a bloke like you with that kind o' sawn-off cock once belonged to SS Assault Regiment Wotan." He gave a deep sigh like a man sorely tried. "Ah well, it'll soon be frigging Christmas. Peace on earth and all that crap. All right, let's get on with the show. – '*Oma*'!"

Von Dodenburg's temporary grandma needed no urging. Urgently, she clapped her big horny paws together. The door opened immediately and a series of females, some still patting the snowflakes off their shoulders, entered.

"*Gruss Gott!*" the one in the lead, a huge woman, chortled, "Great God!"

"Yer, when yer see him," Schulze answered cynically. The rest of his words died on his lips as she opened her home-made blanket coat to reveal her figure beneath. "By the Great Whore of Buxtehude!" he gasped, "where the dogs piss out of their ribs. Look at them tits! All that meat . . . and no frigging taties!"

The whore smirked and looked around at the circle of brutalised faces in the glowing red light thrown out by the stove, the cellar's only form of illumination. "What's this?" she exclaimed scornfully. "Frigging choir outing! A lot of five against one, the whole lot of 'em." She made an explicit and very obscene gesture with her clenched right fist. "Oh, well, perhaps a couple of 'em at once 'll make up for one good man."

Now as Schulze started to hand out 'flatmen', filled with potato schnapps, the whores started to pick out their partners, laughing and giggling in the manner of the professional 'pavement pounders' that they were, fighting off grasping claws and hands trying to get up their skirts with the ease of women who had been doing so since they had first allowed some dirty-minded schoolboy to lower their drawers.

Matz rubbed his little hands together in delight. "Cor, am

I gonna make a pig o' mesen now! I'll have her for starters." He indicated the massive woman.

Schulze shook his head. "Gerda the Guzzler is reserved for yours truly. Besides we ain't got enough gash to go round for everybody. We'll have to toss for 'em."

"Toss for'em?" *Oma* growled. "The way things is going, I think I'm tossing already." He laughed crudely.

Gerda the Guzzler shot him a cold, imperious look. "Watch your language arse-with-ears. Remember there *are* ladies present." With one hand, barely looking down as she did so, she punched a drunken ex-corporal who in his enthusiasm was trying to wriggle his penis through his flies while at the same time attempting to pull down her huge knickers with his free hand.

Schulze beamed around the circle of excited male and female faces in the ruddy light of the flickering flames, their wavering shadows thrown in grotesque distortion on the dirty cracked walls. "Just like the good old days, comrades!" he chortled. He raised the bottle of potato schnapps clutched in his big paw. *"Hoch die Tassen, Kameraden. Die Nacht wird kuhl."*\* With that he took a tremendous slug at the raw schnapps. The dye had been cast. The rescue could finally begin.

---

\* 'Up the cups, comrades. The night's going to be cold.' *Transl.*

# Chapter Five

Von Dodenburg ended the count. Now he had to move, and move fast. The guard peered through the Judas hole into his cell, as his comrades did into all the cells of those condemned to death and wearing the red jacket, every ten minutes. Now he had exactly that number of minutes to fake the ailment which he hoped would get him into the 'dock' as Schulze called it.

Hastily, not taking his eyes off the hole in the door for one moment, he pulled the stolen razor blade from beneath the hard horsehair pallet on the concrete slab which was his bed. He hesitated only for a fraction of a second. Then he drew the sharp blade across the veins of his upper arm – it had to be there to be able later to pull down the sleeve of his red jacket and hide the wound from which he had drawn the blood. Swiftly he walked over to the noxious piss bucket, encrusted with lime and smelling to high heaven. He pressed the gash from which his blood was already beginning to seep and held the arm over the enamel bucket, already half full of his own urine and faeces. He had reasoned that at first sight, blood-stained urine and faeces would look more alarming and dangerous. The blood started to drip into the bucket more swiftly.

Three minutes had passed. He had seven left. He had spent enough time on the bucket. He flashed a look at it. The human waste was now swimming in bright red blood.

It looked very realistic to him. Hurriedly he pulled down the red jacket sleeve to hide the wound and jerked at his shabby pants.

He squatted as low as he could go, holding onto the bunk with his left hand. He paused. What he was going to do now was highly dangerous if he got it wrong. He had heard of prisoners having to have the phial cut out surgically on the operating table because they had made a mistake and the metal tube had jammed in the anus.

"*One . . . two . . . three*," he counted off the seconds, his eyes still fixed on the Judas hole. Then he started. Spreading his legs as wide as he could, squatting on his haunches, he felt gingerly for the top of the tube inside his rectum. As he did so that ditty which Schulze was fond of singing came to his mind, "*Tight as a drum . . . never been done . . . queen of all the fairies.*" He dismissed it angrily in the same instant that the tips of his fingers touched the warm metal.

He was sweating heavily despite the coldness of the cell and he knew why. This was the moment of truth. He said a silent prayer and then holding on to the end of the tube with the tips of his fingers he started to draw it from his rectum. There was no pain, but he imagined there was. His brow contorted, as if he were in mortal agony. Outside he heard a soft footfall. The guard was coming down the corridor. "Come on," he commanded himself, "get the frigging thing out and have done with it!"

Now it was half way out of his body. He strained, as if he were suffering from severe constipation, and pressed down hard. At the same time, his damp, hot fingers held on to the tube, as if his life depended upon it. But perhaps it did. The soft footsteps were coming nearer. His time was running out. "Great crap on the Christmas tree," he cursed in despair. "Come on . . . *for frig's sake* come on—!"

There was a soft plop and the tube dropped into his palm.

He wasted no time now. With fingers that trembled violently he unscrewed the cap, spilling a little of the viscous liquid from the container in his haste. The footsteps had paused at the door. There was a soft cough like a butler might make before knocking on the door of his master's study.

Hastily von Dodenburg raised the tube to his lips. The smell was over-powering. His stomach churned. For a moment he thought he was going to be sick. Forcing himself, he swallowed the mix, feeling it trickle down his gullet unpleasantly, as he drank the revolting stuff. Then it was down. At the door, the Judas hole was beginning to squeak (he had forced concrete dust beneath it earlier on to make it more difficult to open). His stomach was now in a turmoil. There was a loud rumbling. He broke wind twice, three times, four times. Now there seemed no stopping his guts from taking over. He sensed the overwhelming urge in his lower gut. Frantically, he ripped open the buttons of his trousers. The *Amis* had taken away his belt immediately he had been sentenced in case he attempted to commit suicide.

The Judas hole was almost open. He swayed to the bucket, trying to hold himself back till he reached it. He gave a tremendous fart, staggered to a stop over the bucket and in an instant his guts exploded.

Outside there was a faint gasp. A voice said, "Shit on the shingle! What a helluva of a stink. Christ, that guy's insides must be rotten!"

"Help me!" he cried piteously. "I'm bleeding from the rectum . . . Help me!"

"Rectum?"

"Arse," he quavered, making his point quite clear.

"Holy mackerel!" There was a jingle of keys as the guard fumbled with the lock. Next moment the door was flung open in alarm as von Dodenburg collapsed on the floor, almost overturning the blood-filled bucket, his yellow rump smeared disgustingly with watery faeces and blood. In real pain now, his stomach on fire, his rump heaving back and forth as he still could not control the evil fluids spurting in a stream from his rectum, von Dodenburg cried weakly, "Blood . . . blood everywhere . . . !"

Covering his nose tightly against the smell, gagging as he did so, his pistol forgotten, the guard threaded his way through the mess to the bucket. "Wow! he exclaimed as he saw what it contained . . . "Buddy," he stuttered, "Your guts . . . they're falling apart!"

Von Dodenburg looked up at him, his face ashen, eyes bulging out of their sockets with the searing pain that seemed to be tearing his innards apart, and said weakly, "Ulcer . . . ulcer burst . . . get me to hospital . . . at once!"

The guard pulled himself together. He knew the Kraut had to survive long enough to end on the gallows. That's what the Great American Public wanted. They were told that every morning by the OD when they came on duty. And the guy was obviously dying right in front of him. "Hold on brother!" he yelled. Don't frigging croak on me – *please*! I'll get the medics. Now hold on . . ." Hurriedly he left the cell and hit the emergency button just outside on the wall. A high-pitched alarm ran through the cell block. It was intended to warn the prison that an attempt to escape was being made. But it served this particular purpose well enough. As von Dodenburg slipped into a faint, urgent feet came running down the gloomy grey corridor. Voices rang out in alarm, someone shouted an order and suddenly things were happening *fast*.


Shroeder looked in alarm at the ashen face of his prisoner on his cot in the spartan prison ward. Behind him, McDougall looked angry. He was muttering to himself until Schroeder, angry as well as alarmed, turned round and snapped, "What the Sam Hill's the matter, McDougall – talking to yourself like some goddam old broad!"

Shroeder didn't impress McDougall. Already he was in touch with the illegal Jewish Haganah organisation, helping them to smuggle German weapons out of the country for the fight in Palestine. Once he had dealt with von Dodenburg and his killers, he, too, would be off to the Holy Land to take part in the sacred struggle against the British and the Arabs. So he said almost carelessly, "Just this, Colonel. That SS bastard is due to be strung up by Woods tomorrow. I want him dancing at the end of the rope – there's gonna be no excuse, no getting away from that." He said the words firmly, even decisively, as if he were in charge.

A hot retort sprang to the fat colonel's lips. Then he thought better of it. The Kikes were everywhere back in the States. Perhaps McDougall, or whatever his goddam real name was, had pull in Washington. He'd better play it by ear. "Yeah, I'm with you there." He turned and faced the little orderly, his white jacket stained by the red vomit that von Dodenburg had brought up. "You spikka da English?"

The little Popov, his round, high-cheeked face full of that winning cunning which had enabled him to survive when thousands of his Red Army comrades, who had been captured with him by the Germans back in 1942, had died of torture and simple starvation, beamed at the American and replied, "*Boshe moi . . . da*. I speak *nmetski*?" He spat on the ward floor at the mention of Germans and French language, American. He extended his pudgy, none-too-clean hands like a fawning head waiter welcoming a rich client who tipped generously. "You are wishing to know, gentlemens?"

"Where's the doctor? . . . The doctor – American – in charge of this ward?" Schroeder demanded.

The Popov's steel-toothed smile broadened even more. "Doctor gentleman in *lab* . . . making tests." He pretended to be shaking a test tube over a Bunsen burner.

Schroeder relaxed a little. "Good," he said, "And this man here?" He indicated an apparently unconscious von Dodenburg, who had a large white porcelain bedpan stuck under his skinny rump.

"*Horoscho*," the Popov answered hastily. "Good now . . . Sickness nearly over." His fat face revealed nothing of his fears. The American doctor was out like a light in the little office to the rear. After he had smuggled the girl into him and the cautious, bespectacled American had tested her for both types of VD before 'fornicating', as he called it, on the surgery table, the American had hit the bottle of 'American-style genuine Scottish whisky' *hard*. He had passed out like a light. All the same, the Popov was worried. He knew his drunks. Sometimes they would wake up from their stupors and start looking for more alcohol. He hated to think about the naked doctor, minus his steel-rimmed GI spectacles, wandering down the corridor, the used contraceptive still attached to his flaccid organ.

The Popov need not have worried. Schroeder was reassured. He handed the Popov a half-empty pack of Camels, worth a small fortune on the black market, and said, "See that he's on his frigging feet by 0800 hours tomorrow morning. Then we hang him." As the Popov bowed and scraped at the rare gift, Schroeder turned and faced McDougall, "Come on, Captain," he urged, "let's get out of here. It's as cold as the morgue. Besides, I need a stiff shot after this business."

Von Dodenburg and the Popov waited till their footsteps had died in the corridor and all was silent again save for the moans of the would-be suicide in the side room. He had tried – and failed – to cut his throat with a piece of broken glass. The SS officer opened his eyes cautiously and found himself looking at the beaming face of the little Russian ex-POW. "All gone," he hissed happily. "*Slav krasnaya armya . . . Heil Stalin\* . . .*" His grin broadened.

"So what do they think?"

"Ulcer . . . gut ulcer," the Russian answered, pressing his fat lower belly and wincing in great pain seemingly. "Too sick to run." He winked. "*Horoscho?*"

"*Horoscho?*" von Dodenburg agreed, lapsing into Russian like all the 'front swine' who had spent years in Russia. "What now?"

"You friends . . . They come." He threw a glance at his cheap black market wristwatch of which he was inordinately proud. "Two hours." He held up two pudgy, dirty fingers to make his meaning quite clear. "Now you get ready, Comrade Officer."

"Ready?"

The Popov indicated the bundle in the corner. "Clothes . . . civvie clothes. And this." As if by magic his hand dived into his voluminous pocket and reappeared clutching a German Army Walther P38 9mm pistol.

Despite his pains and aching left arm, von Dodenburg whistled softly as he palmed the little 34oz weapon, feeling its comforting weight, happy to have a weapon in his grasp once more. He checked – it was loaded.

"One up the spout," the Popov said urgently, using the front swine's expression.

"Yes," von Dodenburg nodded, his emaciated face suddenly grim yet purposeful, for he knew this was his last chance. If he failed now, he'd be dead, courtesy of Master-Sergeant Woods, in twelve or so hours. "Trouble?"

The Popov shrugged eloquently like a ham actor in the last act of a third-rate play. "Perhaps . . . perhaps not. Your

---

\* 'Long Live the Red Army'. *Transl.*

Sergeant Schulze," his hands carved an enormous shape in the air so that von Dodenburg knew whom he meant, "He good man, tough man."

Von Dodenburg nodded. "You can say that again. Allus with his hooter in the shit and still coming out smelling of roses. All right, come on – help me with those civvie duds." A little weakly he clambered out of the cot, leaving the blood-stained sheets behind him. In the single room the would-be suicide still moaned, *"Let me die . . . let me die for God's sake. . . . PLEASE!"*

Von Dodenburg bit his botton lip grimly. To die – that wasn't so easy, he told himself. Then he got on with the slow business of dressing himself.

A hundred yards or so away, with the snow still coming down in courtyard as if it would never stop, Major Sharpe awoke, startled. Instantly he was wide awake, heart pounding excitedly, fully aware that something was going on.

It was the same feeling he had experienced on that beach in Crete after a week-long fighting retreat, when he had woken from an exhausted sleep to find that the brass had crept away in the darkness to be evacuated to Egypt, leaving the 'unimportant mouths', as they were always called, to their fate. Later he had felt the same sensation before the battle of Knightsbridge and above all at El Alamein, when he had awoken to know that something terrible was going to happen to him on the morrow. It had.

Mary-Ann had somehow sensed his inner tension, for she shifted uneasily in his arm and whispered hoarsely, "Do you want me?"

"No," he answered in a whisper, "There's something going on."

She sat up, naked, wide awake immediately. *"What?"*

He repeated what he had just said.

"How do you know?"

"I just feel it," he answered lamely and reached for the automatic beneath his pillow. Even now with the war over he still stuck to his cautious habits.

"Do you think it's him?"

He knew whom she meant. "Yes, von Dodenburg, I'm sure. I know he's not had a fair trial—"

"He's been goddam railroaded by that fat creep Schroeder!"

"Agreed. All the same, Mary-Ann, we can't let him escape. We don't want him, however innocent he might be, to become a symbol, a rallying point for the Jerries in the years to come. They'll become a problem whichever way you look at it. Aft all they are a great nation in the heart of Europe and you can't keep 80,000,000 down for ever. So we can't allow them to have Nazi saints, as it were, in the years to come. We've got to stop him, even if—" He didn't finish his sentence. Instead, his face grim, he tapped the pistol now stuck in the waistband of his slacks. *"COME ON . . . !"*

# Chapter Six

Now the three-day long snowstorm had reached its peak. The snowflakes were falling from the night sky in white sheets and the wind howled in an eerie fury, slamming the flakes against the dirty barred windows of the prison. In their boxes and at their posts, sheltering in whatever cover the doorways afforded, the guards felt completely cut off, isolated by the snowfall, each one plagued by his inner uncertainties and apprehensions, as if he were the last man alive. It was a night of elementary fury, as Nature raged against mankind. It was almost as if the elements were preparing the scene for the hanging soon to come – stark, white, relentless and without mercy.

In the corner guard tower, a wooden structure balanced on three stork-like legs which shook and trembled in that mighty wind, the fearful young guard in his black ankle-length Army slicker cursed the Bull once again for having posted him to this remote tower opposite the hospital and for giving him 'the graveyard shift' – twelve to two – as well.

Inside the prison, its walls heavy with clinging snow that had already flung itself against the ancient stone and lodged there, the Kraut prisoners were still in bed, warm and asleep, while he perched on top of his swaying tower, fearful that it might collapse at any moment. "Christ, what a frigging life!" he cursed miserably to himself as the tower trembled violently once more. Why wasn't he tucked up in bed with one of those fat Kraut whores that the big guy – Schulze or whatever his frigging name was – provided the GIs with for a pack of Camels?

The prison clock chimed the quarter. Even above the howl of the wind, he heard it. It startled him. He jumped and then told himself that in ninety minutes he'd be relieved. Then he'd be able to get at the bottle of rye he had stashed away in his bedroll in the guardhouse. Fuck Bull and the big NCO's objection to his MPs drinking while on guard duty.

The thought of Bull decided him. The big bastard moved silently for a guy who weighed well over 200lb and it was his habit when he was guard commander to sneak up on his unsuspecting guards and put them on report if they weren't carrying out their duties correctly. He took a deep breath and shouldering his MI carbine more firmly, stepped out of the cover of his box which housed the machine-gun, into the raging snowstorm. The wind took his breath away. "*Christ on a crutch*!" he gasped, fighting for air. "What a frigging night—" He stopped short suddenly. There was someone out there next to the platform! In a sudden gap in the falling snow he was sure that he had seen someone at the base of the platform, crouched low and menacing.

"What should I do?" he asked himself uncertainly, as the snow closed in again and the gap was blocked by the thick, wet, whirling, white flakes. Was he seeing things? He was sure he wasn't. If that was the case, should he clamber down the rickety wooden ladder and call Bull in the guardhouse? But if there *was* somebody there waiting for him in the shadows—! He didn't think that frightening thought to an end. And if there wasn't and he called the Bull out on a false alarm, there'd be hell to pay. The big bastard of a noncom would never let him live it down. What the Sam Hill was he going to do?

Protectively, perhaps without even thinking, he dropped to one knee. Putting the condom off the muzzle, which protected the barrel from dampness, he rested the weapon on the outer railing. He jerked the bolt back and clicked the safety off. If there *was* anyone out there, he'd blow his goddam head off, he told himself with sudden resolution. No goddam messing! "Okay, buddy!" he snarled through gritted teeth, peering through the whirling white gloom, "let's be goddam having you—"

He never finished his terrible threat. As the huge, threatening shape loomed up out of the gloom, the young guard opened his mouth to scream. But the scream ended in a thick, muffled grunt as a terrible killing blow smashed into the back of his head. His skull splintered like a soft boiled egg struck by a heavy spoon. He was dead before he hit the snow.

On Schulze's signal from the watchtower, a barely glimpsed flicker of a storm lantern off and on three times, the handful of ex-Wotan troopers moved swiftly and silently into action. Veterans that they were they did so without a single order being given or expected. Expertly they sealed off the hospital, taking out the handful of completely surprised sentries with silent, lethal blows. Then they watched the remaining guards opposite covering the main entrance, walking their beat in miserable, muffled silence, plodding through the knee-deep, fresh snow totally unaware of what had happened only yards away.

Cautiously, assisted by the little Popov, whose normally ever-present peasant grin had vanished, von Dodenburg made his way down the dimly lit ward. Outside, the wind continued to howl and rage and, von Dodenburg hoped, it would cover any sound they might make.

Von Dodenburg's legs felt like rubber. He felt he might collapse at any moment. He realised that everything would depend on Schulze's men and the assistance of the little Russian hospital orderly. He hadn't the strength to make decisions, or fend for himself. It took all his strength to just keep upright and walking. Next to him, the Popov whispered encouragingly, "Not long now, Comrade Officer . . . not long. He forced a grin, displaying those shining stainless steel false teeth of which he was inordinately proud.

"Yes, I know," von Dodenburg answered tensely, concentrating all his strength on just keeping going. "Thanks."

They started to crawl past the closed door of the outer office. Yellow light escaped from beneath the door and he could hear, through the static of a transatlantic broadcast, an excited announcer proclaiming, *"Folks, it looks as if it's gonna be a triple hitter after all . . . Jones is now on first base . . . but you can believe me, he's not staying there very long . . . The pitcher's beginning to wind up . . . In the bleachers, the crowd's going crazy . . . !"*

Von Dodenburg didn't understand anything of what the announcer on the other side of the Atlantic was saying. But he was grateful to the man in that 'Land of Unlimited Possibilities'.* The noise he made covered any of theirs.

"Not far now," the Popov comforted the weak patient, "Not far. Then General Schulze, he look after you."

Von Dodenburg did not even have the strength to comment on Sergeant Schulze's sudden post-war promotion to 'general'. He confined himself to a faint nod as they shuffled closer to the door and freedom. But it was difficult, damned difficult. A black veil threatened to overcome him time and time again so that he desired nothing more than to slip down and sleep. But he knew that it would be fatal. He had to be

---

* Expression used by the envious immediate post-war Germans for the fortunate Americans. *Transl.*

out of this place in a few minutes or it would be evil-faced Sergeant Woods and his noose . . .

Defiantly, Sharpe and Mary-Ann, coming up behind him, clinging desperately to his one hand, fought the violent wind. Time and time again it buffeted them like a blow from an invisible fist as they ploughed across the snowbound courtyard, threatening to throw them off their feet. They gasped and panted. The terrible storm seemed to be snatching the very air from their straining lungs, but they didn't give up and seek the nearest cover as all sensible people were doing. For now their vague suspicions had turned into reality. Even with the storm raging and howling all around them they were aware of vague sounds and movements which they knew were out of place on a night like this. Someone besides themselves was up to no good out there in the night.

They staggered to a stop at the base of the stork-legged watchtower, the wood groaning and creaking like a live thing in pain. Sharpe released his grip on Mary-Ann's hand – and she immediately took hold of the nearest leg in order not to be blown away by the wind – and cupping it around his mouth yelled, "Hey, up there – what's going on?"

There was no reply.

Sharpe told himself the wind had snatched his words away and the guard above hadn't heard. He tried again – still no answer. Behind him, Mary-Ann cried, "No one can have fallen asleep in a racket like this. It'd wake the dead!"

He felt the simile was not well chosen, but didn't remark upon it. Instead he switched on the khaki-coloured GI torch attached to his lapel and flashed it upwards. The beam of the flashlight had difficulty in penetrating the whirling white gloom. Finally it did, however. For an instant he caught a glimpse of the empty glass cubicle in which the machine-gun and searchlight were housed. It was empty. But before the snow closed in again, he spotted the dark shape of a man lying sprawled at an awkward, unnatural angle outside of the box. It had to be the guard.

She had seen it, too, for she shouted. "It's a GI, Tom! They've nobbled him, the bastards!"

He didn't need to be told who 'they' were. 'They' could be only the men of SS Wotan, come to rescue their ex-CO. That is why he had gotten himself into the least defended part of the prison – the hospital wing. "Come on," he hissed urgently, "Try not to take any chances." He knew she was armed and, if necessary wouldn't hesitate to shoot it out with the heavy .45 Colt.

She said nothing as they plunged forward into the night. But already she had clicked down the big automatic's safety. She was ready for action . . .


Sergeant Bull's mood was as wild and as angry as the storm-tossed night. The whore that had been offered him at 'Papa Schulze's Hometown Cathouse', as the big German called it in his new 'American', had not turned out the way he had been promised. They had danced – even though he was already very drunk – the 'Trembling Fox', as she called it. Then he had bought a couple of bottles of German rotgut, contemptuously throwing two packs of Camels to cries of awe from the Krauts on the beer-wet table. For a while, things had been vague until he had found himself in her two-room 'apartment' – a former kitchen in a bombed-out ruin, partitioned off by sacking. "All right baby!" he had growled, slumping onto the only chair, "I've paid ya. Show us ya tits."

She had been drunk, too, and perhaps – for a whore – a little excited. She had stripped naked despite the cold outside. In the dusk-red light cast by her red knickers draped over the bedside light she had lain back on the divan, invitingly holding up her heavy breasts to him, a mocking look on her drunken face as she had spread her legs. In an excited voice – unusual for a whore – she had invited him to enter her *"Now!"*

He had ripped his pants off somehow and his drawers and then he had towered above her, his flaccid organ hanging uselessly. But nothing had happened. He had drunk too much.

At first the whore hadn't noticed. Perhaps she had thought he was teasing, and she had pressed her full breasts even more, forming a deep, inviting cleavage between them, wriggling her nubile body feverishly as if she couldn't wait to be penetrated. *"Los . . . schnell . . . come quick, schatzi!"* she had gasped and it sounded as if she really meant it.

He had tried, but to no avail! "It won't work!" he had stammered drunkenly. "The goddam thing won't come up . . . too much frigging booze!"

It had been then that she had started laughing. At first it had been only quietly, increasing however until finally, tears trickling down her cheeks, she had been rolling back and forth on the divan, as if she had just heard the world's funniest joke.

It was then that he hit her.

He had punched her straight in the face, like he might have done with some truculent prisoner. Her nose had smashed and blood had squirted in a scarlet arc. She had screamed with pain and in total disbelief she had cried, "You hit me!"

"Yeah and I'm gonna hit ya some more – *CUNT!*"

Now, as he plodded through the driving snow back to the prison, his mood as black as the night, his mind raged at her last words – flung between sobs – at him as he had left. "No can get it up . . . Not like my black friend . . . Washington Lee, he got a big one . . . He get it up the way I like . . ." For a few moments he had been tempted to turn back and really whip the shit out of her, but he had decided against it, he might kill the cock-sucking nigger whore.

But even as he raged inwardly, his big paws dug deep into his pockets, his eyes narrowed to slits against the driving snow, he was becoming aware that something was happening at 'his' prison, as he always thought of it: faint whispers, stealthy footsteps, the click of metal striking metal.

Suddenly it dawned upon him and he gasped to the night, "*Jesus*! *The krauts are trying to break out*!"

# Chapter Seven

"Going for a little hike – on a night like this, Kraut?" Bull asked silkily, his drunkenness vanished, as he stepped from the shadows near the entrance to the hospital wing, his Colt in his big hand.

Weakly, von Dodenburg turned round. The Popov had left him there, whispering "Comrades here in shake of elephant's tail". But this wasn't Schulze or Matzi. There was no mistaking the harsh voice of Sergeant Bull. Von Dodenberg tried to pull out the pistol, but Bull beat him to it easily. A grunt, a chop of his right fist and the weapon fell from von Dodenburg's grasp to the snow. He tried to bend and pick it up again. Bull beat him to it again. With one massive kick, he sent the pistol flying into the darkness, saying as he did so, "OK, Kraut, who's helping you trying to dodge the necktie party, eh?"

Von Dodenburg didn't understand 'the necktie party', but crouching in the shadows, Sergeant Schulze did. He didn't need a crystal ball to know that Bull's appearance was putting all his carefully laid plans to naught. A great burning rage started to well up inside him. "*Holy bim-bam!*" he cursed to himself. "I'm going to bring that asshole around the corner* if it's the last frigging thing I do on this earth."

He launched himself forward.

---

* German slang for murder. *Transl.*

"What—?" Bull began. Too late. A massive shape had detached itself from the shadows.

"You're the guy who runs the cathouse," Bull began to mutter as he went down to his knees in the snow with the impact. Again Schulze cut him short, this time with a fist like a steam shovel that slammed into Bull's upturned face. The bear-like American's nose splintered audibly. Blood spurted from the shattered nostrils, dripping to the the snow in scarlet gobs.

Desperately, knowing that the other man was going to kill him, Bull attempted to level his Colt. Schulze's foot lashed out – and missed. Groggily, the blood streaming from his shattered nose and down into his throat, threatening to choke him, Bull pressed the trigger.

There was a sharp crack. It was followed by a hollow boom in that stone chasm. A spurt of scarlet flame and a slug whined off the wall. Crazily, his hand wavering, Bull tried to fire again. Schulze didn't give him a second chance. He dare not fire. There had been enough noise as it was. Instead, he sprang forward and with all his weight behind him he slapped his brute-like shoulder into Bull. The big American NCO gasped. But he didn't go down, though the sickening blow had forced him to one knee. Again Schulze levelled a kick at the American's face with his cruelly shod boot.

Automatically, the veteran of many a tavern brawl squirmed to one side at the very last moment. Schulze, carried away by the force of his kick, staggered forward and screamed as Bull grabbed his genitals, found them and cruelly twisted them.

Schulze went reeling into the snow, the Bull still holding him in that sadistic vice. In a minute he knew he was going to be sick – and worse. Already great scarlet and silver stars were exploding in front of his eyes. He was going to black out!

Desperately, as the two giants writhed back and forth in

the snow, gasping and panting, von Dodenburg sought for a weapon, knowing that he had to deal with Bull, or else it would be too late. Somehow, his mind racing with fear and apprehension, he found the pistol in the snow. Schulze was making strange sobbing noises at the back of his throat. Bull, for his part, was screaming curses as he towered above the downed Schulze, his free hand about to smash into the German's face to put him out for good. Von Dodenburg hesitated for a second, then he steadied his grasp and pressed the trigger. The pistol exploded in his right hand. Bull gave one last scream, which seemed to echo and re-echo for ever. The back of his skull flew apart. In the welter of red gore and brains the shattered bones gleamed like ivory. Slowly, the American collapsed onto Schulze's chest.

*That single shot did it.*

Wild, confused firing broke out everywhere. Scarlet flame stabbed the white gloom. Tracer zipped back and forth like a kind of lethal morse. There were cries of alarm and anger. Sirens began to wail urgently. Orders were rapped out. Everywhere in the grey, stone, faceless building, lights began to flash on. In an instant all was crazy, confused chaos.

"*There he is!*" Sharpe yelled above the sudden racket. "*VON DODENBURG!*"

With the muzzle of his pistol he indicated the two figures, one gigantic and tremendously broad-shouldered, the other weak and tottering, outlined in the silver light of a searchlight sweeping the courtyard.

"I see him!" Mary-Ann cried back and started running clumsily through the deep snow.

"Careful . . . Mary-Ann . . . careful!" he cried desperately. But she was no longer listening. A dark shape detached itself from the wall and fired at her. Ineffectually, the slug howled off the wall close to the running figure. Without seeming to aim, the American woman snapped off a shot.

A scream and a shocked gasp of agony. The dark figure's hands fanned the air, as if climbing the rungs of an invisible ladder. An instant latter the unknown assailant hit the snow face first. Mary-Ann ran on.

Sharpe staggered after her. He snapped off controlled shots to left and right from his automatic. He didn't know whether he was firing at friend or foe. All that mattered was that she should come through safely. At that moment it was all he cared about in the wide world. "*MARY-ANN!*" he howled after her like a demented creature, "*GET DOWN!*" But even as he shouted the one-armed British officer knew she wasn't listening. Once she had felt sorry for the German SS man because of the injustice being done to him. But no longer. Now her Jewish soul cried out for retribution: retribution and revenge for the 2,000 years of suffering that her race had suffered at the hands of people like von Dodenburg.

Mary-Ann seemed to bear a charmed life. As the fire fight intensified, the snap-and-crackle of angry small-arms fire echoing and re-echoing round the inner walls of the prison courtyard, she zig-zagged through the deep snow. Again someone fired at her. She returned the fire without stopping. An unknown man slipped to the ground – dead before he reached it. Frantic with worry, Sharpe tried to cover her, attempting to out-guess the men firing from every doorway and opening. But even as he did so he knew that a tragedy was in the making. However much he prayed and hoped he knew she wasn't going to make it. She had been doomed from the first day she had come to this damned place, full of new hope and determination, knowing that soon she would put a decadent, old Europe behind her and return to the land of her forefathers. *She was going to die!*

\* \* \*

"Oh, my balls!" Schulze moaned pitifully, as Matz hobbled up to the two of them. "I swear that the *Ami* arse-with-ears has pulled them right off! I'll never get another diamond-cutter in all my born days."

"Heaven, arse and twine!" Matz cried, his voice revealing his joy at seeing his old CO once again despite the desperate situation in which they found themselves. "Who frigging well cares about them frigging pigeon's eggs? Here, sir . . . lean on me. We're going out. *Los!*"

Schulze forgot about his aching balls which seemed to be on fire. He, too, realised that they had only minutes before the *Amis* summoned up reinforcements. "Get yer frigging yeller keester out of the way!" he cried to Matz. "Here we go, sir!" He bent and as von Dodenburg fainted, picked him up in his brawmy arms as if he were the merest child and started to carry him to the now open gate.

"Stop them!" Mary-Ann cried wildly, the wind tearing the words out of her mouth. *"It's him! He's getting—"*

The burst of Schmeisser fire at close range caught her completely by surprise. She stopped in her tracks. She didn't go down, though her knees crumpled with the shock of that savage impact. Across her chest, half a dozen freshly stitched buttonholes suddenly started to spurt blood. She began to waver, trying to shout the alarm, but unable to do so. Inside her brain, she raged. "No," an angry Old Testament voice rasped, "they shall not escape. No . . ." the angry voice seemed to go on and on for ever, trailing away into infinity until she could hear it no longer. Like the legs of a new-born foal, hers started to give beneath her. She was going down, the noise, the shots, the cries receding farther and farther away. Abruptly she experienced absolute calm, as if she had known from the day she had been born that this would be her fate. Then she was dead.

The shooting had finished. The MPs had brought up the spotlights. They shed their cold, unfeeling light on the body-littered courtyard. Somewhere someone was crying piteously in German, "Help me . . . oh, help me . . . I . . . I think I'm blind! For God's sake help me . . . !" But tonight God was looking the other way.

Inside the prison the guards were crying harshly, "Okay, number off you Krauts . . . Let's have your assholes. Number off . . . ONE . . . TWO . . . THREE . . . !"

In the middle of the yard, Sharpe and McDougall stared down at her slumped body, looking like a bundle of carelessly abandoned rags. Someone had tried to cover her with a GI blanket. Savagely, his dark eyes blazing with rage, McDougall had torn the blanket from the helpless, puzzled GI's hands, crying, "Leave her . . . leave her . . . Let everyone see her as she is . . . !" The scared GI had stumbled away into the surrounding darkness.

For what seemed an eternity, unaware of the coming and goings of the MPs and stretcher-bearers, the two them had stared at her, until finally McDougall had broken the heavy, brooding silence. "See what happens to us when we mix with you people!"

"You people?" Sharpe had said, "How do you mean?"

"Gentiles," McDougall pronounced the word as if it were a great curse.

In a way, Sharpe had understood.

Now, as the stretcher-bearers came their way again, having dealt with the wounded and ready to carry away the dead, Sharpe asked tonelessly, "What shall we do with her?"

It seemed to take McDougall a long time to answer. Finally he said, *"We do?"*

Sharpe did not need to ask what he meant. His role in their lives was over. He would return from whence he had come. Probably he'd die sooner or later in some place like Bognor Regis or Cheltenham: a crusty white-haired ex-officer, typical of his kind, who expressed forceful opinions at the top of his voice on all and sundry to anyone bored enough to listen. And she, Mary-Ann? Never would they bury her in this accursed Germany, he knew that now with the certainty of a vision.

He frowned and, awkwardly with his one hand, he thrust the pistol back into his waistband, saying "I won't wish you luck because I don't like you – never did. But," his voice faltered and he felt the hot tears well up in his eyes, "look after her please, for me!"

McDougall didn't respond. For a minute or two Sharpe continued to stand there. In the end he turned silently and began threading his way through the dead. A moment later and he was gone.

# Envoi

Kuno von Dodenburg breathed in deeply and pleasurably. The mountain air cut into his lungs like the blade of a sharp knife. All the same he delighted in its keenness and freshness. After three months hiding in the cellar of Schulze's 'knocking shop', with the hue and cry going on all about his hiding place, it was a sheer tonic to be free of worry and out in God's good fresh air once more.

He turned, savouring every moment of it, as the two others rested on the craggy side of the mountain trail which led to freedom – his brow darkened at the thought – and permanent exile. To his front, long shadows sweeping across it like the wings of giant crows, lay the plain of Italy, with the sun like a blood-red ball to the east. Once he and the proud blond giants of SS Assault Regiment Wotan had held up all the Allies had been able to throw against them in that war-torn country retreating from mountain pass to mountain pass, making the enemy pay for every single metre of ground gained. Now he would soon descend into Italy, a hunted man with every man's hand against him.

But the thought could not spoil his delight and wonder this fine May morning. He savoured the sound of some mountain farmer driving his animals up to the lush grass of the upper pastures, their jingling bells hung around their necks.

How beautiful!

Matz farted. Obviously he wasn't impressed by Alpine

views, however beautiful. He drained the last of his flatman, belched, and said, "Time we was going. The spaghettis patrol up here every three hours. It's getting on for nine."

Schulze looked at his wizened little running mate a little angrily, as if he didn't like his tone. You didn't address the CO like that. "Hold yer frigging hosses," he growled. "Let the CO finish his salami sandwich."

Von Dodenburg stuck the rest of his sandwich in the pocket of his shabby civilian jacket. "Corporal Matz—"

"*Ex*-Corporal Matz," the latter growled sourly.

"We'd better be on out way. But," he shook his handsome head, as if finding it difficult to express himself, "it's funny, leaving Germany like this and knowing that you'll never be able to come back. That you'll die in foreign exile."

"A lot of the lads died in worse places," Matz persisted doggedly, as Schulze shot him a threatening glance saying, "Ain't you just the fucking little ray o' joy this fine morning! Let the CO have his last bit of pleasure." He beamed at von Dodenburg. "We'll all miss you, sir."

"*All*?" Matz sneered. "How many's frigging *all*? Most of the lads went hop in Russian and half a dozen other frigging countries – for what?"

Schulze tried to appease his old running mate, changing his former opinion of what it had all been about. "They weren't bad times, Matzi, admit it."

"Yer, I know what yer gonna say. You've said it before. The beaver, the booze, the bash-on spirit and all that bullshit. But what good did it do us in the end, even those who survived like us? Remember old Sergeant Gierig? Just before we started that Ardennes do, he sez to me I can have his leather jacket – he knew I liked it – if anything happened to him. Well, he bought it, didn't he! And what did I do? I'd known him since we'd been recruits together back in Wittlich in '39. I'll tell yer," he pulled a sour face.

"I sez, where's that frigging jacket – and I hope he didn't cop it in the guts or anywhere to spoil the leather". He spat drily in the white dust of the mountain trail. "That's what frigging Wotan did to us."

Schulze flushed angrily and doubled that mighty fist of his "You're aiming to enjoy a shitty knuckle sandwich in five seconds flat, you Bavarian barnshitter!" he snarled threateningly.

"*Ist doch wahr, Mensch?*" Matz persisted defiantly.

"All right, all right, don't start World War Three," von Dodenburg cut in quickly, forcing a wan smile. He told himself that the old spirit was dead for good. The old Wotan closeness, comradeship, the feeling of utter dependency on each other, was long gone. He would have to live with it. He shook his head, blinking in the slanting rays of the new sun peering over the sparkling, snow-tipped peaks, like a man waking from a long and involved dream. The two old comrades, for whom he would gladly have given his life (as they would have done for him) were like strangers.

He rose to his feet and shouldered his home-made pack more comfortably. They shook hands without feeling and without words. "*Hals und Beinbruch* – happy landings" he uttered the old tough greeting for the very last time. Then he was off plodding down the steep descent which led into Italy. Once, he looked back. But Schulze and Matz had already vanished. He was alone at last . . .